By SHAE CONNOR

All in a Day's Work (Multiple Author Anthology)
Cabin on the Hill
Chicago
En Fuego
Grand Adventures (Dreamspinner Anthology)
Model Student
Of Holiday Spirits, Wake-Up Calls, and Happily Ever Afters
Playing Ball (Multiple Author Anthology)
Sand & Water
Sharing Christmas
Unfortunate Son

Published by DREAMSPINNER PRESS
http://www.dreamspinnerpress.com

UNFORTUNATE
SON

Shae Connor

Dreamspinner Press

Published by
DREAMSPINNER PRESS

5032 Capital Circle SW, Suite 2, PMB# 279, Tallahassee, FL 32305-7886 USA
http://www.dreamspinnerpress.com/

This is a work of fiction. Names, characters, places, and incidents either are the product of author imagination or are used fictitiously, and any resemblance to actual persons, living or dead, business establishments, events, or locales is entirely coincidental.

Unfortunate Son
© 2015 Shae Connor.

Cover Photography
© 2015 www.feedyoureyes.net.
Cover Model
© 2015 Travis Irons.
Twitter: @Travis_Irons
Cover Design
© 2015 Paul Richmond.
http://www.paulrichmondstudio.com
Cover content is for illustrative purposes only and any person depicted on the cover is a model.

ISBN: 978-1-63216-530-5
Digital ISBN: 978-1-63216-531-2
Library of Congress Control Number: 2014951983
First Edition January 2015

Printed in the United States of America
(∞)
This paper meets the requirements of
ANSI/NISO Z39.48-1992 (Permanence of Paper).

AUTHOR'S NOTE

First and foremost, I owe a deep debt of gratitude to Travis Irons, who allowed me to both pick his brain and use his body to develop the basis for Trevor Hardball—and for Evan Day. His willingness to open the doors to his life and his work made this book possible, but more important, his friendship makes my life richer.

Although I did use Travis's physical appearance and some of his personal experiences to help construct the framework of this story, I want to be very clear that the events and people described here are fictional. This is not a biographical work. As the disclaimer on the copyright page says, any specific resemblance to real people or events is coincidental.

Thanks also to Cody, Teresa, Perry, Joey, Bryan, Devon, Kat, my "long-suffering sister," and all the others whose insight and support contributed to this story. Particularly special thanks to my crack editing team for keeping me in line: D. M. Grace, Tia Fielding, CJane Elliott, Charley Descoteaux, and J. P. Barnaby.

Finally, a tip of the glittery hat to the legendary Armorettes, the Infamous Camp Drag Queens of the South, whose work inspired the drag troupe in this story. The Armorettes' fun and fabulous shows go so much deeper than entertainment: since they first got started in Atlanta thirty-five years ago, they've raised over $2 million for HIV/AIDS support services. Find out more about the Armorettes, including information on performances and how to donate, at armorettes.com.

For my friend Derek

Chapter 1

"Yeah, take it… fuck yeah… you know you want it…."

Trevor moaned and opened his mouth wider, his lips stretched to their limit around the thick dick between them. A big hand gripped the back of Trevor's head hard, holding him in perfect position to have his face fucked. A string of words Trevor mostly ignored fell from the other man's mouth. Trevor just relaxed his mouth and throat and let himself be used.

Behind him, another set of hands held Trevor's hips just as hard while another hard dick thrust into his ass, filling Trevor's hole just to the brink of pain without pushing him too far. Spit-roasted between two sweat-soaked, muscular bodies, Trevor let his mind turn over control to his body and his instincts, and lost himself in sensation.

"Shit, man."

The fucking from behind stopped, and Trevor was jerked out of the fantasy he'd been building for himself. "Damn condom's slipping again." Jackson, the guy who had his cock in Trevor's ass, yanked out with no warning, making Trevor wince. He turned his head in time to see Jackson stripping off the latex. "You got another kind or something?"

Mick, the face-fucker, laughed and stepped to the side, his still hard cock bouncing wetly in the cool air as he smirked at Jackson. "You got some extra-smalls for Jack-off here, boys?"

"Fuck you." Jackson's voice was mild, not angry, and Trevor was glad for that. He hated being on set with guys who went off on testosterone-fueled rants, especially for no real reason. It wasn't like condom troubles were any kind of rarity in porn.

"Since we're stopped anyway, let's reset, guys." That instruction came from the director, Brent, another model who was in the process of making the switch to the other side of the camera. "Mick, let's get a cumshot from you. Hit Trevor in the face, and watch the eyes this time, okay? Trevor, you good?"

Trevor nodded, rocking his head from side to side and giving his mouth a few stretches. Trevor was always good, always ready for another round, another shot, another angle. Whatever it took to get the job done and get another paycheck in the bank.

Kneeling on the end of the mattress, waiting for the crew to finish adjusting things around him, Trevor breathed in the smells of sweaty men and raw sex. *Jesus.* Whatever else went on in his life, he'd never get sick of that scent. Just a whiff was enough to get his dick hard. A room full of it, like this one, could almost get him off with nothing else.

"Okay, ready." Mick nodded at Brent's words and moved in closer, stroking his cock just inches from Trevor's face. Trevor balanced himself with his hands on his thighs, mouth open slightly to catch a blast or two once Mick let it fly. If sex was his favorite smell, cum was his favorite taste.

While cameras recorded from several angles, Mick jerked himself hard and fast, moaning and cursing, his free hand planted on his flank, out of the way of the shot. Trevor watched Mick's face closely, five years' experience and a number of previous shoots with Mick having taught him the signs of impending orgasm. He closed his eyes just seconds before the first wet streams hit his face, one and then another right into his mouth, and he hummed and swallowed before licking around his lips to capture even more of that flavor. Unlike some of Trevor's scene partners, Mick always tasted clean and a little sweet, never funky or bitter. Trevor knew he should savor it while he had a chance.

Mick rubbed his cock over Trevor's face, picking up more of his cum and bringing it to Trevor's mouth for him to lick off. Trevor followed Mick's lead, not that he minded at all, and it was another minute or two before Mick took a step back. "Good?" he asked, the question directed to Brent.

"Perfect," Brent replied. "Okay, let's take a break. Everybody back on set in fifteen."

Trevor uncurled himself from the bed, shaking out his legs where they'd started to go numb. Even with his regular workouts and plenty of practice on his knees, holding any position for a long time got uncomfortable. He could handle it, of course. He was a professional. But damn, was he glad they took plenty of breaks during most shoots.

He crossed the loft to the corner where he'd left his bag, dug out his cigarettes and lighter, and headed toward the balcony. It was too chilly and damp to go outside—and he'd need clothes for that anyway—so he just slid the door open far enough to let the smoke out and lit up, leaning against the wall and staring out over the gray Atlanta skyline. He liked his hometown, though he much preferred it bright and sunny, like it was most of the year. Today, clouds and rain had set in, and the weather dragged Trevor's mood right down with it.

Maybe he needed a change of scenery. He had friends in Fort Lauderdale. Florida was sunny pretty much all the time.

He chuffed out a semblance of a laugh around a puff of smoke. *Yeah, no.* Too many porn stars down there, too much partying. Trevor liked most of the guys he worked with well enough, but he didn't want to be pressured into spending his free time with them.

The sounds from behind him, where cameras and props were being reset, faded into white noise. He could hear the more distant sounds of cars passing by, a plane flying overhead, a siren in the distance. Off to his left, he could see the green edge of Piedmont Park, an oasis in the middle of Midtown where he spent many hours walking or just chilling out. Even on a Saturday, only the diehards would be out there in this weather—runners and dog walkers, for the most part.

Trevor took a last long drag from his cigarette and bent to snuff it out against the concrete floor of the balcony. After five years of experience, he knew how to time his breaks pretty well, so he wasn't surprised when Brent spoke just as he pushed the door shut and turned his back to the glass.

"Okay, let's get Trevor and Jackson now. Trevor, hands and knees, and Jacks, try to keep the condom on this time, okay?"

Trevor half smiled as Jacks flipped Brent off. The two had been friends for years, but never a couple, since Brent was gay and Jacks nominally straight. Trevor figured that was probably why they'd been able to stay friends for so long. He couldn't think of a single former couple in the industry who'd managed any more than staying cordial after a breakup.

Back on the bed, Trevor got himself positioned and arched his back, lifting up his ass for Jackson. He knew he looked great like this; he'd seen himself doing it often enough, even taken some pictures of his own. Jackson settled one hand on Trevor's hip and used the other to guide his resheathed cock into Trevor's hole, which was still loose and wet with lube.

Trevor groaned and pushed back against the intrusion, relishing the blend of burn and pleasure, as he always did. Shooting a scene wasn't anything like having sex in private—Trevor much preferred one-on-one with no cameras—but it damn sure didn't suck. Except in the good ways.

Jackson shifted behind him and tightened his fingers on Trevor's hip. "Ready?" he asked, and Trevor nodded. The exchange was unnecessary and they both knew it. Trevor was always ready.

"Okay, camera rolling… action!"

Jacks followed orders, starting off with just a few long, slow thrusts before he began to piston into Trevor, hard. Trevor braced his arms more firmly and pushed back, moving his hips into Jackson's thrusts. Brent loved his bottoms to be active, which was great for Trevor, because he loved it too. He and Jacks had worked together several times over the years, so it took only seconds before they were moving in perfect harmony, each collision of their hips pushing a low grunt out of Trevor.

The one thing Trevor hated about working with Jacks was that the man almost never made a sound unless prompted. That might work in private, but on camera, the noises were just as much a part of it as the visual. Sure enough, a few thrusts later, Brent's voice broke in.

"Great action, guys, but we need some vocals, Jacks."

Jacks immediately began moaning, muttering "fuck" every few thrusts, just barely loud enough for the sound equipment to pick up. Trevor fought not to roll his eyes; the only thing worse than Jackson's silence was the fakeness of his sounds. Trevor let his own voice loose, hoping to offset Jackson with something a little more real. Unlike some performers, Trevor often had to hold back when he was being fucked on camera, especially if the top managed to hit the right angle to peg his prostate—something Jacks usually did.

Dropping his head to let it hang loose, Trevor groaned loudly and pushed back harder, the sound of flesh slapping together joining with their voices to create a mishmash of noise that Trevor didn't find very sexy but the viewers would probably love. Jacks improved things by going back to mostly groans, and Trevor settled in for a long fuck. Jacks had always said he was never one to get off fast, and if that was true, then being gay for pay couldn't be making things any easier on him. That was part of what made him well-suited for porn, though. The longer he could hold off, the more time they'd get on camera in one stretch, which would make editing for the final scene that much easier.

Trevor didn't know how long they kept up the pace, but his ab muscles were getting sore by the time Brent called out, "All right, one more setup, guys," and Jacks stop thrusting. He pulled out too quickly, though, and Trevor winced at the sharp pinch.

"Damn, man, that's twice! Gimme some warning!" Trevor rolled onto his back and shot Jacks a glare. The other man had the decency to look sheepish.

"Sorry, man," he said. He looked over at Brent. "On his back to finish?"

"Yeah." Brent wasn't looking at them directly, his gaze instead intent on the camera screen. "Mick, let's get you back in here too. Lie down next to him so you can kiss him and jerk him off while Jacks finishes fucking him. Okay?"

The three men moved into the requested positions, careful, as always, not to block the cameras, and they got back to work. Trevor turned his mind off and just let his body do the work. The way they were situated, Brent wouldn't need them to shift to get his cumshot, so he just let it happen. A dick in his ass, a tongue in his mouth, and a hand on his cock were plenty for him, even under these artificial conditions.

He let the orgasm build in him, mouth open to let out the words and moans he didn't try to hold back. A part of him never shut off during a scene, no matter how good the sex, even though after nearly five years, making things good for the camera had become instinct as much as his body's natural reactions. He'd been good at this from the start, but with experience, he'd reached the point where he hardly had to think about what he needed to do.

He enjoyed himself, sure. The sex was nearly always good. But it had been so long since he'd truly been able to let go during sex that he'd almost forgotten how it felt.

That was the thought on his mind when he finally came, spurting long ribbons of white across his chest and abdomen. He gasped and moaned, body shuddering as Jacks kept fucking him through the orgasm, until Brent said something. Trevor's ears were still ringing, so he didn't hear the words, but he knew it would be an instruction to move on to Jackson's cumshot while Trevor's was still fresh. That would save them the trouble of creating fake semen with lube or lotion later.

Jacks pulled out much more carefully this time, and Mick slid his hand through the wetness on Trevor's body, rubbing the cum around while Jackson jacked off over them both. Trevor expected Jacks to take a while to come, even after the long fucking sessions, and sure enough, the cum had cooled on Trevor's skin by the time Jacks sucked in a breath and spurted across Trevor's body and Mick's hand. Trevor pushed out a moan and bucked up, knowing the intervening time would be edited out, making it look like they'd come one after the other. Mick bent to kiss Trevor again, openmouthed and with a lot of tongue, then shifted to do the same to Jacks.

"And... cut. Great job, guys!"

Brent's words broke things up that quickly, and the three men separated. One of the production assistants tossed a couple of towels toward the bed, and Trevor snagged one to wipe the sweat and two layers of cum off himself. He'd take a quick shower before leaving the apartment, but the air-conditioning on his wet skin had him getting chilled, so he wanted to get some of that off as quickly as possible.

Rolling to sit up, Trevor shot a quick grin at his scene partners. "Thanks, guys." He turned his head toward Brent. "Good shoot, Brent?"

Brent nodded, his gaze trained on the playback screen on his camera. "Looking good from here. Think we got plenty, between this and the backup."

"Great." Trevor's legs were steady enough by then to stand up and head to the bathroom. Mick followed him, smacking one large hand hard into Trevor's right asscheek.

"Always good working with you," Mick told Trevor. He turned to face Jacks. "Okay with sharing a shower?"

Mick knew from experience that Trevor never extended his scene activities once the cameras quit rolling, like a lot of models did. He'd have a better chance of getting some action from the straight guy.

Trevor walked on into the bathroom alone. Mick and Jacks could have their fun once he was finished and headed out for a drink. Or several.

MUSIC POUNDED in Evan's head, almost but not quite loud enough to drown out his own thoughts. *That's what liquor is for,* he thought, tossing back his third shot and then nodding to the bartender for another before the burn even hit his stomach.

He took a last, long drag on his second cigarette of the night, blowing out smoke in a thick, steady stream as he crushed the butt into the ashtray on the bar in front of him. There weren't many bars left where you could still smoke inside, which was part of the reason he came to Logger's. Stupid name, heavily redneck clientele for a gay bar, even in the South, but he could drink and smoke and still be able to pick up some company if he got desperate enough.

He and desperate had gotten to be pretty good buddies the past few years.

Another full shot glass and a longneck Bud appeared on the wood in front of him. He gave the bartender, an older guy named Tony, a raised-eyebrow look and got a shrug in response. "Figured you wouldn't want to waste something good on a whiskey chaser."

Evan nodded and picked up the shot glass. "Fair point." He tossed back the whiskey and set the glass back down before reaching for the beer and half turning to look out over the crowd. Sipping at the piss water, he searched the room for anything halfway decent. Preferably something not wearing flannel or a trucker hat.

"Hey, you're Trevor Hardball, right?"

Preferably not someone who knew him as *that*, either.

Evan pasted on the best somewhat-sexy smile he could manage and turned to the man standing at his left. "In the flesh," he said. "Having a good evening?"

Bland and neutral, the way he always went into these things. You never knew when a fan encounter might go south—*been there, done that*—so better not be too friendly or too dismissive.

This time, the man just smiled and held out a hand. "Thought so." His smile widened as Evan shook his hand. "Just wanted to say I'm a fan of your work. A lotta the guys doing porn are all fake, but you come across as real genuine. Makes it a lot hotter."

Like many of the bar's patrons, the man's drawl doubled the syllables in most of his words. "Thanks." Evan took back his hand and reached for his beer. "Nice to get feedback."

"I follow you on Twitter too. Love the shots you post." The man's gaze ran down Evan's body, lingering at his crotch before returning to his face. "You got an amazing body. Not all overpumped like some guys."

Evan sipped his beer, swallowed. "I may be dancing at Rooster's next month," he said. "You should come by and say hi."

Unlike some people, this man got the hint—*not to be rude, but I'm on my own time now*—and nodded. "Will do. You have a great night, now."

"Thanks, you too. Nice to meet you."

Evan turned back to meet Tony's amused gaze, lifting his beer and an eyebrow in tandem. "What?" he asked just as glass met flesh.

Tony shook his head and set the glass he'd been wiping under the edge of the bar. "Just funny to see you turn it on and off like that. Flip a switch and it's like a whole 'nother person."

Evan shrugged. "Kind of is," he agreed.

And kind of not, his mind supplied. Porn had been his life and livelihood long enough that the edges blurred even for him. The only thing he knew for sure was that he liked sex. Whether he truly liked the kind he had on set was a different question, but usually, yeah, it was good. And when it wasn't, well, he just faked it. It might not be Hollywood caliber, but acting was still part of the job.

And a job it was. Not that he'd had many options after he got kicked out of the Corps.

Evan shook off the thought. Not one he liked to dwell on.

"Oh shit!"

A high-pitched half shriek was Evan's only warning before something—some*one*—tumbled halfway into his lap. Evan only just kept himself from leaping up, which from the look of things, once he could focus, would've resulted in his unexpected visitor landing in a pile on the floor. As it was, the smaller man was in danger of slipping off Evan and going down hard, and not in the fun way.

Evan set his beer on the counter and wrapped his free hand around the arm of the guy who'd fallen quite literally into his lap. He stared down at the riot of loose, blond-tipped curls against his chest. The kid's hands were scrabbling then, trying to get some kind of grip so he could get back on his feet, or so Evan supposed, though he didn't seem to be making much progress in that direction.

Finally something caught, the kid got his feet back under him, and he stood up. Evan kept his hands up protectively on instinct, just in case, but the kid just shook his head, hair a blur of motion, and then looked at Evan straight on, as if he'd meant to do that all along.

"I'm so sorry, honey," the kid said, and Evan thought he couldn't have been more than nineteen. Never mind that they were in a bar; it wasn't like a fake ID was hard to get. "I don't know what happened there. I was just coming over to get another club soda and, *bam*, there went my feet, right out from under me." He smiled, teeth bright white against his lightly tanned skin and full, deep pink lips, and held out a hand. "Where are my manners? I'm Riley Yeats."

Without conscious thought, Evan found himself sliding his fingers around Riley's, feeling long, fragile bones beneath soft skin. "Evan," he said. "Evan Day."

In his peripheral vision, he caught the widening of Tony's eyes. He *never* gave out his real name to strangers. He had no idea why he'd done it now, but it wasn't like he could take it back.

"Well, Evan Day, I'm very glad to meet you." Riley gave Evan's hand a quick squeeze and then climbed onto the next barstool— climbed quite literally, since the dang things were difficult for Evan to handle, and he was nearly six feet tall. Riley couldn't be more than five-foot-six in his bare feet. *Or in flip-flops*, Evan thought as he glanced down at Riley's feet, now hooked on the rail that ran around the chair a foot off the ground. Metallic gold flip-flops? Evan didn't even know they sold such things. And was that glittery pink nail polish on his toes?

"So let me buy you another of whatever it is you're drinking there, Evan," Riley was saying when Evan tore his gaze away from Riley's tiny, shiny feet. "It's the least I can do after throwing myself at you." Riley smiled at Tony. "I'll have a club soda with two lemon and two lime slices, please, and whatever the gentleman wants."

Tony nodded toward the beer, a question on his face, but Evan decided he was about done for the night. "I'll have the same as him."

Riley gave him a long, appraising look. "Don't think you have to not drink on my account, honey. Just because I don't doesn't mean I mind if others do."

Evan blinked. "No, I—I didn't know you don't drink. I'm just done drinking for tonight."

Riley studied him for a few more moments before turning back to the bartender. "Okay, then, make it two club sodas, please."

Tony nodded and started on the drinks, and Evan pulled out another cigarette, figuring he'd get one more smoke in with the soda. Riley shook his head.

"Those are bad for you, you know."

It was all Evan could do not to crack up. Shit, on the list of bad-for-you things he'd done, cigarettes barely broke the top ten.

"Yeah, I know," he said. "Don't do it a lot. Probably should quit." *Probably won't.*

He lit up and took a good, deep drag, aware of Riley's gaze still on him. He blew out the mouthful of smoke—considerately away from his unexpected companion—and knocked the ash into the glass dish that already contained his previous butts. "So if you don't drink," he asked, "why are you hanging out in a bar?" He lifted the cigarette back to his mouth, held between two fingers, and raised an eyebrow in question.

Riley shot him a grin. "Believe it or not, I like the music."

Evan's other eyebrow shot up to match the first. The country-gone-dance (or was it dance-gone-country?) fusions the bar preferred were an acquired taste, to put it mildly. The current soundtrack to their conversation was some kind of club version of Shania Twain's "Man, I Feel Like A Woman," and before that had been a mash-up of a classic twangy hit he didn't know the title of combined with Lady Gaga's "Born This Way."

"Yeah, I know." Riley headed off his comments. "It's not *all* I like, not by any means. But it's certainly unique, wouldn't you agree?"

Their club sodas arrived just then, and Riley smiled at Tony before lifting his glass from its napkin coaster and toward Evan. "To being unique?"

Evan couldn't help the smile. "I'll drink to that," he said, and they did.

The song changed as Evan swallowed, this time into something both straightforward and easily recognizable, at least to anyone with any knowledge of modern country music: Garth Brooks' "Friends in Low Places." Every bar or group Evan had ever been in when this song played had turned it into a sing-along, and tonight was no exception. Voices of varying quality rose around them, including a not-bad baritone from Tony, but Evan and Riley sat it out in silent agreement. Evan smoked between sips of his lemon-lime flavored soda. Riley just sipped his drink, one leg bouncing incessantly, though not in time with the music in any discernible way.

What with all the singing, the noise level had risen much too high for conversation, so they didn't talk. Their eyes met occasionally in the mirror behind the bar, but unless Evan's instincts were deserting him—not entirely out of the question—the interest in Riley's never strayed past the friendly. It felt... well, it felt strange, actually. Not only had Riley shown no sign of recognizing him by his profession, he'd shown no sign of coming on to him, either. Those two things nearly always went hand in hand, and that was a big part of the problem. Trevor could bed any guy he wanted anytime he wanted, but Evan? Evan rarely even got the chance to be himself, much less try to figure out if another guy was after him, or looking for the guy they thought they knew from his films.

By the time the song ended, Evan had finished his cigarette and his drink, and his eyelids were starting to sag. He didn't often go out after shoots, which took a lot out of him, but he'd needed the unwind time today. He turned toward Riley and smiled.

"Think I'm ready to head out," he said. "Thanks for the drink."

Riley tipped back his glass to drain the last of the liquid and then set it neatly back on the napkin. "I think I'll walk out with you, if you don't mind." He slid down from the high stool and extracted a bill from the front pocket of his skinny jeans to toss on the bar. "Thanks, Tony." He gave the man a bright smile and turned back to face Evan. "Shall we?"

It appeared they would.

CHAPTER 2

ANOTHER REASON Evan spent time at Logger's was that he could walk there from his apartment. The streets even had sidewalks all the way, and in good shape, which was by no means the usual even in the relatively walkable neighborhood of Midtown.

What Evan didn't know was how far Riley had to go.

"Do you need a ride somewhere?" The question was out before Evan knew it was coming. He didn't know what he expected to do about it. Call a cab, he supposed, although he also supposed Riley could handle that on his own.

"No, I'm parked just around the corner." Riley pointed that direction and smiled up at him. "Would you like a ride? While I don't mind other people drinking, I do have a problem with them then driving."

Evan had to smile at the teasing note behind the clearly all too serious words. "No worries, I'm on foot."

Riley touched Evan's forearm with cool fingers. "Well, then, I'd be all too happy to see you home safely." And really, how could Evan say no? Even if he'd wanted to, as tired as he suddenly felt, a ride would be fantastic.

That kicked up a few notches when he got a look at Riley's car, a shiny-new deep blue BMW coupe. Evan couldn't help a low whistle, and Riley gave him a pleased smile before pulling away to walk to the driver's side. He clicked open the locks and paused as he opened his door to catch Evan's eye. "No smoking inside."

Evan nodded his agreement, not that he'd planned to light up in the five minutes it would take to get to his place, and slid into the passenger's seat. Soft, cushiony leather caressed his body, and he sighed at the unaccustomed luxury. He didn't live big, and he made enough money from his jobs, but he traveled so much that he hadn't bothered to upgrade his car accordingly. Not that he'd spend quite this much, but if he'd cared to, he could do better than his six-year-old sedan.

"It would help to know where I'm going."

Evan had already gotten used to the seemingly constant teasing tone in Riley's voice. It made him wonder if the man ever got angry at all.

"Eleventh off Juniper. Straight up Piedmont and to the left."

"I'm familiar." Riley backed out carefully and started in that direction. "I'm not that far myself. Piedmont Lofts."

"Wow." Those were the priciest lofts in the area by far, right on the edge of the sprawling urban park that sat at the center of Midtown. Not surprising, considering the luxury of the car they sat in, but it made Evan wonder how a borderline-legal twink came into that kind of money, at least without a sugar daddy hovering nearby.

"Wow indeed," Riley said, gaze staying on the road in front of them. Streetlights flashed like lightning across his pale skin. "All inherited, I'm afraid. I can't lay claim to having earned it, unless growing up with my family counts."

Family. That flipped the switch for Evan. Yeats Arts Center. Yeats Boulevard. The Yeats Business School at one of the local universities. *That* Yeats. One of the old-line money families whose legacies were tightly woven into the tapestry of the city.

"Oh." Evan wasn't sure what else to say that wouldn't be trite, or stupid, or both. Riley had been the one living with that family name all his life. He'd surely heard it all.

"Yeah, *oh.* Mason O'Reilly Yeats III, at your service. I'm the black sheep, but the only scandal worse than having a flamingly gay heir would be the publicity fallout kicking him out of the family might cause." He shrugged one shoulder. "So I got my trust fund on schedule, and for the most part, they pretend I don't exist, and I return the favor."

14

Riley's voice was matter-of-fact, but even though the teasing tone never dissipated, the underlying tension was obvious. Evan wasn't about to dig deeper into that, though. He'd just met the guy.

"Trust fund?" he asked instead. "Don't you usually have to be, like, twenty-five for those?"

"Twenty-one for mine," Riley replied. "But either way, I'd be covered."

Evan stared at his profile. "You can't be over twenty-one."

Riley laughed. "Try twenty-seven. Guess that skin-care regimen really *is* doing the trick."

Evan shook his head, still staring. "I never would have guessed you were older than me. Seriously. You should share your secrets for staying young."

"Moisturizer, sunblock, clean living, and daily orgasms."

Evan almost choked. "One of those things is not like the others."

Riley had relaxed by then, and his grin was decidedly wicked this time. "Oh, but it is. Endorphins are very good for you, and what better way to get them pumping?"

"I hear some people work out." Including Evan—not that he needed them to replace orgasms most days, but even acrobatic sex wouldn't give him the cut hips and abs gay porn viewers wanted to see.

Riley pulled up at the walk-in gate to the side of Evan's apartment building. "I hear some people sleep with the opposite sex too, but that doesn't mean I'm tempted."

Evan reached for the door handle, but Riley stopped him, again with a hand on his arm. "I'm having a picnic in the park for lunch tomorrow. You're welcome to stop by. I'll be near the dog parks."

Evan shrugged. "Sure." Not like he had a packed schedule. "Should I bring anything?"

"Just your smiling face, honey." Riley's hand slid away. "Sleep well."

WHEN THE blast hit, Evan didn't have a chance to move or to think before he was flying through the air, ears ringing. He landed on his

*side in the sand with enough force to push all the air out of his lungs,
and it seemed like an eternity before he could make himself move
enough to look back toward the road.*

*The transport was on its side, fully engulfed in flames. Bodies lay
in all directions, some moving, most not. Men swarmed the scene, from
the transports that had been in front and behind them, a few
scrambling toward the vehicle itself, where Evan could see at least one
more body still trapped, flames licking all around.*

*He dragged himself up and limped toward the transport as fast as
he could, gaze roaming wildly, searching for Lucas.* He's fine, he's
fine, *his mind chanted.* He's got his breath knocked out, like you did,
but he'll be up and moving soon. He's fine, he's—

Desperation for breath dragged Evan out of the nightmare of a
memory. He gasped in air like he was the one dying. Trembling,
covered in sweat, Evan tried to slow his breathing and his heart rate. He
looked at the clock, saw that it was only fifteen minutes before his
alarm would go off, and reached with a shaking hand to turn it off.

He pushed himself to his feet and stumbled toward the shower,
leaving his grief to the night.

BY THE time Evan stepped outside, he'd nearly shaken off the residue
of his nightmare. The weather helped. In contrast to the gloom of the
day before, it was one of those rare, glorious late May days in Atlanta
when the sun shone brightly in a clear blue sky but the heat and
humidity stayed under control. The front that had brought in the
previous day's rain had left this in its wake, and as Evan walked down
Eleventh Street from his apartment toward the park, he could almost
feel his skin soaking up the sun. His last spray-on tan had faded—gay
porn viewers liked their guys cut and tanned, but Evan didn't relish the
idea of skin cancer—so he'd have to be careful to keep from ending up
a lobster. He had an appearance tentatively set up in Boston in a month,
but he didn't think they'd like him to take it *that* seriously.

His flip-flops, sporty and black in sharp contrast to the shiny gold
ones Riley had worn the night before, slapped against the pavement in
time with Evan's slow walk. Riley hadn't told him a time to show up,

so Evan figured if he was early, he'd just stretch out and watch the dogs play. He'd thought about getting one of his own, but as much as he traveled, it would be a little unfair.

Familiar faces greeted Evan on his walk. He'd lived in the same apartment for going on three years now, an eternity for someone his age in Midtown—and several eternities within the gay community. But he liked recognizing his neighbors and the people who worked nearby. Some just nodded when they saw him, others smiled and waved, and a couple even stopped what they were doing and came over to say hi, shake his hand. He even got a quick hug from half of the lesbian couple who ran the coffee shop on the corner. It may or may not have helped his case that he bought a giant hazelnut latte from them nearly every time he walked by.

Fresh cup in hand, he continued across Piedmont Road and into the wide-open green fields beyond. Unsurprisingly for such a day, the park teemed with activity. Runners, walkers, dogs, kids, softball on the fields to his left, what looked like a cutthroat game of Ultimate Frisbee up ahead—people roamed everywhere he looked. The fact that a substantial portion of them were hot, shirtless men did absolutely nothing to detract from the scenery along his route.

He followed a group of dog walkers to the dog park area, watching as they let their charges loose to play with the other large animals in the first area. Beyond, smaller dogs roamed another enclosed section, with owners standing among them or off to the side, chatting. Chatting up, in some cases, from the looks a couple of the men were exchanging.

A fair number of those out enjoying the weather were pretty clearly gay, or at least not straight. Evan saw more than one pair of men or women holding hands or otherwise attached to each other. His gaze followed one couple, strolling along with arms around each other's waists, the shorter man's head tilted to rest on the shoulder of the taller man. Something in his chest twisted.

"Evan!"

The call came from off to his right, and he tore himself away from the picture of domestic bliss and searched out its owner. Riley stood a dozen feet away from the edge of the small dog park, waving one hand in a clear "get over here!" sign. Evan hadn't realized his shoulders were tense until they relaxed as he walked over.

"Glad you could make it!" Riley practically bounced on his toes, his feet bare this time but his toenails still glittery and pink. "I hope you like cheese, because I'm afraid I went a wee bit overboard there. I have Jarlsberg, Edam, and Brie, and I absolutely could *not* resist the red-rind cheddar. There's freshly baked ciabatta, and some lovely wild plum jam, and the ginger ale is amazing—I had a sample of that. And of course I picked up some peaches. You can't go to a farmer's market anywhere in the South without buying peaches. It might as well be law."

Evan was laughing by then. He couldn't help himself. Riley had an old-fashioned picnic basket, of all things, and he'd spread out what looked like a vintage quilt for them to sit on. A small cooler sat open with several bottles and ice filling it, and... were those *cloth* napkins? With *napkin rings*?

Riley lowered himself gracefully onto the quilt and patted the empty spot next to him. "Have a seat, sweetie." As Evan did, Riley reached into the basket and started pulling out packages wrapped in wax paper or cloth, along with a sharp knife. "I didn't bring glasses, since the ginger ale is in bottles. I much prefer drinking from a glass, but it seemed much easier this way. I hope you don't mind."

"Not at all," Evan replied, feeling at a loss next to Riley's ebullience. Before he knew it, a small feast was laid out on a tray in front of him, and Riley was slicing the bread.

"Help yourself to whatever looks good, honey." Riley shot him a quick, flirty look. "Of the food, at least. No running off with whatever tasty treat might wander by."

That surprised Evan. Sure, Evan might look, but he wouldn't abandon a date, although now that he thought of it, he wasn't sure that's what this was. Evan gave Riley a closer look. He wasn't Evan's usual type, but he was cute, in a 100 percent twinky way, and he was nice, which was always a good start. Other than that one glance, though, which seemed like a joke, Riley hadn't actually shown any of the usual signs of interest.

Without even realizing it, Evan had filled one of the small plastic plates Riley had provided with cheese and bread, and Riley handed him an open bottle of ginger ale. Setting aside the remainder of his coffee, Evan took a sip, smiled, and took a larger one.

"This is good stuff," he said, and Riley gave him the same semiflirty look he had before.

"I wouldn't steer you wrong." He reached over to pat Evan's knee. "I am so completely *not* a morning person, but I drag myself up to go to the farmer's market every Saturday as soon as they open for the season. It's always worth the trip. I brought home four or five bags this morning, and it took me an hour to get it all sorted and washed and put away. I went a little overboard on the tomatoes, but, God, they just taste like heaven when they're fresh like that. I can never resist."

Evan shrugged and spread some Brie on a piece of bread. "I don't like tomatoes."

Riley's eyes widened. "Oh, honey, you must not have had good ones, then. They are just sweet and juicy and perfect this time of year." He patted Evan's knee again. "I'll have you over for dinner and show you. It's almost better than sex."

Evan snorted. "I have trouble believing that."

Riley's lilting laughter rang out across the fields. "I did say *almost*. Although a perfect summer tomato probably does beat out the blander brands of sex. Not that I've had to suffer through that many of those, thank the gods of gaydom." He popped a square of cheese into his mouth, eyes twinkling with mirth.

Evan shook his head. "Somehow I didn't picture you as a sex fiend." He took a bite of bread topped with a thick smear of the softened Brie, stifling a groan as the rich flavor hit his taste buds.

Riley reached for his bottle of ginger ale. "It's one of my very favorite pastimes. Right up there with cooking, eating, and flirting."

He gave Evan one long, appraising look and then batted his eyelashes, literally, at Evan over the top of his bottle as he took a sip. Evan thought that he had the flirting part pretty down pat, at least. His body thought so too, and Evan had to shift to accommodate his suddenly interested cock.

"So you know that my lot in life is to live off my family's money," Riley said. "What do you do, Evan?"

19

Evan used the bite of bread and cheese in his mouth to decide how honestly to answer. *If he doesn't know*, he decided, *I'm not going to tell him. Not yet, anyway.*

Evan swallowed. "Modeling," he hedged. "Nothing fancy, probably nothing you've seen. But it's enough to pay the bills."

Riley's next look was even more frankly appraising than before. "I'm surprised. I wouldn't have guessed model, but only because I would have thought of Paris runways, and that doesn't exactly mesh well with someone who drinks whiskey and beer at Logger's."

Evan shook his head at that image. "No, nothing like that. More like… stock art, I guess is the best way to put it. I fly out for a shoot tomorrow."

Riley gave him a raised eyebrow but didn't dig. Instead, he reached for another small container and popped off the lid, holding it out so Evan could see the neat slices of peach lying inside. "Help yourself. I taste tested. It's amazing."

Evan had yet to see a fork, so he reached in with his fingers to pick up a slice and lifted it to his mouth. Juice oozed down his palm, but he ignored that and bit off about half the piece. Rich, sweet flavor burst across his tongue, and his eyes fell closed as he chewed and swallowed before popping the rest into his mouth.

"That might have been worth the cost of the entire shopping trip."

Evan opened his eyes to find Riley's focused on his mouth. As Evan watched, the tip of Riley's tongue came out to lick his lips, and a shiver ran through Evan. God, it had been so long since he'd been flirted with like this, sensual and gradual rather than blatantly sexual. Riley might not be his usual type, but his growing interest and frank appreciation definitely amped up his appeal.

Well, two could play at that game. Watching Riley's face, Evan slowly licked the sticky residue of the peach from his fingers, ending by sucking on his thumb longer than necessary. Riley swallowed and licked his lips again, gaze never leaving Evan's mouth, and Evan only barely resisted the urge to reach for him. His cock was certainly getting with the program fast, growing heavy and warm against his thigh.

Riley lifted his eyes to meet Evan's gaze. "I think I should cook dinner for you tonight," he murmured. "After we spend the afternoon having an appetizer or three."

Evan smiled slowly. "Or more," he added, watching heat flare in Riley's eyes. Yeah, he could get into this. He could *really* get into this.

THEY DID finish their picnic in the park. Riley never stopped flirting, but he dialed it back from eleven while they ate and then packed up the containers and leftovers. They even lay back side by side on the blanket and soaked in the sun for a while, exchanging comments about the cute dogs and hot men they saw pass by their spot.

Finally, Riley sat up and then rolled smoothly to his feet. "My vitamin D meter is full," he said, bending to pick up the picnic basket. "I'm ready to fill up something else."

His body jumping to attention, Evan stood as well before lifting the blanket and shaking it to knock off the grass and dust. He folded it loosely as Riley watched, his gaze focused and hot, and when Evan was finished, Riley reached for his hand and started walking, dragging him along, a willing captive.

"I hope you don't have any objections to my place." Riley's speech was fast, clipped, laced with impatience. "I know it sounds counterintuitive, but I much prefer bringing men there to meeting them somewhere impersonal or invading their spaces. I find being surrounded by familiarity allows me to relax and focus on them, rather than worrying about how recently the sheets were washed." He laughed lightly. "Yes, I will admit to being a bit fastidious about such things. But I do like my creature comforts."

Evan didn't try to interrupt. He just followed and listened to Riley chatter on as they crossed the side street and climbed the wide, curved stairs at the front of the Piedmont Lofts building. Riley paused and dropped Evan's hand long enough to punch in a code to unlock the front door, which Evan opened, and then Riley was pulling him again, across the high-ceilinged lobby to the elevators.

Inside, Riley finally stopped talking. He put his mouth to better use, lifting on his tiptoes to press his lips against Evan's. Evan curled his free hand around the back of Riley's neck, the silk of Riley's blond curls tickling his skin as they kissed.

Evan forgot sometimes how much he loved kissing. On camera, kisses were so often glossed over, just a checkbox to be marked off on the way to the fucking. In private, though, Evan liked to kiss the whole time, unless one or both mouths were busy elsewhere. Having his mouth fucked by a tongue and his ass fucked by a hard cock could make him come faster than almost anything.

He moaned into their kiss at the thought. He didn't think Riley was a top, but, God, he sure hoped he was at least somewhat versatile, because as much as Evan would enjoy fucking him, he'd love to get fucked for real too. He'd spent the day before getting fucked for the pleasure of the viewers. Today, he wanted it for his own pleasure.

The elevator dinged, and Evan reluctantly untangled himself from Riley as the doors slid open. His breathing rough, Riley led the way across the wide hallway to his door, once again letting Evan's hand go just long enough to get the door unlocked and open. Once they were both inside, Riley turned the deadbolt, set the picnic basket and his keys on the table next to the door, and wrapped himself around Evan again, this time with both hands and a leg.

Evan leaned against the closed door for support as he and Riley tried to devour each other with a voracious kiss. One of Evan's hands found its way back into Riley's soft hair, and the other cupped his perfect bubble butt and gave it a squeeze. Riley ground his hips against Evan's thigh, and Evan's hole clenched in anticipation at the size of the hard shaft he felt. Holy *hell*, he was definitely in favor of getting that inside him, versatile or not.

Riley must have read his mind, because he pulled out of the kiss and grinned up at Evan, rolling his hips again. "I hope you're flexible," he said, his lilting voice gone raspy with arousal. "Flip-flops aren't just something I like to wear on my feet."

Evan grinned back. "I think it's time you show me your bedroom."

CHAPTER 3

EVAN CAME awake from a light doze to the feel of Riley's mouth around his cock, one of the best wake-up calls he'd had in ages. He moaned and reached under the covers to slide his hands into Riley's curls. *Fuck*, he could suck cock like a pro. And Evan would know.

They'd sucked each other off earlier, after making out and playing around for a while, and then Riley had cuddled up and suggested a nap before round two. Looked like Riley was ready to go again, or so the tongue lapping at Evan's balls seemed to be telling him.

Riley's mouth disappeared, and the covers moved before Riley's head popped out. He grinned at Evan. "Fuck me," he said, and Evan had to laugh.

"Whatever you say."

Evan watched as Riley reached for a condom from the bowl on his night table. The (big) bottle of lube had already gotten some use, since their sixty-nine had come with bonus ass fingering on both sides. Riley grinned down at Evan as he settled across his thighs and ripped open the package. "Don't think I'm not still planning to turn this around at some point."

Evan reached for the condom and rolled it down over his cock with practiced ease. "I'm counting on it." He grabbed the lube and gave the latex a generous coating, then held his cock up straight. Riley didn't waste time, shifting up to hover over him for only a second before lowering his lithe body one slow, delicious inch at a time.

Evan moaned when he bottomed out inside. "Hot."

Riley gave him a dirty grin. "We're just getting started, honey."

The next fifteen minutes were an exercise in self-control like Evan hadn't experienced in years. Riley moved like a dancer above him, his hips rolling in slow counterpoint to the steady, fast pace he set. Strong muscles bunched and flexed in his thighs as he lifted himself up and then dropped back down, driving his body hard against Evan's, sending shockwaves out along every nerve ending. Evan ran his fingers up Riley's legs, feeling those muscles move, the light dusting of near-invisible hair like fine-grain sandpaper against his oversensitive skin.

This was what Evan had been missing: real sex. No cameras or direction, just two bodies coming together in whatever ways brought them the most pleasure. It didn't matter if no one could see where Evan's cock breached Riley's body, or whether Riley hid his cock from view when he bent forward to kiss Evan hard. Which he did, and often, and it made Evan want to wrap his arms around Riley and hold him there, fuck up into his tight hole until they both came, and then not let go.

He shook off the unwelcome, too-intimate thought. Instead, he braced his feet flat against the mattress and brought his own muscles into action, thrusting up each time Riley's body dropped toward his. He wriggled his hips, changing angles until Riley gasped and a mottled pink flush spread across his chest.

"Yeah," Riley breathed out. "That's it."

Evan grinned, though it felt like a grimace, and worked that same angle, knowing he was getting just the right spot inside Riley's body. Riley had been fairly quiet until then, but his prostate must've been the volume knob, because his noises got louder and more wanton until he finally grabbed his dick and started rubbing the head. Evan wrapped his fingers around Riley's hips and pounded him even harder, watching him lose control until Evan's own orgasm wouldn't be denied another second. His vision blurred and he groaned loudly, spurting three, four times inside the condom, his body jerking from overstimulation as Riley clamped down on him hard and his cum landed on Evan's stomach and chest.

For a long minute, they stayed frozen, Riley still perched on Evan's cock, one hand on the mattress next to Evan, the other holding his dick. Their harsh breathing echoed around them, until finally Riley moved, lifting his body off Evan's and rolling onto his side on the mattress. Eyes partly hidden by his dampened, curly bangs, he looked up at Evan.

"You're pretty fucking good at fucking."

Evan laughed roughly and reached down to yank off the condom. "You're pretty fucking good at riding," he returned as he tied off the latex. He turned to the side far enough that he could see the wastebasket and tossed the used condom away before rolling back to lie flat. The ceiling fan rotated slowly ahead, cooling the sweat on his skin. Evan let his eyes fall shut and breathed deep, enjoying the smell of sex and the warm lassitude stealing over his throbbing body.

Riley shifted on the mattress. "I'm going to take a quick shower, honey, and get some dinner going." A hand landed on Evan's leg. "You rest up. You earned it."

Evan smiled as Riley's lilting laughter trailed behind him. The bed and pillows were soft, the room cool, and Evan let himself drift off, content.

"WOW."

Evan stood in the entryway between the dining room and hall, having followed his nose from Riley's bedroom. He felt underdressed in the clothes he'd tugged back on after a quick-and-dirty cleanup, even though Riley was dressed just as casually as he carried a steaming dish in from the kitchen. He shot Evan an easy smile. "Hungry?"

Evan nodded, his attention still on the table, which was covered with a shimmery, cream-colored cloth and set with sparkling, silver-rimmed china, silver flatware, and crystal goblets. Deep red cloth napkins sat folded on the plates, and two matching candles burned in silver candlesticks.

"You didn't need to do all this." It was all Evan could think of to say, but Riley just laughed and stepped over to tug Evan into the room by one hand.

"This is what I do, honey," he said, directing Evan into the seat at the end of the table before taking his own seat next to him. "I like making things nice, and since I don't have to work for my money, I have the time, so why not?" He nodded toward the ice bucket sitting to one side. "If you'll pour the wine, I'll serve our plates. I hope you like seafood. This is one of my favorites, and it's so easy to make."

Evan poured the wine as directed, letting Riley's chatter wash over him as he took a sip of the sweet Riesling and watched Riley dish up what looked like enchiladas with a side of asparagus and large, fluffy rolls. He lifted an eyebrow at Riley. "Seafood... enchiladas?"

"Crepes," Riley corrected, setting down the last serving plate and pushing the butter dish Evan's way. "Not to say that I have anything against enchiladas! I had chicken and cheese enchiladas in Puerto Vallarta that would break your heart, they were so good, and I've been trying to find a recipe to do them justice ever since. I haven't quite gotten there yet, but I have one that's very close. Do you like Mexican food?"

Evan had just taken his first mouthful of crepe and blinked as the creamy, smooth flavor flowed over his tongue. "Mmmmm," he said as he swallowed. "This is amazing. Yeah, I love Mexican, Spanish, Tex-Mex, all of that. Lucas always said—"

He stopped, his eyes widening as he realized what he'd said. *Holy shit*. He couldn't remember the last time he'd said that name out loud. His stomach twisted, and he had to force himself to take another bite of the crepes. He forced a smile. "These are great, though. Did you have them in Mexico too?"

He hadn't fooled Riley, he could tell from the look on his face, but to his relief, Riley just shook his head. "Key West," he said. "Conch and shrimp there, but conch is so hard to find here, so I use lobster instead. But it's almost as good with whatever you have on hand. It's great for using up leftover fish and such." He smiled. "This is all fresh, though. I'm not feeding you what I didn't eat yesterday or anything."

Evan took another bite, concentrating on the rich flavor and pushing aside the thoughts he couldn't let intrude any further. He swallowed and took a sip of wine. "Puerto Vallarta, Key West... do you travel just to collect recipes, or is that a side benefit?"

Riley patted his lips with his napkin. "I travel for work." He shrugged one shoulder. "I know I don't actually *have* to work, but I can't do nothing. I've tried it." He shuddered. "I do design, of whatever kind strikes my fancy. I'm not much of an artist, but I can put together rooms, parties, clothes. I take jobs that appeal to me. Mostly I work for friends, or for charities. They get a bargain because I don't charge them much, and I get to have fun."

Evan nodded and kept eating. He hadn't realized how hungry he was, and the crepes were amazingly good. Riley didn't seem to mind. He kept right on talking around his own mouthfuls, telling Evan about a charity event he'd worked on a few weeks earlier. Evan remembered seeing an ad or an article about it, something with the art museum. Not his kind of thing. He liked art, and he'd been to the museum, but he figured the rich people gave them plenty of money. He'd rather put his more limited funds toward groups that needed it more.

Before he realized it, he'd finished eating, even wiping up a bit of the cream sauce with the last piece of bread. He finished his second glass of wine and wiped his mouth. "That was amazing," he said, setting down his napkin and giving Riley a smile. "I've been to Key West too, and nothing I ate there was as good as that."

Riley practically glowed from the praise. Evan thought he might have even seen a slight blush, though it was hard to tell, since Riley already had a hint of sun-kissed pink on his face and possibly some residual flush from their bedroom activities. Riley stood and began gathering up dishes. "Let me get this all put away, and—"

Evan stopped him with a hand on his arm. "You cooked and set all this up. The least I can do is clean up."

Riley smiled at him, his eyes suddenly shy, and Evan's heart flipped in his chest. Was this a glimpse of the real Riley, hidden under all the teasing and devil-may-care attitude? Evan knew all about building walls to protect a soft core. Had Riley done the same thing?

"I'm just going to rinse these, honey." Riley moved away, and his expression slid back into its usual expression. "I have a housekeeper to deal with the rest of it. No need to put yourself out."

Evan gave in, not willing to push over something that just wasn't that big a deal, especially when this was just supposed to be a hookup. *On the other hand*, he thought, as he helped carry their dishes into the kitchen, *when was the last time a hookup did more than make scrambled eggs and coffee for breakfast the morning after?* A picnic lunch and a gourmet-quality dinner made this far from a typical hookup.

Still, he left Riley to his rinsing, and he'd just finished wiping his hands on a kitchen towel when his phone vibrated in his pocket. He dug it out and looked at the number but didn't recognize it. Not unusual. He got calls from studios and their directors fairly often. He shrugged and answered.

"Hello?"

"Hello, Evan."

Evan's knees nearly gave out. He hadn't heard the voice in years, but it wasn't like he'd ever forget it.

"Mom?"

Evan saw Riley shoot him a curious look over his shoulder. He stepped out of the kitchen and around the corner. "How did—" He cut himself off from asking how she'd gotten his number. He'd had the same one for years; he wasn't sure, but it might not have changed since the last time they'd talked. Either way, he didn't want to start things off with an argument. "I mean, it's nice to hear from you, Mom. How are you? Is anything wrong?"

"We're fine, dear." Her voice shook, just enough for Evan to hear it. "Could we… could we see each other, Evan? In person?"

Evan's body jolted inside, as if he'd touched a live wire. The last time he'd seen either of his parents, his father told him he was a disgrace to the family name and no son of his. The words hadn't come as a surprise. Being gay would've been bad enough for his conservative parents, but being dishonorably discharged from the Marine Corps as a result might carry an even heavier weight. He'd never expected to see them again unless by chance.

"I…. Mom, are you sure?"

"Yes, dear. I know it's a surprise, but I think we have some things to talk about."

Evan's mind raced. "I'm… I'm on the road now, but I'll be back in Atlanta in a few days." The lie came out without him even realizing it. It wasn't much of a stretch, since he'd be leaving for his shoot in Fort Lauderdale the next day.

"I can meet any time this week. Would you be free for dinner Friday night?"

Five days to get used to the idea. Evan thought he might be able to handle that.

"Okay," he agreed. "Can you…. If you want to pick a place, just text me or call and leave a message if I don't answer."

"I will." She paused for a long moment. "It's wonderful to hear your voice, Evan. I'll be looking forward to seeing you."

Evan was sure he gave some kind of reasonable response before he hung up, but it wasn't until he slid the phone back into his pocket that he realized he was trembling all over. He leaned against the wall in Riley's nicely decorated hallway and watched his hands shake.

"Honey, are you okay?"

Evan lifted his head to find Riley standing a couple of feet away, a blend of concern and curiosity on his face. Evan managed a jerky nod.

"Yeah." He pushed off the wall. "Just an unexpected call. I haven't heard from my mom in… a long time."

Riley shifted on his feet, and Evan could almost see a wall go up between them. "Well, I'm happy for you," Riley said, his voice light, lilting, and obviously false. "It's been great having you, but I do have a few things I need to take care of. Do you need a lift back to your place?"

Wow. Evan blinked at the blatant dismissal. He shook his head. "No, it's not far. I can walk it."

Riley's expression softened. "I'm sorry. I didn't mean to sound like I was kicking you out. I really *do* have an appointment later, though. Oh!" He brightened and half turned toward the kitchen. "Let me give you a few things to take home. I can't possibly eat all these peaches and tomatoes before they rot."

Evan followed, confused by Riley's sudden changes in mood. He watched as Riley moved between cabinets and refrigerator, pulling out several items and sliding them into a green canvas bag.

"Here you go," he said, holding out the bag by its handles. "Tomatoes, peaches, cheese, and even a bottle of that wonderful ginger ale. Don't worry about the bag," he added, waving his free hand. "I've got dozens. Can't seem to resist buying them everywhere I go!"

Evan took the bag, still not sure what had just happened between them, but he smiled anyway. "Thanks for the picnic and dinner and... everything." He took a chance and leaned in for a kiss, which Riley accepted. "See you around?"

Riley smiled again. "I'm sure you will," he said, back to his flirtatious self. "I know I'll be keeping an eye out, now that I've had a sample."

CHAPTER 4

RILEY'S PARTING shot helped, but Evan couldn't shake off the lingering feeling of rejection. He'd hoped to spend a little more time with Riley, maybe get a turn at bottoming. At least Riley had seemed interested in getting together again, so Evan always could try again.

Still, his steps dragged as he trudged up Eleventh toward home, the new-penny brightness of the day tarnished as night snuck in. He thought about stopping by one of the bars he passed as he walked through the heart of Atlanta's "gayborhood," the pounding music and flashing lights designed to draw people in.

But he didn't feel up to all that tonight. He didn't much relish the idea of sitting alone with his thoughts, either, but at least it would take less energy. He still needed to pack, anyway, and his flight left at ten the next morning, so he'd need to be up no later than eight to get to the airport.

Dodging a group of twinks dressed in tight shorts, tank tops, and brightly colored sneakers, Evan turned the corner toward his apartment building. This was one of the times he was glad he'd been able to find a place cheap enough that he hadn't been forced into having a roommate. Sure, the apartment's "one-bedroom" description had been shaky at best, considering only a half wall separated the "bedroom" and "living room." A glorified studio, in reality, but it worked for him.

He slipped inside the tiny entryway of the building, skipping the mailboxes and heading up the flight of stairs to his floor. The building was quiet, not unusual for a Sunday night, since it was inhabited mostly by other young gay men who were probably out getting in the last gasp of the weekend at bars like the ones he'd passed up on his walk. Evan got inside his apartment without running into anyone, locked his door, and stopped off in the kitchen to grab a beer. He popped off the lid and tossed it on the counter before wandering over to sit on the bed. He pushed a few of his collection of a half-dozen pillows up against the headboard to cushion his back and leaned back, sipping at his beer and staring at the plastic stars that glowed on the ceiling. Some previous tenant had put up constellations all over the space, the Big Dipper directly above the bed and Orion above the sofa, and the landlord hadn't bothered to try to remove them. Evan didn't care. There were worse things in the world than stars on your ceiling.

Unbidden, Evan's mind wandered to a different view of the stars, on a dark night in the desert. He'd been on sentry duty, guarding his platoon mates while they slept in their tents, when his relief had arrived in the form of Lucas Chavez.

"Hey, hombre, your turn to hit the hay." Lucas grinned at him, teeth shining in the moonlight. "I kept the cot warm for ya."

Evan remembered the warmth, not from the bed, but from the feeling that Lucas's smile gave him. He'd wanted to kiss the curve of those lips, but even with no one else in sight, the danger of exposure or worse was too great. Instead, he'd let his fingers brush along Lucas's thigh as they switched positions. Lucas didn't say a thing, but the swift intake of breath told Evan everything he needed to know.

Lying on his bed in comfort, drinking his beer, he let himself remember.

IT WAS Evan's third day at Parris Island when he first realized he was gay. He'd dated girls back home, but mostly because everyone else did, and with all his studying, he didn't really have time for a relationship anyway.

On his third day in South Carolina, he met Lucas Chavez.

Lucas was an inch or so below Evan's height, broader and more muscular, but still lean overall. His skin was the color of toasted sugar, a warm, rich shade of brown that made Evan want to lick him to find out if he tasted as sweet as he looked. Lucas's smile was bright white against his skin, his hair and eyes black as night. Evan tried not to stare, but Lucas woke up parts of Evan's mind and body he hadn't even known existed.

He knew then exactly how much trouble he was in.

He saw Lucas only a handful of times in boot camp, though he knew he'd always carry the image of him at the ceremony marking the end of their basic training. Just as their drill sergeant had promised three and a half months earlier, they'd been transformed from children into Marines, and Lucas had looked every inch the part, all hard muscles and tight discipline from the high-and-tight haircut under his cover to the tips of his shining black boots.

Evan and Lucas had gone their separate ways after that, though Evan had carried the image of Lucas's smile with him. He jacked off to it more than once, though he couldn't bring himself to do any more than that, not that the desert and the Marine Corps left him much time for even the acceptable forms of R&R.

It was on the way to his second deployment in Afghanistan a year later that Evan was astonished to find himself on the same flight as none other than Lucas Chavez. Lucas hadn't changed much, just a bit more honing and bulk to his already perfect body, as much from adding another year of age as from the hard, physical work of being a Marine in a combat zone. Lucas grinned when he saw Evan.

"Hey, hombre. How you manage out there in the desert without goin' up in flames? All that lily-white skin."

Evan didn't know if he should be amused or offended, but Lucas's crooked smile and the wink he gave made Evan smile and relax. Lucas, he learned, was on his first trip to Afghanistan, after a deployment in Kuwait.

"Crazy country, hombre." Lucas shook his head and leaned in closer, lowering his voice so the people around them didn't hear. (Evan tried to ignore the looks they got at the airport, two men in desert-drab fatigues. Everyone stared.) "You know they pay, like, ten cents a liter for gas? Get a couple gallons for a buck. Sure makes me wish I had a couple oil rigs back home in Texas like some folks do. 'Course, then I wouldn't need to be sweatin' in the desert for a livin'."

Evan could have listened to—okay, watched—Lucas talk for the entire trip halfway around the world. Layovers and all, Atlanta to London to Landstuhl, ten-plus hours in the air and nearly fourteen in transit by the time they landed in Germany. There they stopped, still a good eight hours out of Kabul, stranded by a freak early October snowstorm that grounded their flight overnight. Lucas turned on the charm at the USO office and managed to get them rebooked on a flight late the next morning and nabbed a room at the hotel nearest the airport.

When they got to their room, Evan didn't expect anything more than some conversation and a decent night's sleep. He was shocked when, after locking the door firmly behind them, Lucas dropped his duffel on the floor, took Evan's face in both of his rough hands, and kissed him like it was the most natural thing in the world.

Because it was.

That night, Evan learned who he really was for the first time. Lucas taught him everything he knew, even though he admitted readily it was just the tip of the iceberg. But when Lucas slid his fingertips firmly across that spot inside Evan's ass and sucked Evan's dick hard, Evan swore he'd found all the answers he'd ever need. Nothing had ever felt so good, and when Lucas jerked himself off until he spurted across Evan's stomach and chest, Evan just wanted to stay locked up in that tiny room forever.

Forever lasted only ten hours.

HE LURCHED into chaos. Someone grabbed his arm, and he looked up to see a young female medic looking into his face. Her mouth moved, but he couldn't hear a thing. Concussion deafness, *his mind supplied, and he shook his head at her, dazed. She ran her gaze over him, a hand down his arm, and he winced when her fingers pressed against his elbow. She reached for his other arm, saying something again that he couldn't hear, but he pulled away and turned back toward the men, desperate, looking for the only person he cared about in that moment.*

The men at the transport had pulled the body away from the flames, and one of them looked up in time to meet Evan's eyes. The way

34

the man's eyes widened, followed by the slow shake of his head, didn't register with Evan at first. When it did, Evan's knees buckled.

No. *He didn't know if he was making any sound; he still couldn't hear, not even inside his own head. But he could feel his throat searing, and as he staggered closer, he could see Lucas's face, eyes wide open, staring up at him, a mask of death.*

Evan fell to the sand, arms reaching out, wrapping around his best friend, his lover, the man he'd never be able to hold again.

EVAN TORE himself out of the dream, jolting upright in his bed at the images seared onto his brain. Lucas had bled out into the Afghan sand, body singed and charred by the fire, and Evan couldn't do a damn thing to stop it. His arms ached as if he still held his lover's body, still screamed out denials into the arid air.

He'd thought losing his brother to an Iraqi IED the worst moment of his life, until another bomb in another desert proved him wrong.

Skin clammy with sweat and remembered horror, Evan dragged himself up and into the bathroom. He turned the shower on as hot as he could stand and stripped off his damp clothes before throwing them into the hamper in the corner. He pushed the shower curtain back, stepped into the tub, and moved under the spray, letting it pound down on his body and wash away the physical evidence of his nightmare.

If only he could shower away his memories.

Determined to shake it off, as usual, Evan reached for the shampoo and went through the lather, rinse, repeat process on autopilot. He followed that with body wash, scrubbing away the last remnants of sweat on his skin, and then he stood under the spray again, letting the heat loosen the tight muscles in his back and shoulders.

When the water started to cool, he forced himself to shut it off. After drying off from head to toe and brushing his teeth thoroughly, he grabbed his toiletry bag and checked it for the necessities—travel shampoo and shave gel, razor and blades, toothbrush and toothpaste, condoms and lube—before heading into the bedroom.

Another week, another city, he thought, tossing his carry-on onto the bed to pack for his trip.

THE FLIGHT to Fort Lauderdale left on time, arrived early, and didn't bounce around a lot in between, which was better than average. The whole trip—via sidewalk, MARTA, "plane train," and 737—took just under three hours, not counting the waits in the security line and at the gate. Evan had made the trip so many times he could almost do it blindfolded, though he imagined the TSA agents wouldn't find it funny.

The cab line was nonexistent, so in minutes Evan was headed to the studio-slash-house for his shoot. Manclub kept a steady stream of models flowing in and out of their sprawling oceanfront location, which had setups for everything from poolside shoots on the patio to a dungeon playroom in the basement. Two large bedrooms with en suite bathrooms handled the bulk of the work, though, and smaller bedrooms at the end of the house served as sleeping space for the models. It was all very efficiently run, and Evan had never had a problem during the shoots there, but he'd never been interested in the exclusive contracts some of the models had, either. He'd had an agent for a few years at the start of his career, but now he handled his own bookings. He preferred to keep as much control as he could.

It took only about twenty minutes to get to the house, and Evan paid the cabbie a little extra because he'd actually made an effort to help with Evan's suitcase, even though he hadn't needed it. The three-day shoot would pay well, and with everything else covered for the trip, he could afford to be generous.

As he walked toward the front door, Evan forced himself to make the mental shift into Trevor Hardball. He didn't have to put on a completely different persona like some porn models did, but he'd need to remember to answer to—and use—the right name for the next few days. By the time the door opened in response to the doorbell, he'd settled into the switch.

Rod Zane, the studio's second-in-command—which meant he was the one who really kept things running—greeted Trevor with his trademark lopsided smile and one-armed hug. "Hey, Trev, glad you're here. Come on in. Good to see you, as always!"

Trevor stepped inside and gave a small smile in return. "Good to see you too."

Rod, who wore a small square-cut swimsuit that showed off his hard abs, nodded down the hall. "Drop your bag and we'll go over the shoot. You remember where everything is?"

"I should." Trevor laughed. "I've been here enough!"

Rod grinned widely. "You could be here more if you'd ever take that exclusive!"

Trevor shook his head. "You know I'd just cause trouble, man. I'm a loose cannon!"

"Suuuuure you are." Rod smacked his shoulder lightly. "Go on and get settled and meet me out by the pool. Too gorgeous a day to spend inside if we don't have to."

Trevor nodded and headed down the hall to the back bedrooms. One door was closed, but the other was open and the room looked empty, so he went into that one and dropped his bag on one of the two double beds. The bedrooms were set up like stripped-down hotel rooms, with two beds covered in tropical-print bedspreads, nightstands with lamps and clocks, and a long dresser on one wall with a decently sized flat-screen TV on top. He knew that if he looked in the nightstand drawers, or in the bathroom vanity drawers, he'd find a stash of condoms and lube. Get a group of young, mostly gay men together in a house filled with sexual energy, and it was inevitable that some of it would spill over outside the shoots.

Trevor changed into his own swimsuit and switched out the sneakers he'd worn on his flight for the flip-flops that everyone wore in Florida before he headed back down the hallway and through the open glass door onto the patio. Rod had stretched out on one of the lounge chairs, and Trevor grabbed a bottle of water out of the ice-filled cooler sitting nearby before heading over to sit on the chair next to Rod's. He kicked off his flip-flops and swung his legs up to stretch out, letting out a sigh as the warmth of the sun soaked into his skin.

Rod laughed. "Feels great, doesn't it?" He sighed happily too. "Wish I could get paid to just lie here like this. Maybe take a dip in the pool or the ocean now and then."

Trevor smiled. "But you've got a job to do."

"Yep." Rod turned his head toward Trevor. "This one's pretty simple, though. We'll do some promo stills tomorrow, so don't lay out here too long or you'll be all red. Then there's the party at Club Hurricane tomorrow night, and they're looking for a couple of extra dancers, if you want to rack up some extra cash. Not required." He laughed. "Well, the party is a promo, so it's part of the deal, but the dancing is extra."

"Got it." Trevor shrugged. "I didn't bring anything for a show, but I can shake my ass in my underwear."

"They'll probably have some kind of promo stuff for that too, so you might not have to wear your own. Anyway, primary shoot on Wednesday, and we'll do any pickup stuff we need before everyone heads home on Thursday. Then we're done."

Trevor nodded. "Who am I shooting with?"

"Lex Kent, mainly," Rod answered. "Sam Silver and Aron Fox are booked too, but it'll be two separate shoots. We might do some stills or crossover if we have time, but we have a big shoot scheduled over the weekend, so we need some time in between to get some editing done and set up for that."

Trevor nodded. He didn't know Lex or Aron, but he'd worked with Sam a few years earlier. Considering Sam was a tall, muscle-bound black man who tended to be paired with blond twinks for the contrast, he expected Aron to fit that mold, but then, he'd been surprised before. He'd find out about Lex when he showed up, he supposed. He'd known barely half of his scene partners before the shoots. In many cases, the men came into the industry, got their rocks off and made a little cash, and then moved on. Models who made a career of it like he had were the exception, not the rule.

Rod fell silent, and Trevor lay still, letting the sun's rays soak into his skin, the warmth loosening tight muscles. Trevor liked to travel, but cramming his long legs into a coach seat for even a short flight was never fun. He suffered through, though, saving up his miles for business-class upgrades on cross-country flights and for the occasional fun trip. He'd spent last Christmas on the beach in San Juan thanks to a year's worth of flights for shoots.

A doorbell sounded, much too clearly to be the standard front doorbell, and Trevor opened one eye to look at Rod, who shrugged in response. "We finally rewired it to be sure we could hear it from out here," he said, swinging his legs over and pushing to his feet. "Has a switch so we can turn the whole thing off during shoots too."

Handy, Trevor thought as he closed his eye. He wouldn't have thought about the problems something as simple as a doorbell could cause, but he guessed that trial and error would teach those lessons, if nothing else. He'd never particularly wanted to work behind the camera in porn, but he supposed it could be interesting, working out little details like that.

After a few minutes, a boisterous laugh rang out from the doorway, and Trevor opened his eyes and glanced toward the house. He froze. The man standing next to Rod, nodding at whatever the man was telling him, had dark caramel skin, black hair, and a sleek, lightly furred body that Trevor felt like he already knew intimately. This must be his scene partner, Lex. Trevor's stomach clenched.

Lex could've been Lucas's brother.

Not his twin, though. Trevor could see differences even without being up close. The longer hair, for one, though Trevor too had long lost the military cut. Lex's skin was darker and his body hair more sparse than Lucas's, though Trevor didn't know if either might be the result of tanning beds and manscaping rather than nature. He appeared to be taller than Lucas too, probably exactly Trevor's height.

He's not Lucas, Trevor told himself. *He's just a guy*.

A guy Trevor would have to have sex with. On camera, where he had to stay focused and in control.

Trevor's stomach twisted again, and he dropped his head back against the chaise and blew out a breath. *It'll be fine.*

With enough repetition, even a lie could become the truth.

CHAPTER 5

THE ONLY thing that kept Trevor from getting blasted Tuesday night was the knowledge that he had to film the next day. The stills shoot that afternoon had been slow torture. Everywhere he turned, there was Lex, wearing next to nothing, his smile too much like Lucas's for Trevor's comfort. He'd gotten through the four hours of photography on pure grit and determination, coming out the other side mentally and emotionally exhausted.

When they got to the club, Trevor strapped on every bit of acting ability and charm he possessed and smiled his way through the event, selling shots to fans from the floor and taking tips from them when he took his turn dancing on a raised platform. The shot money would be pooled and divided up later, after the club got its cut, but the dancing tips went into his duffel bag every time he took a break and slipped into the back room to suck down some water. He ended up taking a few shots, bought by overeager club patrons, but between the water and the dancing, he barely felt a buzz.

He knew several of the other performers in the bar that night had more than just alcohol in their systems. Even if he hadn't seen pills changing hands, he'd learned long ago what went on behind the scenes at these events. Hell, he'd indulged himself more than once, but the aftermath never seemed to make up for the high. Liquor and maybe some poppers sometimes were plenty for him.

When the club finally shut down at two in the morning, Trevor's ears rang and his head throbbed from overstimulation. He craved a cigarette like crazy too, especially since he had to deal with the downside of staying mostly sober: having to help manage his costars who'd overindulged. Trevor helped Rod get everyone loaded into the van Manclub had rented and pulled himself into the front passenger seat as Rod slid behind the wheel.

Trevor tipped his head to the side to rest against the door and closed his eyes, the van's swaying lulling him nearly to sleep by the time they got back to the house. Thankfully, everyone in the back had sobered up enough during the drive to get themselves inside, so Trevor just stopped by the kitchen to grab a bottle of water before walking to the back bedroom where he'd left his bag.

He got there to find the second bed had been claimed by Lex.

Trevor's stomach sank, but he forced himself not to react. "Good night?" he asked, moving over to set his water on the table between the beds and then toeing off his shoes.

"Haven't counted the take, but not too bad." Lex flashed him a grin, teeth bright white against his dark skin. "Nice to have a crowd that into the show. Usually a lot more dry back home."

"Where's home?" If he was going to work with the guy, he'd be polite, at least.

"Houston. Well, Monterrey, technically, but don't nobody know that but me and my mamma." He laughed. "She got across the border when I was just a baby. No one ever asked. Just figured I was her anchor baby."

Trevor wondered if the studio knew, or cared, about Lex's immigration status. INS wasn't likely to come knocking on their door. "Yeah, Atlanta's pretty dry on club dates." He pushed off his shorts and tossed them toward his bag where it sat next to the wall. "I'm kinda beat, man. You mind if I shower first? I'm just gonna rinse off and then sleep."

"No problem." Lex dug in his bag and pulled out a zippered plastic bag full of green leaves. "Aron and me gonna meet on the patio for a smoke. Sure you don't wanna join us?"

Weed was one thing Trevor didn't mind at all, and on a different night, he might've accepted the invitation. Not this time, though. Not when he'd have to look at Lex and try not to think about Lucas.

41

"Nah, you guys enjoy. See you in the morning."

He stripped his tank top over his head and dropped it on his bag as he walked toward the bathroom. He'd have enough to worry about tomorrow. Tonight, he just wanted to sleep.

"UP AND at 'em, boys!"

At the pounding on the door and yell from the hallway, Trevor groaned and pulled a pillow over his head. It couldn't be morning yet. He'd *just* fallen asleep, hours after Lex had stumbled back in, high as a kite on God knows what but humming happily under his breath.

He reached out a hand and snagged his cell phone from where it lay on the bedside table. Squinting, he read the time: 10:23. *Dammit.* He had to be ready to shoot at noon, and between showering, shaving, douching, and fighting others for bathroom time, that would take an hour, minimum.

He sat up slowly and waited for the room to stop spinning. The handful of shots he'd had the night before all seemed to be hitting him now, no matter how little biological sense that made. He needed caffeine, but coffee and bottoming were a bad combination for him. Maybe someone had some Excedrin or something he could borrow.

Bracing himself, Trevor pushed to his feet and stumbled toward the bathroom, pausing to drop his briefs next to his duffel bag and grab his toiletries bag on the way. He turned on the shower full blast and peed while the water warmed up, then climbed under the spray and just let it soak him down for a few minutes.

Finally, he dug out his shampoo and body wash and scrubbed himself down from head to toe, paying particular attention to his groin and ass. He rinsed off and let the water pound against his stiff shoulders for another couple of minutes before turning the shower off and climbing out to grab a towel.

He hated douching, but enemas were the best way to keep things from getting messy on set, so he took care of that bit of unpleasantness as quickly as possible. He finished up with a careful shave and a long session with his toothbrush, scrubbing away the remnants of last night's partying.

He was surprised no one had tried to come in while he was busy getting ready, but when he got back to the bedroom, he found out why. Lex was still curled up under his covers, dead to the world. *Great*, Trevor thought, dropping his towel and pulling on fresh underwear. *Now I get to try to roust my scene partner out of bed on top of everything.*

"Hey, Lex," he started. "Time to get moving. We start in, like, forty-five minutes." Nothing. "Lex?" Trevor stepped closer. "You in there?"

He shook Lex's shoulder, and Lex flopped like a fish. Trevor's stomach clenched. "Lex?"

He shook again, harder this time, and Lex fell onto his back, revealing the puddle of vomit he'd been lying in. Trevor flinched away for a second, but then the medical training from his military time kicked in, and he jumped forward.

"Lex?" He was yelling now. "I need some help in here!" He leaned close to Lex's nose, stomach rebelling against the smell of vomit, alcohol, and urine, and placed a hand on Lex's chest. Lex wasn't breathing, and Trevor couldn't feel a heartbeat. "Somebody call 911!" Trevor shouted as he set himself to start chest compressions.

He'd only counted out six compressions when Rod walked into the room. "What's going—Lex?" He ran to the side of the bed.

"Call 911!" Trevor demanded again, never slowing down his work. He saw someone else appear at the doorway. "Call an ambulance!" The person at the door disappeared, and Trevor hoped like hell they were finally going to call someone, though he knew it was probably too late for Lex. He wasn't responding, and Trevor had no way to know how long he'd been under.

Memories pushed at the corners of his mind, and he pushed them back, hard. The last time he'd done this had been during basic training, working on a dummy as part of the standard medic training that all recruits underwent. He'd thought about going the medic route for his career field, but they'd been full up when he enlisted. The last time he'd been face-to-face with Marine medics had been in the desert, as they worked futilely over Lucas's body.

"Hey, don't you need to, like, breathe or something?"

"Been too long since I was trained." Trevor never stopped working. "Compression alone works too. They changed the guidelines a few years ago."

Another person joined them. "Liam is on the phone with 911. You need relief?"

Trevor's arms were burning. "Can you do rescue breathing?"

"Yeah." The other man—Sam, Trevor finally realized—climbed onto the bed and tilted Lex's head, positioning it to open his airway. He pinched Lex's nose shut and nodded. Trevor paused his movements, and Sam bent down to give two short puffs of air. He lifted his head and Trevor went back to his compressions.

"Do thirty," Sam said, reaching for Lex's wrist to check for a pulse. Trevor counted under his breath, then paused for Sam to breathe again. He didn't try to keep track of how many rounds of compressions and breathing they did, but he was just about to ask if they could switch places or someone could take over for him when there was a commotion in the hallway and then—thank God—paramedics were dashing into the room.

Trevor dragged himself away from Lex's body and fell onto the other bed, his arm and shoulder muscles screaming at him. He'd be sore for days, probably, but he pushed that thought away. Lex still wasn't breathing. He'd never felt anything like a heartbeat. He looked at Sam, who stood on the far side of the bed, back against the wall. When their eyes met, Sam shook his head, and Trevor's heart fell into his stomach.

Jesus Christ. Why hadn't he checked on Lex before he got in the shower? He might have been okay if he'd been found an hour ago, when Trevor first woke up. He would've had a better chance, at least.

Someone put a bottle of water in Trevor's line of sight, and he took it without thought, opened it, and drained half of it in one long draught. He shivered, suddenly cold, and reached to pull the bedspread around himself. He watched the activity with a sort of clinical detachment, mentally cataloging and naming the procedures and equipment he recognized. One of the paramedics continued chest compressions, but a breathing bag had been inserted, and a second person provided breaths at a steadier rate. A third worker called out numbers and relayed information through her radio. The leads to an emergency defibrillator had been placed on Lex's chest, but the defibrillator unit lay to one side, unused.

He knew when the guy doing the compressions paused that he wouldn't be starting back. He scrutinized the readouts, looked at his coworkers, and shook his head.

Trevor's head pounded and his stomach twisted. He couldn't be there any longer. He shoved the blanket away, ignored the hand that landed on his arm, and left the room.

He didn't know where he was going. Outside seemed like a good idea.

He stopped at the edge of the pool and stared down at the water. A light breeze rippled the surface, and the late-morning Florida sun painted the vibrant blue with flecks of shimmering gold. Trevor's brain told him the image was beautiful, but he didn't feel it. He might as well have been looking at a landfill.

Lucas's body, broken and burned, lay limp in his arms. Lifeless. Spirit gone, taking Evan's heart with it.

"Trev?"

A hand landed on his arm again, and Trevor let it stay. "Hon, we got your bag moved into the other room." Rod's voice stayed low and gentle, so unlike his usual boisterous self. "Why don't you come get dressed?"

Trevor swayed toward the water. "What about the shoot?"

Rod's fingers tightened. "Don't worry about the shoot, hon. We'll take care of things for you. Come on in and get dressed, have some breakfast. Okay?"

Trevor nodded once. "Okay." But he didn't move until Rod slid his hand down to wrap around Trevor's and tugged him back toward the house.

MANCLUB GOT Trevor on a flight home late that night. They'd briefly debated going ahead with the shoot the next day, reworked into a threesome instead of two pairs, but abandoned that idea when no one could stay on task long enough to make the arrangements. Instead, Trevor left Fort Lauderdale on the last flight back to Atlanta

Wednesday night, arriving just before midnight and barely making the last MARTA train to Midtown.

As the train emerged from the downtown tunnels and phone service kicked back in, an e-mail notification alert sounded. Trevor pulled up the e-mail and didn't recognize the name at first, but then he remembered seeing the guy mentioned online from time to time.

Dear Trevor, the message read. *We would like to book you to shoot a scene with Erato in two weeks. We shoot in my apartment in northern Atlanta. As you may have heard, Erato is dedicated to filming scenes that focus on intimacy and emotion. We encourage kissing, touching, and physical closeness, even when it results in camera angles that are less than optimal under the usual standards for adult films. We try to book scene partners based on compatibility, and your name was suggested by a mutual friend to work with Adam Manning, who we've already booked. Our rates are within standard range for a straightforward shoot (no kink and minimum stills) and are negotiable. If you are interested, please contact me as soon as you can so that we can finalize our plans.*

The e-mail finished up with a phone number. Trevor rarely turned down shoots, but he was too tired to figure out if he was free in two weeks. He'd deal with that in the morning. The train was pulling into his stop, and it would take all of his mental and physical energy to walk the several blocks home.

Fifteen minutes later, he unlocked his apartment door and stepped inside to a sauna. "Ugh," he muttered. He always set the thermostat to keep the unit from running a lot when he left town, but that made coming home a miserable experience sometimes. He kicked the temperature down and waited for cool air to start blowing before he dragged his bag into the bedroom, where he toed off his shoes, stripped to the skin, and then fell onto the mattress in the dark. He needed water, and he needed to pee, but his body had had enough.

He slept.

BUT NOT for long.

In some ways, the nightmare was familiar: harsh sun, gritty sand, and Lucas's crumpled body. But a bright, crystalline-blue pool glimmered next to the overturned transport, the medics working on Lucas wore not desert-sand BDUs but dark blue polyester pants and shirts, and Marines standing to the side mingled with jockstrap-wearing twinks.

Evan looked down at the body in his arms and saw Lex's face, eyes wide and smile a rictus, frozen in death.

The scream tore his throat as he woke, and he gasped for breath. Images tumbled through his mind—sand and sun, fire and water, sex and skin, Lucas and Lex in life and in death.

He thought the top of his head would blow off from the pressure.

Evan scrambled for the bathroom, making it there in time to spew what little he had in his stomach. More bile than anything else hit the water, and he gagged again at the smell before flushing the mess away. Closing his eyes, he forced himself to breathe slowly and deeply, fighting off another wave of nausea, until he thought he could move without losing it again.

He stood carefully and washed out his mouth at the sink. He wanted a shower, but the way his head pounded told him something to drink and maybe to eat should probably come first. He padded into the kitchen and found a bottle of Gatorade in the door of the refrigerator. He didn't remember where it came from, but it was still sealed and the expiration date was a month away, so he opened it and took a few sips. Once it seemed like they'd stay down, he drank more deeply, bracing one hip against the counter.

He tried to keep his mind clear, with only partial success. When he'd first seen Lex and his resemblance to Lucas, he'd been worried about how he'd react to filming with him. Evan shook his head, his mouth twisting. Instead, he'd ended up with another layer added to the worst moment of his life. Now he had images of *two* dead men in his own personal horror show.

And that didn't even count his brother, whose body he hadn't seen.

That thought reminded Evan of his dinner with his parents. He had an extra day now, with his trip cut short, which just meant that much more time to build himself into a giant knot of anxiety. He needed something to fill the time. Something more than sleep, which was fast encroaching.

Unbidden, Riley's smiling face flashed into his mind. Evan hadn't thought of him on the trip, too distracted by everything else, but maybe he'd try to hook up with him again over the weekend. Evan cursed under his breath when he realized he hadn't thought to get Riley's number, but he did know where he lived.

He shook his head. He'd figure it out in the morning. He drained the Gatorade bottle, tossed it toward the trash can, and headed back to the bathroom. A quick shower to wash away the grime from travel and the sweat from his nightmare, and maybe this time he'd actually make it until morning.

A BUZZING noise dragged Evan from sleep, but it took him a couple of minutes to figure out it was his phone ringing. By the time he found it where it had fallen on the floor between his bed and night table, the call had gone to voice mail, but the screen still showed the caller. COCO LAMÉ, the screen read, and Evan rolled his eyes, redialing the number and remembering the dinner a couple of months back when his best friend, Cory Lassiter, had laughingly grabbed Evan's phone and changed his contact to his shiny-new drag name.

"Hey, honey, I didn't wake you, did I?" Cory sounded truly sorry, a rarity for him, and Evan had to smile.

"Yeah, but I should probably have been awake for a while." He glanced at the alarm clock and saw it was after ten. "What's up?"

"I just got your message about what happened in Florida and wanted to check on you." *I left a message?* Evan thought. He didn't even remember calling. "I can't imagine having to deal with that," Cory said. "Are you okay?"

Cory clucked at him like the mother hen he had a tendency to be with everyone, but particularly with Evan. The seven-year age difference played into that, but also the fact that Cory had mentored Evan's older brother on their high school football team and stepped into a brotherly role after Charlie died.

"Yeah," Evan repeated. He reached behind him to rearrange his pillows and then reached for the bottle of water on the bedside table. "It was pretty fucking crazy, man. He just…." Evan shuddered, unwilling to relive the scene again. "I can't believe it."

"I can't either." Cory blew out a quick breath. "Listen, honey, I'm having some people over for a cookout tonight. I didn't ask you because I thought you were gonna be gone, but since you're back, you want to come? Might help to be around people."

Evan's shoulder relaxed at the thought of a low-key evening spent with Cory and his friends. "Yeah, that sounds good," he agreed. "What time and what should I bring?"

"Anytime after five, and whatever you want to drink, babe. I'll have burgers and all the trimmings. Jimmy's even making dessert."

Evan did smile at that. "Jimmy's in town?"

"Just for a few days. He finally hired some help he can trust not to ruin the place while he's away." Jimmy, Cory's longtime boyfriend, owned and ran a private, rustic, and clothing-optional resort an hour east of Atlanta. Evan didn't know how the couple handled living mostly separate lives—Cory managed his own small advertising firm in downtown Atlanta, though he spent many weekends with Jimmy—but it had worked for them for years. Jimmy had also been leaving the porn industry just when Evan was getting started, and his advice and insight had made a world of difference.

"Well, if Jimmy's there, I'm definitely coming." Cory blew a raspberry at him for that one, and Evan laughed. "I'll bring some Corona and limes, how about that?"

"Perfect. And a swimsuit. The weather's too nice not to go for a swim."

"Pffft." Evan laughed again. "You know you just wanna skinny-dip, anyway."

Cory crowed out a laugh of his own. "Gotta make it look spontaneous!"

"Pervert." Evan's smile softened. "I'll see you at five. Call me if you need me to pick up anything, okay?"

"Will do. Later, love."

Evan ended the call, still smiling. Cory was the one person in his life who always left him smiling, no matter how bad things got. And Cory had seen Evan at his lowest moment, heartbroken and homeless after the Marine Corps threw him out, so he knew how bad things could get.

Evan shook his head at himself. All the bad memories he'd held back for so long had been resurfacing since his mother had called, and the episode in Florida had only made things worse. For the first time, he looked forward to dinner the next night. He didn't expect it to go well, not by any means, but at least then it would be over, and maybe his mind would stop tangling him back up in old, frayed knots.

It had taken him far too long to escape those the first time around.

Blowing out a breath, Evan climbed off the bed and headed for the kitchen. A bowl of cereal, a shower, and he'd be ready to face the day. Or as ready as he'd ever be.

CHAPTER 6

THE SMELL of charcoal burning filled the air when Evan climbed out of his car in Cory's driveway. He reached back in to grab the beer and bag of limes from the passenger seat before slamming the door and heading up the path to the gate beside the house that led to the backyard. His flip-flops smacked softly against the concrete, but he could tell by the music and voices drifting around the house that no one would likely hear him coming.

As soon as he rounded the corner of the house, though, he saw Jimmy, and Jimmy saw him at almost the same instant. "Oh my God!" Jimmy yelled, bounding over toward Evan. Evan hardly had time to set down the beer before Jimmy launched himself into Evan's arms, nearly toppling them both back onto the grass. Evan got one foot behind him and a double handful of Jimmy's ass and managed to keep them upright.

Jimmy's mouth landed on the curve between Evan's neck and shoulder and sucked so hard Evan figured he'd have a hickey. When Jimmy finally pulled his mouth free with a loud *pop!* he lifted his head to grace Evan with a shit-eating grin. "How you doin', loverboy?"

"Much better after *that* greeting."

Jimmy laughed in reply and planted a wet, smacking kiss on Evan's mouth before unwrapping himself and sliding back to stand on his own two feet. And it was quite a bit down—Jimmy was only five-foot-five, but built like a brick shithouse, all muscle and covered with tattoos and salt-and-pepper hair. Nearly fifteen years older than Evan, he had more energy in his little finger than Evan managed in total most days.

"Grab that beer and come join the party, babe." Jimmy didn't wait for Evan, bouncing his way back over to Cory, who grabbed him for a hot, wet kiss, complete with plenty of moaning and groping. The contrast between the men was sharp—Jimmy short but built, and Cory, at six-foot-two, muscular but lacking Jimmy's level of gym dedication and as a result going a bit soft around the middle as he headed toward his midthirties.

Evan shook his head fondly at the pair and smiled as he retrieved his beer and headed over toward the pool. He saw a few familiar faces, but he expected many of the partygoers to be strangers or people he'd met only once before. Jimmy and Cory had an impossibly wide range of friends from all walks of life, and both of them loved a good party. And "good" for them meant filled with people who'd join right in with whatever craziness they came up with. Considering the all-male makeup of the attendees, Evan was betting on some nakedness to happen later in the evening.

Cory greeted him with a hug and kiss, not as physical as Jimmy's hello but no less enthusiastic. "Cooler's by the pool, hon, and you know where the knives and cutting boards are in the kitchen. Make yourself at home."

Evan did, nodding to the familiar folks and giving small smiles to the others on his way inside. He sliced up a lime and put the slices in a plastic bowl before carrying everything out to the pool, where he added his bottles to the already full cooler, saving one for himself. He popped off the top, took a big swig, and then pushed a lime slice down into the bottle.

Several of the poolside chairs were open, probably because a good half-dozen guys were already splashing around in the pool. Evan pulled his phone and keys out of his pockets, kicked off his flip-flops, and put his things under the back end of a cushioned chaise, well away from the water, before settling into the seat, beer in hand. He closed his eyes to soak up the late-afternoon sun, its warmth seeping through his skin and down to muscle and bone. His tension melted away, and he relaxed for the first time in days.

"Evan, right?"

Evan tried not to be annoyed at the interruption. He was, after all, at a party. He opened his eyes and turned his head to his left, where one of the familiar faces smiled back at him.

"Hey." Evan sat up a little straighter and took a sip of his beer to give himself a second to remember the guy's name.

The guy just smiled wider. "Taylor," he said. "We only met once, about a year ago. Probably the same 'opening of the pool' type party, actually. Anyway, I'm freakishly good at remembering names. Throws people off a lot."

Evan smiled, and it actually felt genuine. "Kind of a weird superpower."

Taylor laughed and lifted his beer in salute. "That it is." He looked around. "Hard to remember names for people I haven't met, though. I don't think I know more than four or five people here."

He gave Evan a hopeful look, and Evan shook his head. "Sorry, can't help you there. Other than the hosts, I know about as many as you, and I could maybe tell you two other names, if I thought about it hard."

Taylor's smile never dimmed. "Oh well. I guess I'll just introduce myself. If nothing else, can't beat a night of burgers and beer."

"And swimming."

Taylor's face did fall then. "I, um... never learned to swim. Can't bring myself to do more than sit on the side and stick my feet in."

Evan had grown up with a backyard pool and couldn't even remember not knowing how to swim, but he just shrugged. "Well, if you feel brave and want a lesson later, let me know."

Taylor grinned again. *Did he ever quit smiling?* Evan thought. "Might just do that," Taylor said. "Assuming we're not all shitfaced later."

Evan lifted his beer. "Guess we should work on that."

Taylor laughed and brought his own beer up to take a long draught. Evan watched his throat work as he swallowed, let his gaze roam down Taylor's bare chest, lightly tanned and dusted with brown hair. He waited for his body to react, but nothing happened. Not even a spark.

He gave a mental shrug. He was here to have dinner, not get laid. And if he *did* decide he wanted to get laid, he already had Riley in mind for that job.

Taylor had turned away by then to chat up one of the guys hanging on the edge of the pool. Most of that guy's body was beneath the surface, but his face, shoulders, and arms told a tale of regular visits to the gym, not to mention a tattoo parlor or two. Evan had two tattoos of his own. The small USMC in block letters on his upper right arm that he'd gotten after his first deployment drew a lot of attention when he went sleeveless—especially among gay men—but the design on his back carried more personal meaning: the image of folded hands sat above a simple caption: "Father, forgive me."

Evan flexed his back, almost as if he could feel the words etched into his skin. He'd gotten the ink not long after he'd started his porn career, but he no longer felt he needed forgiveness. After raising him in church and telling him God loved everyone, his family had abandoned him because of his sexuality, something he couldn't change and didn't want to. He still wanted to believe that God loved him, but he sure had a hard time feeling it.

"Hey, boys, it's time to suck down some buns and dongs—I mean dogs!"

Jimmy's playful call got everyone laughing and moving toward the grill. Evan waited, though, letting the others gather up and wait their turn in line. He leaned back in his seat and sipped his beer, enjoying the smell of grilled meat and the lingering rays of the sun.

A shadow fell over his body. "C'mon, boy, get your fine ass over here and get some grub before it's all gone."

Evan squinted up at Cory. "Just waiting for the crowd to clear out a little first."

Cory laughed and held out a hand. "Well, come join the party, then. You need more socialization."

"I get plenty of socialization on set."

"Getting fucked does not equal getting socialized." Cory made a "c'mere" gesture, and Evan gave in. He knew Cory wouldn't leave him be, so he might as well go along. It was easier than fighting him. That was how their entire friendship had been, and Evan doubted it would change anytime soon.

Evan set his beer down and grabbed Cory's hand, and then he let out an extremely unmanly shriek as Cory yanked hard. Evan went flying toward the edge of the pool, and before he could even make an attempt at stopping his momentum, he plunged into the water.

Laughter filled the air when Evan surfaced, spitting out water. "You asshole!"

Cory just laughed harder. "Just thought you needed a little bath before dinner," he managed between giggles. "Y'know, clean and fresh!"

Evan shook his head and ran a hand over his face. Water filled his sinuses and ears. "A little warning next time would be nice." He swam the few feet to the ladder and pulled himself up, water sluicing off his body. As soon as he reached the pool deck, he paused to strip off his tank top and shorts. He'd make Cory throw those in the dryer so he'd be able to wear them home. Good thing he'd emptied his pockets and worn his swim trunks under his shorts.

Evan held his wet clothes in one hand and grabbed a towel from the stack sitting nearby with the other. He ran the towel over his body as he walked toward the grill, where he stopped next to Cory and thrust his dripping clothes against the other man's chest.

"You got 'em wet," he said. "You get 'em dry."

Cory just laughed again. "That's what he said!"

Evan rolled his eyes. "That doesn't even make sense." But Cory was off already, headed toward the house, where Evan hoped his clothes would make it into the dryer. The line for food had dwindled by then, so he grabbed a plastic plate and started filling it. Besides the burgers and hot dogs and a huge selection of trimmings, the food table held coleslaw, three kinds of potato chips, and even a bowl of fruit salad. Evan took a little of everything, though he stuck to the barbecue-flavored chips, and carried his loaded plate back over to where he'd left his beer.

"Hey, Ev, honey?" Evan turned to where Jimmy was settling into a chair at the patio table halfway between the house and the pool. "Would you let me have one of your Coronas?" He grinned, ever irrepressible. "I feel like drinking some piss, and you know Cory doesn't like watersports."

Evan shook his head even as he smiled and turned toward the cooler. "You want a lime?"

"No, thanks, babe. If I want it fruity, I'll just stick my finger in it!"

Cory's voice came from over by the food. "That's what he said!"

"No." Evan pointed the neck of the unopened bottle at Cory, trying to fight back a smile. "You only get one 'that's what he said' a day, and you already burned it earlier. Try again."

Cory huffed and planted his hands on his hips. "My house, my rules!"

"That's what he said!" Jimmy crowed, before collapsing against the back of his chair in a giggle fit. The laugh Evan had been fighting burst out, and he walked over to put the beer on the table in front of Jimmy.

"Behave yourself and eat," he told the other man, who by then was wiping tears of mirth from his eyes. "And no snappy comebacks to that one or I'm taking my beer back!"

"Yes, dear." Jimmy reached for the beer as Evan headed back to his chair. His own bottle still sat where he'd left it, and as he picked up his plate and lowered himself into his seat, Taylor appeared and retook his previous spot in the next chair.

"Oh my God, I am so hungry!" Taylor popped a chip into his mouth and crunched noisily while he picked up his burger. "I had a bowl of cereal when I got up and haven't had a single bite since then. I need some *meat!*"

That's what he said! went through Evan's mind, followed by, *Great, now I'll have* that *in my head for the next few days.* He rolled his eyes as he bit into his own burger. As much as he loved Cory and Jimmy, they could drive him absolutely batshit crazy sometimes.

And you wouldn't have it any other way, he told himself. As if he needed the reminder. Cory and Jimmy weren't just his best friends; they were his only friends. His only *real* friends, anyway. Evan didn't spend much time hanging out with other porn models. He rarely went to industry events, and when he had shoots or appearances, he preferred keeping to himself during downtime. Of course, like a lot of porn models, Evan had pseudofriends everywhere, people who followed him on Twitter and Facebook, sent him fan mail, came to his live events and had their pictures made with him, and then felt like they knew him.

The truth was, while there were a handful of other models and fans he'd talked to enough that he'd probably consider them to be friends of a sort, none of them had anything close to the kind of insight into his life that Cory and Jimmy had. None of them had spent time with him, talked him through the bad days, supported him no matter what. Hell, since Cory and Jimmy were the reason he'd gotten into porn in the first place, without them, none of the others would know him anyway.

That was why he was here, surrounded by a dozen strangers and near-strangers, drinking beer and eating burgers in a suburban backyard. He would do almost anything for these two. Coming to a cookout barely even registered on the scale.

The group stayed mostly silent while everyone ate, just a few compliments thrown in the direction of the hosts and the requisite smartass replies. Low music came from just inside the screened-off patio door, upbeat but neutral, nothing like the hard, driving dance music that tended to be so popular in most groups of gay men. Probably Cory's playlist, Evan thought. He liked throwbacks, especially from the '70s and '80s, while Jimmy was the one who kept up with the latest hits, even though Jimmy was older by six-plus years.

Evan felt himself relax as he ate and drank, knots he hadn't even realized he was carrying loosening and falling away. To say he'd had a shit week would be the understatement of the century, and he still had dinner with his parents to deal with. But sitting in Cory's backyard, full of good food and surrounded by good people, he could let go of it all.

It was a good day.

EVAN STOPPED drinking after three beers, though he went back for another burger after taking a turn in the pool. The water was still too far on the chilly side for him, so he didn't stay in long. He dried off so he wouldn't get cold as evening fell, and settled back into his seat with his second plate of food.

"God. I wish I still had your metabolism."

Evan smiled over at Jimmy, who hung off the side of the pool, arms folded on the tiled edge. "You've got nothing to worry about."

"Tell that to my trainer." Jimmy shook his head. "I swear, if I still lived in the city full-time, I'd strangle him in a week. He's always talking about protein intake and body fat percentages and acting like I'm going to stroke out if I eat a steak now and then, just because I'm not in my twenties anymore."

"And if it wasn't for the gray hair, which you know looks hot, no one would guess you weren't in your twenties anymore." Evan had heard Jimmy's grousing before and knew it was never that serious. Very little could get Jimmy down for more than a few minutes.

Sure enough, before Evan had gotten halfway through his burger, Jimmy had wrapped his arms around one of the twinks Evan didn't know, wrestling and groping him playfully. Water splashed around them as the kid squealed, and Cory's big, booming laugh came from over Evan's shoulder, where Cory still sat at the table.

"Show us that ass, Jimmy!" Cory called, and Jimmy followed orders, wrangling the twink around so he could get his tiny little trunks pushed down. He held the kid with one hand and gave his butt a few smacks with the other, laughing as the boy wriggled and squawked between peals of giggles. Evan shook his head and finished off his burger before leaning back on the chaise with his last beer. He knew what would come next. When everyone else left, the twink would stay behind, and Cory and Jimmy would have their fun with him. Evan doubted it would last any longer than the night. It rarely did.

A shadow passed over the sun, and Evan shivered in the sudden cool. He glanced up to see clouds gathering, likely heralding one of the evening thunderstorms that popped up most days from April through the end of summer. Sure enough, a low rumble of thunder rolled, and Cory's voice sounded again.

"All right, boys, time to get out of the pool." A chorus of dissent followed, but Evan knew Cory wouldn't be denied. "Nope, sorry. Pool is closing for the night. Everybody out, and y'all help me get this stuff moved inside before the heavens open up."

Evan set aside his plate and grabbed his phone, keys, and shoes, slipping back into the flip-flops. With his clothes still drying, he had no pockets for his phone and keys, so it was a bit of a balancing act to gather up his plate, two empty bottles, and half-gone beer to get everything safely inside.

He'd spent enough time at Cory's that he knew where to find things, so as the others helped bring things in, Evan sorted it into trash, recycling, refrigerator, or wherever else it needed to go. By the time the patio was cleared off, the rain had started, and a minute later, lightning flashed. Evan was standing close enough to feel Cory's flinch and reached out to run a soothing hand down his back.

"We're good," he murmured, and Cory nodded, though he didn't relax. With his own bad memories to deal with, Evan understood. A decade earlier, Cory's father, an avid golfer, had been killed by a lightning strike on the eighth green of his favorite course. The result had been a phobia of thunderstorms that Cory fought but had yet to overcome.

The other guys had wandered farther into the house, and Evan heard discussion of video games or strip poker. Riley's face flashed through his mind again, and he cleared his throat. "So, once the storm dies down a little, I'm going to head home." *Or to see if Riley's home*, he thought. If the guy was going to keep showing up in his head, Evan might as well try to get to the real thing.

Cory gave him a side-eye. "You're not leaving before dessert," he stated. "Jimmy made lemon meringue pie. Three of 'em, actually, and if you don't help us eat them, I'll eat a whole pie, and...." He puffed out his cheeks and held his arms out to the side in the universal "weight gain" sign, and Evan had to smile.

"I'll stay for pie," he agreed. "As long as there's coffee too."

Cory gave him a wicked grin. "Sure thing, honey. You know where all the fixins are!"

He landed a big, smacking kiss on Evan's cheek and disappeared toward the den before Evan could mount a protest. Sighing, he opened the cabinet and started pulling things out. Going after Riley would just have to wait.

CHAPTER 7

FRIDAY NIGHT, Evan was almost late for dinner. His degree of punctuality came and went, although he was adamant about never being late for professional gigs. But this dinner was kind of important, no matter what came of it. He needed it to start off right, even if it all went wrong in the end.

He walked into the restaurant with three minutes to spare and pulled up short. His mother stood to the left of the entrance, alone, and it caught him off guard. He'd been sure the "we" in "can we have dinner?" had included his father as well.

Apparently not.

Gwen Day's smile had always been the stuff of legend, and the one she gave Evan was no exception. She hugged him before he could decide if he was okay with it or not, but he must've been, because he hugged her right back. Her scent wrapped familiarity and memory around him, and he closed his eyes as his mind tumbled toward oblivion.

"Oh, Evan," Gwen whispered. "I've missed you so much."

His mother's words, as heartfelt as they sounded, pulled him out of his fugue. He broke the embrace as gently as he could manage and took a step back. "I missed you too, Mom," he said. "I never wanted to leave in the first place."

Gwen's smile faded, her eyes clouding. "I know, honey. That's why I wanted to see you. Can we…." She looked around, caught the eye of the hostess. "Let's sit, and we can talk. Okay?"

"That's why we're here," Evan agreed.

He followed her to a table in a corner. She must have made the request of location before he arrived, since the hostess hadn't even checked before heading in that direction. She pulled out her own chair before he could think to offer, something he'd been raised to believe was proper but hadn't really thought about in years. He did wait until she was seated to take his own place to her left. She gave him a small smile.

"You remembered," she murmured, and he realized what he'd done. A viral infection when Evan was ten had left his mother with hearing loss in her right ear. Even five years after they last saw each other, he'd automatically sat on her good side.

He gave a small smile. "Habit." He picked up his menu. "Have you been here before?"

"Oh yes." Gwen smiled and looked around. "A good friend of ours is head chef. I helped her with some of the interior design. It turned out lovely, didn't it?"

Evan raised an eyebrow. His mother had been a full-time wife and mother all his life, apart from charity work befitting a former sorority member and spouse of a well-known attorney. "It's nice," he said, watching her glow with pride. "You've been doing design work?"

She turned her focus back to him and laughed lightly. "Oh, just a bit here and there. I've been at loose ends since...." She trailed off and turned her attention to her menu. "The seafood is my favorite here, but everything is delicious."

His mind filled in the rest of her incomplete sentence: *since you left home*. Wife and mother had been more than a full-time job, but wife alone apparently left something to be desired.

He was happy for her that she'd found something she enjoyed. "Have you been taking design courses, or...?"

She blushed. "I had a certification from decades ago," she admitted. "Beverly, the chef here, has been trying to talk me into updating it." She paused, then shook her head and waved a hand. "I'm sure it would be too much bother."

Evan didn't press, but he knew she had the time, and she certainly showed an interest. If they managed to rekindle a regular relationship, maybe he'd encourage her to take some courses. God knew he'd like to have the time and money like she did.

He turned his attention back to the menu, settling quickly on one of his favorites—grilled rainbow trout. He set the menu aside and took a sip of water, looking around the dining room again. The space felt comfortable, the noise levels low, the design sleek but warm. He thought of Riley and his design interests. Maybe they could…. He shook off the half-formed thought. He didn't even know yet if his mother was here to accept him or make another effort to get him to renounce his sexuality. The idea of bringing Riley into the picture was so premature as to be ludicrous.

Gwen set her menu down, and within moments, a server appeared. "May I take your order?"

Gwen smiled her beauty-queen smile. "Yes, thank you. I'll have the scallops Florentine, and a glass of house chardonnay."

The server nodded. "Yes, ma'am." She turned to Evan. "And you, sir?"

"Grilled rainbow trout," he said, and he nodded at Gwen. "And the same wine, please."

"Excellent. May I get you anything else? An appetizer?"

Evan looked at his mother, who tilted her head winsomely. "A bread basket and some of that wonderful honey butter would be lovely."

"I'll have that right out," the server said. She smiled before turning to head toward the kitchen, and Gwen turned her smile onto Evan.

"I can never resist bread," she confided, reaching for her water glass. "All my friends have done the low-carb and the gluten-free and all that, and I simply can't manage it. I've long ago given up fighting it."

Evan chuckled. "You don't need to worry about any of that anyway," he said. "You still look just as beautiful as you ever did."

Gwen blushed again, which only made her more beautiful. She still had the poise and grace of the beauty queen she'd once been, but unlike many others, she'd let her looks age gracefully. If she'd had any work done, Evan couldn't tell, and he'd seen enough bad plastic surgery to recognize it from three feet away. Aside from deeper lines around her mouth and delicate crow's feet at the corners of her eyes, she could easily pass for decades younger than her fifty-six years. No one would believe that she had a twenty-five-year-old son, much less that she'd had one four years older. And that she'd survived the loss of one and estrangement from the other.

Evan's mood followed those darker thoughts. He dropped his gaze to the deep gray tablecloth, noticing a tiny gap in the fabric just to the right of his knife, not a tear but a flaw in the weaving. *Story of my life*, he thought. *Looks fine from a distance, but get up close and you can see the holes.*

"Honey." Gwen slid a hand, long fingers tipped with a perfect french manicure, to cover Evan's where it sat on the table. "How have you been? I want to hear everything about your life."

No, you really don't, Mom, Evan thought. He shrugged. "Pretty typical, I suppose. I work. Have an apartment. Have friends. Travel sometimes." Gently, so as not to cause trouble, he extracted his hand and lowered it into his lap with the other. "How have you been?"

Gwen was quiet for a long moment, long enough that Evan looked up to catch her with tears in her eyes. "I feel like we're strangers," she whispered. "Like I gave you up for adoption and we're just now meeting. How did—?" A soft sob cut her off, and she fumbled for her purse, found a handkerchief, and used it to dab at her eyes. "How did we let this happen?" she finally finished, and Evan had to fight to tamp down the anger that welled up in him.

"'We' didn't do anything, Mom," he pointed out, proud of how calm he sounded. "You did. You and Dad let this happen. All I did was tell you who I am, and you refused to have anything to do with me."

"We were wrong!" Gwen's eyes glittered. "Oh, God, Evan, there hasn't been a day that's gone by that I haven't regretted what we did. We thought… *hoped* that you'd change your mind and come back. We were stupid and ignorant and thought we were doing the right thing."

Gwen stopped and bit her bottom lip, hard, as if using it to get her emotions back under control. Evan saw their server approaching with their drinks and bread, and he leaned back and nodded in that direction so his mother would understand. She did, and when the glass of wine was placed in front of her, she managed a gracious smile, if not a verbal thank-you.

Once the server was gone, Evan grabbed his wine and drained half of it in one swallow. He set the glass back on the table and focused on his mother. "What made you change your mind?"

Gwen sipped at her wine more delicately, as befit a genteel Southern lady, but her hand trembled. "A lot of things," she murmured. She took another sip and then set down her glass. "But mostly it was your brother."

Pain sliced through Evan. "What does Charlie have to do with anything?"

Gwen's head snapped up and her gaze locked on to Evan's, blue eyes so like his own suddenly hard. "He has *everything* to do with it!" Anger laced her low voice. "I lost one son because of something none of us could stop. I will be *damned* if I will lose my other son if there's anything I can do to keep it from happening!"

Evan's stomach roiled, and his hands clenched into fists. "Charlie always has 'everything' to do with it," he shot back. He shook from the effort of keeping his words steady, of keeping himself from losing control. "Your golden boy died a hero in a war zone, and you've got him canonized in your memory. I spent *five years* trying to live up to that legacy, got into the Marines and everything, but just because I fucked another guy, I lost my lover, my job, *and* my family. You and Dad and the *goddamned* Marine Corps just couldn't handle being touched by the gay."

Uncurling his fingers, Evan reached for his wine glass and drained it even as he pushed to his feet. "Thanks for the wine and the heart-to-heart, Gwen." He slammed the glass down on the table, almost disappointed when it didn't shatter. "Enjoy your dinner."

He turned on his heel and stalked out of the restaurant without looking back.

A PHONE rang in Evan's dream. He tried to answer it, but the buzzing wouldn't stop, no matter how many buttons he pushed. He threw the phone at the wall and it shattered, disintegrating into a million tiny shards of sand that slid down to land at the feet of his brother.

"Hey, Ev." Charlie's smile was lopsided, because half his face was gone. "How've you been?"

Evan gasped himself awake just as his phone quit ringing and the call clicked over to voice mail. He lay on his back and stared at the ceiling, willing away the ghoulish image of his dead brother's mutilated face. When he felt like he could move without throwing up, he rolled over and grabbed his phone to check his missed calls. Two from his mom, both of which he'd ignored the night before, and a new one from Cory. Evan pulled up the call screen and waited for it to connect.

"Hey, honey." Cory's happy voice lifted Evan's spirits even at his worst moments. "I was kinda hoping you'd call last night. How'd your dinner go?"

Evan groaned. "Disaster," he muttered, letting his eyes fall shut. "She made it all about Charlie, and I went off on her and stormed out. Pretty much what I expected."

Cory made a sound of sympathy. "I'm so sorry, babe. I know you were hoping for better."

Evan shrugged one shoulder. "Pipe dreams." He cleared his throat. "So, any other reason you're calling me at o-dark-thirty and waking me up?"

Cory laughed. "It's after eleven, dear heart. It's past time you were awake. We're going out dancing tonight. Wanna come?"

Not really, but Evan supposed he shouldn't sit around and sulk all weekend, either. Not that Cory would let him. "Who's we? Jimmy?"

"And a few other guys are supposed to meet us at Panther. It's leather night, so strap on that hot harness of yours!"

Evan laughed. "Okay, okay. Ten?" That was the usual time they'd meet up for drinking and dancing.

"Absolutely! See you then, honey." Cory made a loud smacking sound and ended the call, and Evan laid the phone on his chest and blew out a long breath, trying to erase the nightmare. With all the practice he'd had over the past five years, it should be easier to get past it.

Tell that to my brain, he thought, forcing himself to get up and hit the shower. He needed groceries, and probably to do laundry. Maybe, just maybe, by the time he headed out that night, his mind would be clear and ready to just have some fun.

A DRIVING rhythm pounded from the building as Evan approached Panther. The dance club had never been one of his favorite places, though at least they'd cracked down on the drug activity that nearly got them shut down a year earlier. They'd gone no-smoking too, and Evan much preferred to have a few cigarettes when he drank. But Cory loved to dance, Jimmy loved to accommodate him, and Panther had the best dance music in town, so this was where they ended up more often than not when Jimmy was in the city.

Inside, Evan showed his ID to the bouncers and then headed for the bar. Sure enough, he saw Cory and Jimmy near one end, Jimmy leaned way over the bar, flirting with the bartender and Cory pressed up behind him, grinding his hips into Jimmy's ass. Evan would bet on Cory being a few shots in already. He didn't drink more than beer often, but when he danced, he always drank the hard stuff.

On a whim, Evan stepped up behind Cory and pressed in close, running his hands down Cory's sides. "Hey, hot stuff, you got the moves," he crooned, raising his voice to be heard over the music.

Cory's head jerked around in recognition, and he smiled. "You know it, baby!" Cory leaned back and raised his arms, and for a few moments, they danced like that, hips moving in sync. The song shifted, and Evan gave one last grind before stepping to the side and sliding onto a barstool.

"Tease!" Cory yelled, waggling a finger at Evan. Evan stuck out his tongue, feeling silly but enjoying it, and turned to the bartender.

"Vodka cranberry with lime," he yelled, handing over a credit card to start a tab, and the man nodded and got to work on the drink. While he waited, Evan turned on the stool and looked around the club. The crowd was thin, but it was early yet for a Saturday. A few dozen people gyrated on the dance floor, but Evan knew that by midnight, the space would be stuffed to the gills. Panther might not be his favorite thing, but it was definitely the place to go if you wanted to dance. And especially if you wanted to dance dirty and take your partner home for the night.

"Where's your leather?"

Evan snorted but didn't look at Cory. "Good thing I didn't listen to you. I checked the website. Leather night is *next* Saturday."

Cory giggled. "Dammit. You're too smart for my own good."

"You know damn good and well I haven't gone off your word since you told me it was superhero night and I showed up in a cape."

"That was an honest mistake!"

Evan gave him a look. "And every time since then?"

Cory threw back his head and laughed until Evan thought he'd never stop. When he finally wound down, he wrapped his arms around Jimmy's shoulders from behind. "C'mon, stud. I wanna dance!"

Jimmy turned his head and grinned at Evan. "Duty calls!" He reached for Cory's hand, and in another few seconds, they were gone.

Evan sipped his drink and watched the crowd surge and pulse under the flashing lights. Hands and hips moved constantly, bodies grinding together while fingers touched and teased. Lots of skin was on display, many of the men peeling off their shirts as things heated up, and several pairs or groups of three were all over each other, to the point that Evan figured they'd end up fucking in the bathroom before much longer.

Been there, done that, he thought, draining the last of his drink. He waved the empty at the bartender. "Can I get another?" He'd have his three drinks right up front and enjoy the buzz while he switched to water so he'd be sober by the time he drove home. Panther was too far from his apartment to walk, and getting a cab on a Saturday night was more headache than he wanted to deal with.

"Hey, I know you!"

Evan turned toward the man who'd spoken. He didn't look familiar, so Evan figured it must be Trevor Hardball the man "knew." A second later, that was confirmed.

"You're Trevor Hardball! I knew it." The man grinned, but something about his expression appeared off.

"In the flesh," Evan said. He held out a hand to shake. "Nice to meet you…?" he prompted, expecting the man to introduce himself, as usual.

Instead, the man's grin twisted into a sneer. "Keep your dirty hands to yourself," he growled. "Probably crawling with germs. Fucking slut. I can't believe your dick hasn't fallen off by now."

Evan rolled his eyes. "They're called condoms, asshole. You should look into it. Idiocy is contagious." He turned back to face the bar, but a second later, a hand grabbed his shoulder and yanked. He almost fell off the barstool, but he got his feet under him in time to duck away from the fist that flew toward his face. His attacker nearly fell over his own feet, obviously drunk off his ass, but before Evan could even react, Jimmy and Cory were there with one of the bouncers.

"You okay, honey?" Cory's voice was laced with concern, and Evan shrugged.

"Yeah, just some drunken idiot making a fool of himself." He watched as Jimmy and the bouncer dragged the guy toward the door. With the kind of checkered history the place had, the last thing the club wanted was the cops coming out to break up a brawl, so they acted fast when anyone got physical in a bad way.

Evan slid back onto his barstool and picked up the fresh drink. "On the house," the bartender yelled, and Evan lifted his glass in acknowledgment. He'd make up the cost with his tip.

Cory leaned on the bar next to him. "What was that all about?"

Evan shrugged as he sipped his drink. "The usual. I do porn, so I must be diseased. Never mind that he probably sleeps with more guys than I do, even counting on set."

Cory laughed. "Gotta love the crazies." His gaze stayed trained on the door as he talked. "I don't know what Jimmy saw, but he was there one second and gone the next, stalking over here. You know how he gets when he's on a mission." He smirked. "I hope Asshole recognized him. It'd be poetic justice for him to get dragged out of the bar by the same kind of guy he attacked."

Evan had to laugh at that. "And by the one who got me started, no less." He glanced around, but no one seemed to be paying them any attention anymore. "Last time I got recognized in a bar, the guy was just a fan." *And then....* Evan shot Cory a grin. "That reminds me. I forgot to tell you about this guy I hooked up with last weekend."

That got Cory's attention. "Oh-ho! Do tell!"

Evan raised an eyebrow and licked his lips. "Much more your type than mine. Hot in bed, though. Might even get a round two." Evan's cock throbbed at the thought. Damn, he should've looked Riley up by now. *Tomorrow*, he promised himself.

"You go, boy!" Cory shoved at Evan's shoulder. "Next time bring him out dancing. I gotta get a good, long look at that one."

A flare of jealousy surprised Evan—*What the hell? I hardly know the guy*—but he pushed it aside as Cory leaned over the bar. "Hey, hot stuff, can I get a couple of waters?" Cory asked, and the bartender nodded and grabbed two plastic cups off the stack behind the bar. Cory turned back to bump his hip against Evan's. "You gonna dance with us, or just sit over here and drown your sorrows?"

Evan took another sip. "No drowning. Just not feeling it tonight."

"Mmm-hmm." Cory gave him an eloquent eyebrow, but before he could push further, Jimmy bounced up to them.

"Hey, lovers." He hissed out the final letter and grabbed a handful of Cory's ass. "Now that we got the trash taken out, let's dance!"

"Just taking a water break, honey," Cory replied, giving the bartender a winning smile and a couple of ones as he delivered their drinks. Cory picked up a cup and handed it to Jimmy. "Here, drink this so we can get back to shaking our asses."

Jimmy took the cup and drained it in one long pull. He slammed the cup down on the bar, though the plastic didn't give the same kind of satisfying sound as glass. "Finish that off, honeychild," he told Evan. "You're comin' with us!"

Evan didn't bother to protest. Jimmy could never be denied.

IT WAS nearly three when Evan dragged himself into his apartment, thankfully not sloshed this time, but beyond exhausted. He stripped on his way to the bed and poured himself onto the mattress, not planning to move for at least twelve hours.

Unfortunately, Cory had other ideas. Evan almost threw his phone across the room when it rang at ten fifteen. He grabbed for it and thumbed the answer button. "What?" he demanded.

"Time to rise and shine, baby doll! We're headed to brunch before Jimmy goes home. Come with?"

Evan rolled onto his back and wished for a painful death. For whom, he wasn't sure. "How in the hell are you this awake?"

Cory laughed. "Oh, we haven't slept. We're running on pure endorphins at this point. We got that adorable bartender to come home with us. Sent him off an hour ago with a big cup of coffee and an even bigger smile."

And probably walking funny, Evan thought. He sighed. "All right. Piedmont Diner?" It was Jimmy's favorite.

"You know it! See you around eleven! Love ya!" Cory ended the call, and Evan stared at the ceiling for a minute before dragging himself up and heading for the shower. Maybe he'd take a nap that afternoon.

CHAPTER 8

THE ROUTE from his apartment to Piedmont Diner took Evan right past Piedmont Lofts. Remembering his promise to himself from the night before, he detoured from the sidewalk and climbed the steps to the door, where he found the buzzer for Riley's apartment. *What's the worst that could happen?* he thought. *He says no, and we go on with our lives.*

"Yes?" Riley's voice came through the speaker much more clearly than Evan expected, no hint of static. But then, the residents of this building could afford the best of everything.

"Hi, Riley, it's Evan." The static missing in the speaker came through in his own voice. He cleared his throat. "Sorry to show up unexpectedly like this, but I was headed to brunch at Piedmont Diner with friends. I thought you might like to join us?"

The pause went on so long Evan wondered if Riley had just walked away, but finally he responded.

"All right. What time?"

Evan grinned. "I'm going over now. I can wait for you, or you can join us whenever?"

A soft laugh came through the speaker. "Oh, I'm a mess right now, honey. I'm barely out of bed. Let me get myself together and I'll meet you."

The thought of Riley in "a mess"—bed-warm, hair tousled, eyes heavy with sleep, like the day he'd woken Evan up with a blowjob—

had Evan's body sitting up and taking notice. "Okay," he croaked out, staring at the speaker as if Riley would materialize from it.

"See you in a few!"

Riley's lilting voice settled over Evan like a blanket, warming him from within. He turned and headed off to meet Cory and Jimmy, but his mind stayed on Riley.

CORY MET Evan at the door to Piedmont Diner, all smiles and hugs, like the big teddy bear he was. "C'mon, Jimmy's already got our favorite table." Cory headed across the room to a booth next to a window that overlooked the corner outside. The location gave a panoramic view of the people passing by, most of them young, hot gay men. Cory sighed as he slid into the booth next to Jimmy and leaned over to watch a particularly nice specimen in short-shorts walk by. "Oh, to be twenty-two and single again."

Evan laughed as he took his seat. "Like that's ever stopped you."

Cory's eyes gleamed. "Jimmy wants me to bring someone out to visit next weekend. Seen any new twinks lately?"

"Not any that I'd be willing to share." Evan envied Cory and Jimmy's relationship. They'd fallen head over heels for each other but never gotten over their shared penchant for cute young things, so every so often one of them would pick out a guy for them to enjoy. Part of Evan wondered what would happen if one of them, or one of their visitors, got too attached, but he figured they'd cross that chasm only when they had to.

As much as he loved the guys, though, no way was he letting these two get hold of Riley. He smiled at Jimmy, who had his head down over a cup of coffee. Unlike his boyfriend, Jimmy took a good dose of caffeine to wake up in the morning. "Hey, Jimmy."

Jimmy gave him a small smile, eyes half-lidded from lack of sleep. "Hey, honey."

Cory grinned at the server who walked up to their table. "Hey, mister." Evan recognized that as Cory's favorite term for someone he recognized but whose name he couldn't remember. "Could you start us off with a pitcher of mimosas?"

"No problem." The young man had tousled, wavy black hair, hipster glasses with thick black frames, and a professionally friendly smile. "Anything else?"

"We'll have another joining us," Evan said, noticing the surprise on Cory's face. "But he doesn't drink, so can you bring a glass of plain OJ?"

"Got it. I'll get those drinks and be back for your order." The server turned and walked away, and Cory gave Evan a mock glare.

"You didn't tell me you invited a date."

Evan shook his head. "Not a date, exactly." He pinned Cory with a look. "But don't go getting any ideas when you meet him, either."

"Mmm-hmm." Cory raised an eyebrow. "Who's this, then?"

Evan shrugged. "That guy I told you about last night. The one I hooked up with last weekend."

Jimmy perked up a little at that. "And you're asking him to brunch? Sounds like more than just a hookup to me."

Evan blew out a breath. "I don't know, okay? He's totally not my usual type. More your type. But I keep thinking about him. I can't explain it."

"Mmm-hmmm." Cory leaned back and crossed his arms over his chest. "You, my boy, are smitten."

Evan barked out a laugh. "Smitten? Really?"

"Yep. You're in deep smit." He grinned widely. "And if you wanna keep seeing this guy, I suggest you think about getting your smit together."

Evan's groan in response was cut off by their server delivering their pitcher, along with three empty champagne flutes and a fourth one already filled with juice. "This is the plain OJ," the server said, setting the glass in front of the empty space next to Evan. "Do you want to order now or wait for your friend to arrive?"

"I'm starving," Cory said. "And I already know what I want. Eggs Benedict with a big bowl of grits. And Jimmy'll have a short stack of pancakes with a side of sausage links."

"And more coffee," Jimmy piped up, tilting his nearly empty mug.

"And more coffee for Mr. Personality over here," Cory agreed. He gave Evan a look. "Ev?"

"You're the only person in the world who calls me that." Evan had eaten here enough that he didn't need the menu either. "I'll have the eggs Benedict too, but with home fries instead of grits."

"Heathen." Cory reached for the pitcher as their server headed off to put in their orders. "You know grits are as much a Southern brunch tradition as the mimosas."

Evan accepted his filled glass. "I like grits fine," he pointed out. "You've seen me eat them plenty of times. I just wanted the home fries today."

He sipped his mimosa and looked toward the door just as Riley walked in. Much like Jimmy, he still looked only half awake, but he'd tamed his curls and wore snug shorts and a T-shirt that showed off his small, lithe body to perfection. Evan knew good and well that if he'd walked by the window, Cory and Jimmy both would've been ogling for all they were worth, and Evan wouldn't have blamed them one bit.

Riley glanced around, and Evan set down his glass and waved to get his attention. Riley saw him and half smiled as he headed in their direction. Evan didn't look at Cory, but he could see in his periphery that Cory's eyes were alight with interest.

"I told you," Evan growled under his breath. "Off. Fucking. Limits."

"Doesn't mean I can't admire," Cory shot back. He smiled his best smile as Riley reached the table. "Hello there," he cooed. "Evan was just telling us he'd invited a friend to join us."

Riley faltered as he stopped. "I'm not party crashing, am I?"

"Oh no!" Cory reached out a hand to touch Riley's arm. "You are absolutely welcome! Any friend of Evan's is a friend of ours. Please, sit." He waved toward the empty space next to Evan, and Evan gave Riley a smile too. Riley slid in slowly and sat a little stiffly.

"Riley," Evan said, "meet two of my closest friends, Cory and Jimmy. Cory's the loudmouth." He laughed softly. "Well, normally Jimmy's a pretty big loudmouth too, but not until he's got more caffeine in."

"Gee, thanks." Jimmy shot Evan a mock glare and then grinned at Riley. "How'd you end up meeting this reprobate anyway?"

Evan lifted an eyebrow and his mimosa glass. "He fell right into my arms."

Riley's cheeks pinked. "It's true," he admitted. "Tripped and landed right in his lap."

Cory crowed out a laugh. "Oh my God, that is *fabulous*! Did he catch you like the heroic stud he is?"

Evan could see Riley relaxing by inches. No one could resist Cory when he turned on the charm. "He did. Kept me from sliding right onto the floor. I bought him a drink to say thanks."

"Awwwww," Jimmy piped up. "Sounds like the setup for a Hollywood blockbuster."

"Evan can be Ryan Gosling," Cory chimed in, "and you can be Jennifer Lawrence!"

"We'll call it '*Meet Cute: A Millennial Romance*.'" Jimmy spread out his hands as if writing the title on the air. Then he collapsed into a giggle fit

"Drink your juice, Shelby." Evan made a hurry-up gesture with one hand at the waiter as he approached with a coffeepot in hand. "You've got too much blood in your caffeine stream."

Cory grabbed Jimmy's coffee mug and shoved it toward the edge of the table. "Fill 'er up, mister!" He grinned at the waiter, who refilled the mug and smiled at Riley.

"What can I get for you, handsome?" he asked.

Riley returned the smile. "Do you still have the spinach and mushroom crepes?"

"We sure do! They are super yummy."

This guy's perkier than a coffeemaker, Evan thought, but he refrained from commenting while Riley confirmed his order and Mr. Perky assured them their food would be out soon. Evan drained his glass and reached for the pitcher. Riley eyed him and then nodded toward his glass.

"Is this a mimosa too?"

"Oh, no, honey," Cory cut in, lips quirking. "Your friend over there made sure they brought you some plain OJ."

Riley gave Evan a speculative look as he picked up the glass. "Thank you," he said.

"You're welcome." For some reason, Evan couldn't bring himself to laugh it off. Instead, he held his glass out, and Riley brought his forward to clink them together.

"To friends," Riley said.

"Hear, hear!" Cory held out his glass, and Jimmy lifted his coffee mug, and the simple toast became a flurry of movement and laughter. By the time everything was sorted out, Cory was refilling his glass, Riley was close to needing a refill of his own, and everyone was relaxed and smiling. Evan swore he could see Jimmy bloom like a flower as his caffeine levels reached the full mark.

"So, Riley," Cory said. "When you aren't falling into a man's outstretched arms, what do you do?"

Riley smiled, and Evan recognized it for the façade it was. "I'm in design," Riley said. "Nothing major, mostly interior work for friends and some referrals." He laughed, a practiced sound. "Mostly I live off my trust fund." Before Cory could react to that, Riley leaned forward. "What about you?"

"Advertising," Cory said. "I have a small boutique agency with a short client list. Jimmy over here"—he nudged Jimmy with an elbow— "is a massage therapist and has a private resort out in the sticks."

"You love my stick," Jimmy told Cory before grinning at Riley. "He's right, though. Oasis is in the middle of the fuckin' boonies. But I love it, and so does this one." He nodded toward Cory. "When he drags himself away from the bright lights of the big city."

"It is pretty gorgeous out there," Evan agreed. "Lots of trees and green. Quiet. It makes a nice getaway."

Perky McWaiter arrived just then, carrying a tray laden with plates, and a food runner appeared behind him with a smaller tray and a tray rack. In short order, they had the food distributed, an order for more orange juice for Riley had been taken, and they were off again. Jimmy reached for the syrup, Cory the salt and pepper, and Evan and

Riley picked up their forks and dug in at the same moment. They looked at each other and smiled a private smile around their mouthfuls of deliciousness.

"Mmmmmm." Jimmy's orgasmic moan drew Evan's attention away from Riley. "Oh my God. I wanna marry the chef. Can I marry the chef?" He batted his eyelashes at Cory, who just shook his head.

"Not this month, babe. You've got too many guests lined up." He turned pensive. "Even though June *is* traditional for weddings."

Evan glanced at Riley to see his reaction to their silliness, but he just smiled, shook his head, and carried on eating. Evan followed suit. Best not to encourage them.

"Oh! I haven't told you!" Evan looked back up at Cory's exclamation. "I got my first headlining gig!"

It took Evan a moment to connect the dots from that to Cory's drag queen persona. "You did? Congratulations, man!"

"Next Saturday at Bernhardt's." He grinned and cut his eyes back and forth between Evan and Riley. "You can come, right? Both of you?"

Riley looked surprised at that, but Evan just nodded. "I'll be in town." He turned his head toward Riley. "Don't feel obligated, of course, but I know Cory would like having a few familiar faces in the crowd. If you're free, that is."

Riley gave Cory a smile. "I think I can make it. I haven't been to a show in a while. Is it the Stilettos?"

Jimmy groaned and laid his head on the table. "Oh, please don't get him started."

Cory ignored him. "Yes. One of my oldest friends used to be a member—he tore up his ankle playing racquetball and can't handle heels anymore—and even with his help, it took me for-freakin'-*ever* to come up with the right persona. Those ladies are fierce! But I've done a half-dozen shows with them, and last week the director told me I could have a shot at the closing spot." He bounced in his seat, rocking his hips from side to side. "Oh, I cannot wait. It's going to be a*maz*ing!"

"Yes, please go." Jimmy's tone was serious. "I wanted to be there, but the group we have coming in this week is a major deal, and there's just no way I can get away." He leaned his head on Cory's shoulder. "You know I'm sorry, babe."

Cory lowered his head to rest atop Jimmy's and reached across with one hand to pat his cheek. "I know, love. It's okay. I'm confident it won't be my only chance in the spotlight."

Evan's chest twisted at the loving display the two of them made. It had been years since... no. He'd never had a relationship like that. He'd loved Lucas, but they hadn't had the chance to grow into the kind of committed couple that Cory and Jimmy were.

They hadn't had a chance at all.

The rich, savory bite of eggs and hollandaise sauce in Evan's mouth turned to soggy cardboard, and he forced himself to finish chewing and swallow. He laid his fork and knife on the table and downed the remains of his mimosa, wishing it were something stronger than alcohol. But that thought just reminded him of Lex, and he wouldn't go there.

Now, drowning his sorrows in sex, on the other hand....

He pasted a smile on his face, under the "fake it 'til you make it" principle, and turned to Riley. "Are you busy later?"

Riley lifted an eyebrow but didn't look away from where he was cutting another piece of crepe. "Actually, I'm flying to Orlando tonight. A friend is moving up here this week, and I'm going to help him finish packing and ride back here with him." He lifted his head and smiled. "And knowing Mikey, it'll take every moment of the week to get him up here. It's taken me two years to convince him to move in the first place."

Jimmy snorted out a laugh. "Sounds like me trying to convince this one into a relationship." He elbowed Cory. "I swear, it was like renegotiating the Treaty of Versailles."

Evan couldn't remember the last time he'd seen Cory blush, but there he went. "It wasn't that bad," Cory insisted. "You wanted room to play as much as I did."

"Oh." Riley put so much meaning into the word that it might as well have been a soliloquy. "I didn't realize you had an open relationship."

"They like sharing twinks," Evan murmured, leaning toward Riley as if sharing a secret. "I had to fend Cory off you before you got here or you'd be in their sights right now."

Riley copied Evan's stance. "Did you tell them how far out of the range of 'twink' I actually am?"

"Absolutely not," Evan said. He turned to grin at Riley, their faces only inches apart. "I never give away ages."

Cory's soft laugh drew their attention. "Trust me, boys, just a couple of minutes and we would've known to keep our hands off anyway."

Riley drew back, as if he'd just realized how close he was to Evan. He forked up another piece of crepes. "I'll admit I've never been all that sure about open relationships," he said. "I've known a few people who've tried it, and it never seems to last. If you don't mind me asking...."

"You have to trust each other implicitly," Jimmy replied. "Cory and I were together for over a year before we even considered being exclusive. And the more we considered it, the more we realized that agreeing to be monogamous would be a one-way ticket to infidelity. So, we talked." He looked at Cory, who shook his head with a wry smile.

"And talked, and talked, and talked. Not to mention a hell of a lot of fucking." Cory laughed.

"That too," Jimmy agreed. "But eventually we found a compromise, and it's worked for... hell, almost six years now?"

Cory gave a put-upon sigh. "Six years. That's like a silver anniversary in gay time."

Riley smiled, and for the first time that morning, it seemed to be real. "What did you decide on?"

Jimmy elbowed Cory, who rolled his eyes but recited, "Play on the outside, not on the inside."

Riley tilted his head. "So, touching, hand jobs, frottage, but no blowjobs, no kissing—"

Jimmy cut him off. "Kissing is fine. People always say 'oh, kissing is more intimate than sex.' That's a load of hogwash," Jimmy scoffed. "Sticking your tongue in someone's mouth is not more intimate than sticking your dick in their ass. Kissing is fun. Fucking is serious business."

Evan's face warmed, and he gave Jimmy a warning look. Jimmy had never outed Evan about his job, but while Evan wasn't embarrassed, exactly, he didn't think he was ready for Riley to know. Jimmy didn't look at Evan as he gave Riley a smile.

"Anyway, that's what works for us. I don't presume to tell other people what works for them." He leaned his head on Cory's shoulder, which wasn't much of a lean for him, considering how much taller Cory was. "The only part we haven't successfully negotiated yet is living together."

"Oh God," Cory moaned. He fixed his gaze on Riley. "Jimmy is a fucking neat freak. Everything has to be in the right place and sparkling clean all the damn time. I swear someday I'm gonna have him committed for extreme OCD."

"Oh, get over it, honeychild." Jimmy shoved Cory's arm with his shoulder. "How much work does it take to throw your clothes in the hamper instead of on the floor next to it? Or put your dirty dishes in the sink?"

"This from the guy who spent three hours Thursday morning scrubbing down the entire kitchen and two bathrooms before our cookout." Cory huffed and rolled his eyes at Evan. "And I have a cleaning lady! But apparently her standards are not up to Mr. Clean's here."

"Her standards appear to include not doing floors, toilets, or stoves," Jimmy shot back. He shook his head. "*Any*way. If we ever do manage to find a boy to take care of us in our old age, he'll have to be better at housework than *this* one."

Riley had a small smile on his face as he watched their interplay. "I'm sure you'll work it out eventually," he finally said. "It's clear that the two of you belong together."

"No one else would put up with them," Evan murmured, and Cory crowed with laughter.

"That's right, honey! The secret to a happy relationship is driving each other mutually crazy."

"And separate bathrooms," Jimmy added, before the two of them dissolved into giggles.

Riley turned to Evan, an eyebrow lifted. "Are they always like this?"

"No," Evan said, reaching for his water glass. "Usually, they're much worse."

MORE THAN an hour later, the four of them finally emerged from the restaurant into the gorgeous late spring warmth outside. Cory and Jimmy were all smiles and hugs as they parted ways outside.

"Come to my show," Cory urged Riley. "It'll be a blast. Bring your friend! He'll love it."

"He probably would," Riley admitted. "But either way, break a leg."

Jimmy groaned. "Careful, he might take you literally. You haven't seen him walk in high heels."

"Shut up." Cory smacked the back of one hand into Jimmy's stomach, then reached out to wrap Evan in a quick hug. "You will definitely be there, right?"

"Wouldn't miss it," Evan promised. Cory pulled back and gave Evan a serious look for a long moment, and Evan tried to look unruffled. He probably didn't succeed, but after all the years they'd been friends, Cory knew when not to push.

"Okay, boys, see you soon! Bye-bye!" Cory grabbed Jimmy's hand, and the two of them headed for the parking lot behind the restaurant. Evan turned to Riley.

"What time is your flight?" he asked. "Do you need a ride to the airport or anything?"

"It's at eight fifteen, and no, thank you. It's covered." He smiled. "I really do need to run, though. I'm not as OCD about cleaning as Jimmy is, but I do like to have the place neat when I get home from a trip. Plus Mikey's staying with me, so I need to make sure I have what he'll need."

Evan took a step closer. "I'd like to see you when you get back." And just like that, Riley closed off. Evan could almost see the door slamming shut, behind the bright façade Riley pasted on.

"Well, we'll try to come to Cory's show, so maybe we'll see you there." He leaned forward and dropped a brief peck on Evan's cheek. "Thanks for the brunch invitation. Have a great week!"

Riley turned and headed toward his building, and Evan could only stand and watch him go.

CHAPTER 9

A WALL of sound hit Evan in the face when he stepped into Bernhardt's the following Saturday night. The show hadn't started yet, so he wasn't all that late, but clearly the place was already ramped up. For once, he welcomed the raw energy surrounding him. He'd had a slow week, just one short shoot with a local company and several more ignored calls from his mother. He'd spent most of his time at home, giving the place a good deep cleaning, goaded into it by the conversation at brunch the previous Sunday.

In short, he'd been bored as hell, and he was ready to cut loose a little.

He walked across the small bar area just inside the door, which only had a few small groups hanging around, to check out the next room over, where the performers would be doing their thing. That room was stuffed. It never had been quite big enough to accommodate the most popular shows, though it helped that the open second floor formed a sort of balcony so more people could watch from above.

Evan caught a glimpse of blond curls at the near end of the bar, so he worked his way over. Sure enough, Riley was ensconced on one of the barstools, one hand wrapped around a glass that Evan was sure held club soda with lemon and lime. He turned his head as Evan approached, and he gave a small smile.

"Glad you could make it," Evan said as he stopped next to him.

"Seemed like a good cause." Riley lifted his free hand. "Evan, this is my friend Mikey O'Malley. Mikey, this is—"

"Trevor. Fucking. Hardball." Mikey's voice held a note of awe, and Evan's heart sank.

Oh shit.

"Riley!" Mikey slapped Riley on the shoulder. "You didn't tell me you were dating a porn star!"

Riley eyed Evan with interest, but no apparent scorn or anger. "That would be because I didn't know, honey. You know I rarely indulge." He gave Mikey a sidelong glance. "Unlike your own interest."

Evan girded himself and stepped into the fray. "Evan," he said, holding out his hand. "Evan Day. I'd appreciate it if you'd keep that between us, though. It's not a huge deal, but—"

"I'm very glad to meet you," Mikey said, his voice serious though his eyes still smiled. "And trust me, I'm not going to spread anything around." He grinned. "Well, I might tell people that I met you, but I'll keep the real-name part of things under wraps."

As they shook hands, Riley caught Evan's gaze. "Mikey and I lived near each other growing up, but his family moved to Orlando years ago," he said. "He's moved back here to go to art school."

Evan nodded and looked back to Mikey. "What type of art?"

"Animation." Mikey practically glowed with excitement. "I know it's kind of weird, but I'm a huge Disney fan, and I'd love to be an animator someday. I've been trying to teach myself, but I wasn't getting very far, and then Riley said if I wanted to study it—"

"Mikey." Riley's reproving tone stopped Mikey short, but somehow, Evan just *knew* what he'd been about to say.

He lifted an eyebrow. "You got a Yeats scholarship, hmmm?"

Riley relaxed at that, and Mikey laughed. "Yes!" Mikey said. "I mean, I took some graphic art at tech school, and I've been working at Disney as a cast member since high school, but ugh, I *really* want to do animation. I got into SCAD"—he referenced the Savannah College of Art and Design, which had a large campus in Atlanta—"but there was no way I could pay for it without a huge amount of debt. Riley to the rescue!"

Evan watched a blush appear on Riley's cheeks. "That's a good thing." Evan let it go at that, but if he hadn't already been... *smitten*, to use Cory's word, with Riley, this gesture would've gone a long way.

The music cut off just then, and the screen on the far wall went dark before it started playing a new video. The well-known intro music for the Stilettos began playing, and the crowd cheered as each of the troupe's members appeared on the screen in all her campy glory. Evan took advantage of the distraction to lean in and request a SweetWater 420 from the bartender, who delivered it with a quick smile and made change in ones for the ten Evan handed him. Evan left a single as a tip and kept the others for the show.

The performers and crowd were off-the-scale hyped up for the show. Evan hadn't been to a drag show in a while, and it had been a year or so since he'd seen the Stilettos' campy, funny take on the genre. The glitz, glitter, and high heels of any drag show were bracketed by emcees displaying crazy makeup designs—several had beards on full display—who spun out corny jokes and more double entendres than Evan could count.

Evan stuck close to Riley and Mikey during the show, watching their reactions with interest. The performers came out in their shining finest and worked the crowd hard, racking up piles of tips for the charities the group supported. Evan added his own money, passing a few dollars to each performer as she passed by his spot at the bar. Riley smiled and applauded, tipped each performer, and let his foot tap along with the bouncing pop songs they lip-synched. Mikey, by contrast, seemed about to vibrate out of his skin, so excited by the spectacle that Evan wondered if he'd ever been to a show like this at all. He supposed he might not have, if he'd still been living with his parents.

Part of Evan envied that innocence. He hardly remembered how it felt to be stepping out into the gay world on his own for the first time. Back then, he'd still been in shock from the way his life had been ripped apart. He'd gone along blindly with whatever anyone around him suggested, and while he rarely let himself think about those days too hard, at moments like this, he remembered how thankful he was to have had support from Cory and Jimmy. Things could've been so much worse.

Another performer finished her Lady Gaga lip-synch with a flourish, and the crowd erupted into cheers as she collected the last of her tips and waved her way offstage. The emcees reemerged and launched back into their trademark banter, laced with suggestive comments and pop culture references. Evan pulled his phone out of his pocket to check the time. With only fifteen minutes left in the advertised performance window, Cory should be up next.

Sure enough, the bearded emcee in the pink dress—cupid's bow lips painted to match—smiled and spoke louder. "And now, ladies and gentlemen, without further ado—"

"Ado, ado, to you and you and you-ooo!" the other emcee singsonged, earning a laugh from the crowd and a backhanded slap to the stomach from her cohort.

"…without further interruption from the peanut gallery, the Stilettos are proud to present, in her debut headlining performance—the fabulous Miss Coco Lamé!"

The music started back up, lights flashed, and then out came Coco in all her flashy glory. She wore a gold-sequined vest with matching fringe over a white, midriff-baring top, though as she moved, Evan could see that the midriff was actually covered with flesh-colored spandex. Her cowgirl-style hat, tight skirt, and boots shimmered with black glitter, and on one hip, she carried what appeared to be a holster trimmed in even more shiny gold.

Evan was too busy trying not to laugh at the overkill to notice the music, but when Riley lifted a carefully groomed eyebrow and leaned closer, Evan leaned in to catch his comment.

"I wouldn't have figured Cory—excuse me, Coco—for a Pointer Sisters fan."

Sure enough, Coco launched into an energetic rendition of "I'm So Excited." She shimmied, she twisted, she pointed and flirted, and the crowd went crazy for it all. Hands waved money at her in all directions, and Coco collected it with hands, cleavage, and that holster, its presence clearly meant for more than just show.

Coco came closer to their end of the bar, and Evan shared a smile with her as she took the fiver he held out and leaned in to give him a kiss on his cheek. She took Riley's tip the same way, and then turned to Mikey, who stood as if in shock, staring.

Riley's eyebrow rose again. "Mikey, honey, you're supposed to tip the nice lady now," he admonished.

Mikey snapped back to attention, a blush rising high on his cheeks as he held out his offering. Coco slithered closer, taking Mikey's wrist and giving an assist for him to deposit the cash directly into her cleavage. Maintaining her grip on Mikey, she pulled him in close for a gentle kiss on the mouth, leaving behind a swipe of bright red lipstick to go with the now deep red of his cheeks. She gave him a final lingering glance and a wink and went back to working the rest of the crowd.

Evan couldn't help smirking at Mikey, who just stared after Coco, dumbstruck. He leaned closer to Riley. "I think your boy might have a little bit of a crush."

Riley laughed softly. "I can't imagine where you could have gotten *that* idea."

THEY HUNG around after the show ended until Cory emerged from the back room, bling shed in favor of jeans and a T-shirt, though some shimmering bits clung around the edges. He grinned when he saw Evan and practically bounced across the room, duffel bag held in one hand.

"Oh my God!" He threw his free arm around Evan in a hug. "Thank you *so* much for coming. That was so fucking much fun!" He backed away to smile at Riley before transferring his attention to Mikey. "Seriously, you guys were awesome. Thanks for being here!"

Riley smiled. "Cory… I'm afraid I don't recall your last name?"

"Lassiter," Cory supplied, gaze never leaving Mikey's.

"Cory Lassiter, this is my very best friend, Mikey O'Malley."

Cory moved closer to Mikey and held out his free hand. "I'm very pleased to meet you, Mikey."

Mikey swallowed visibly. Evan imagined it would've been audible, too, had the music not been so loud. "The pleasure is all mine," he replied as their hands met.

Evan could almost see the bubble form around the two men. He turned his attention back to Riley. "Were you headed home after this?"

Riley finished his drink and set it on the bar. "Actually, yes, I should really be going." He slid off the barstool and shot a look toward

Mikey, who only had eyes for Cory. "I think Mikey already has his ride home handled, but he has cash for a cab if that falls through."

Evan chuckled. "Well, if you wanted some company…."

Riley gave him a smile as fake as the eyelashes Cory had worn during his act. "Thanks for the offer, honey, but it's not a good night." He leaned up to brush a kiss over Evan's cheek. "You have a great night, all right?"

He turned and was gone before Evan could blink, much less muster any kind of protest.

"ANOTHER ROUND?"

Evan's vision blurred as he blinked at the bartender. "How many's that? Three?"

The man—Bill? Tony? Damned if Evan could remember—laughed. "Yeah, I think you're done." He reached for the two empty shot glasses still sitting on the bar. "I've served you twice that many. If you're that far off? I think you're eighty-sixed."

Evan frowned. "M'not drunk enough."

A hand landed on his shoulder. "Yeah, you are."

Evan swiveled his head and tried to focus on whoever had walked up next to him. "C'mon, man." The voice sounded familiar, but his brain couldn't force the name through the alcohol.

"'Nother drink!"

"No." The man had him by the arm now. "We're going home, Evan. I'm taking Mikey home, and then I'm taking you home. Say good night to the nice bartender."

Evan rotated his head back toward the bar. "G'night."

The bartender shook his head. "Good night, man. Hope you're not hurting too much in the morning."

Arm still held in a death grip, Evan stumbled his way up the steps to the entrance and out into the night. It wasn't any cooler outside, but the air was fresher, without the cloud of cigarette smoke and sweat that had pervaded the bar.

"All right, keep moving, now." Evan's mind had cleared a little just from being up and moving around, and he recognized Cory now, though he didn't know who the guy with him was.

"After hours?" Somewhere deep under the alcohol and nicotine haze, Evan knew the answer, but he said it anyway.

"The only place you're going now is to bed. Well, first into my car, and then we'll drop off Mikey, but then? Bed."

Mikey. Oh yeah. The guy with Riley. Riley.

"Wanna see Riley." Evan walked into something. It was the side of a car.

Cory grunted, pushing Evan aside so he could get the door unlocked and open. "Inside," he ordered, and Evan flopped down into the passenger seat, mainly because his legs didn't want to hold him up anymore. He struggled to get them inside, too, but they didn't want to work right. Another set of hands grabbed them and swung them into the car, and Evan sighed, exhausted from the effort.

The door closed, and Evan's head dropped against the window. The cool of the glass felt nice on his temple, so he shifted to press the whole side of his face against it. He heard some noises, some people talking, but he didn't pay any attention.

"All right. Evan, hon, if you think you're gonna barf, try to warn me so I can pull over or at least get the window down, okay?"

The car lurched into motion, and Evan's stomach let him know that barfing might be a distinct possibility. Evan closed his eyes, streetlights and headlights strobing through his eyelids, and drifted.

"Evan, hon? Can you come in with us?"

Evan blinked awake. He turned his head to find Cory looking at him, his brow furrowed in concern. Evan was still drunk off his ass, but he'd sobered up enough to be aware of it, which was an improvement. Of sorts.

"Yeah." He reached for the door handle and got it open on the first try. "Go me," he muttered, pulling himself out and then steadying himself with one hand on the doorframe and the other on the car roof, just to be sure his legs would hold him. They seemed steady enough, so he stepped away from the car, pushing the door shut behind him.

Cory and Mikey met him at the front end of the car. Mikey looked like he'd had a few drinks himself, but Cory's eyes were bright and clear. "Let's get Mikey delivered safely, and then we'll get you back to yours."

He wrapped an arm around Mikey's shoulders and headed up the stairs. Evan followed in their wake, concentrating on *not* tripping and *not* throwing up. Mikey had a code for the secured entrance, so they didn't have to wait for Riley to buzz them in, at least. The elevator ride gave Evan's stomach another adventure, but within a few minutes, Mikey was unlocking the door to Riley's place and Evan was following him and Cory inside.

"Let me get you guys some water." Mikey kept his voice low, and with all the lights in the unit off except the one over the stove, Evan figured Riley must be asleep. He wandered into the living room and fell onto the sofa sideways, legs hanging off at an angle that would probably be uncomfortable soon. But he didn't have the energy to move.

He floated again, hearing soft noises off in the distance and his own breathing inside his head.

"Hey, man. Let's get you up."

Hands were on him, and he whined as Cory pulled him into a semisitting position. "Drink," Cory said, pushing a bottle of water in front of him. Evan took it and sipped, then tipped the bottle up to drink deeply, suddenly dry as a desert.

"Whoa, man." Cory manhandled the bottle away from him. "Let that settle first. Last thing we need is for you to—"

Too late. Evan lurched to his feet and ran for the bathroom. As he crouched over the toilet, retching up everything he'd drunk that night and a couple of spare body parts, he had a fleeting thought of thanks that he'd been there before. At least he'd known where to go when his stomach rebelled.

Someone laid a cool cloth across the back of his neck, and once again a bottle of water appeared in front of him. "Thanks," he rasped.

"Thanks for making it to the bathroom."

Evan jerked his head up toward Riley and immediately regretted it when the tile spun. He lunged for the toilet again, dry heaving and spitting. He broke into an all-over sweat and immediately began shivering in the cool air.

The cloth slid away from his neck, and a moment later, a towel was wrapped around his shoulders. "Rinse your mouth," Riley instructed, holding out the water again, and Evan did as instructed, rinsing and spitting into the toilet. He reached with a shaky hand to flush and then sat back on the thick bath mat that had cushioned his knees.

"Thanks." He swallowed and took a tiny sip of water to soothe his ravaged throat. "Sorry."

"Not necessary." Riley leaned against the vanity, arms crossed. "Any particular reason you felt the need to drink yourself into oblivion tonight?"

Evan shrugged one shoulder. Even if he'd wanted to get into everything—which he didn't—he still had too much alcohol coursing through his system to make any amount of sense.

Riley sighed. "Right. Well, I'm not going to leave you on the bathroom floor, but I don't relish the idea of having a mess like this in my bed. Mikey decided to go home with Cory—against my protests, but he's a grown man—so the guest room's open. I'll get it ready while you stay here and make sure you're done being sick. Okay?"

Evan nodded once, not about to risk more movement than that. All he really grasped was that there was a bed he could sleep in, even one without Riley in it. The thought of dragging himself home in this condition was more than he could stand.

He stayed there, face against the cool of the tile wall, and waited for his stomach to settle, or not, as the case might be. It didn't improve, but it didn't get worse, either. By the time Riley returned, Evan actually felt like he might be able to walk far enough to climb into bed.

"All right, let's get you up." Riley held out a hand, but Evan ignored it, pushing himself carefully to his feet. Riley raised an eyebrow before turning and heading back into the hall, and Evan followed, keeping one hand on the wall to steady himself. He made it safely to the bed and lowered himself to the mattress, curling up on his side.

"Shoes." Evan managed to toe them off, the sound of them hitting the floor probably not as loud in reality as it sounded in his head.

"You'd probably be more comfortable if you could get your jeans off."

Evan smiled at that, or tried, at least. "You gonna help?"

Riley snorted. "You're on your own there, honey."

Evan blew out a breath and started fumbling with the button. Thankful he hadn't worn button fly, he got the zipper down and shoved at the denim, eventually managing to work the jeans down and off. He might as well have run a marathon for how wrung out the process left him feeling.

"All right. Water on the table here, and a bottle of ibuprofen for when you wake up needing it. And I put a wastebasket right here in case you get sick again."

Evan made a noise he hoped sounded like acknowledgment. A moment later, he felt something soft and warm cover him.

"Sleep it off, honey." Soft lips brushed his temple. "See you in the morning."

Evan slept.

CHAPTER 10

"Ow."

The word spilled from Evan's mouth before he even knew he was awake. Sunlight streamed through the sheer curtains at the window of the unfamiliar room. Shielding his eyes with one hand, he squinted and looked around, trying to remember where the hell he was. His gaze landed on the bottles of ibuprofen and water on the nightstand.

Oh yeah. Riley's.

Evan groaned and buried his face in the pillow, even though it smelled of stale sweat and alcohol. Images of his behavior the night before flipped through his mind like a slideshow, and he cursed his memory. Why couldn't he be a blackout drunk and just forget it all? Oh, no, he had to remember what a complete ass he'd made of himself.

Dreading the whole idea of it, Evan forced himself to get out of bed and face the music. He sat up first and reached for the bottles. After shaking out three pills, he cracked open the water to wash them down. He forced himself to drink all of the water, slowly, even though his stomach didn't much like the idea. Then he climbed to his feet and grabbed his jeans, which were draped over a chair against the wall. He had to brace himself for balance to get into them, and he didn't bother zipping them up, because he'd need a bathroom stop before he went far.

He grabbed his shoes and headed into the hallway. The smell of coffee wafted toward him from the kitchen, equally enticing and nauseating, but he resisted long enough to make his pit stop. The cloth Riley had used the night before still lay over the edge of the sink, so after relieving himself, Evan used it to wash off his face and neck. A travel-size bottle of mouthwash sat on the glass shelf on the wall next to the mirror, so Evan took advantage of that bonus amenity, rinsing and spitting twice before wiping his mouth and bracing himself to face Riley.

He walked into the kitchen in his socked feet, pausing to set his shoes down at the edge of the tile floor.

Riley stood at the stove, stirring what looked like a pot of oatmeal.

"Hey," Evan said.

"Good morning." Riley didn't move. "Help yourself to coffee."

He sounded normal, but the rigid way he held his back told another story. Evan couldn't blame him, after the way Evan had rolled in the night before. He moved to the coffeemaker and poured himself a cup, then stirred in a lump of sugar from the bowl on the counter and added a healthy splash of cream from the small pitcher sitting nearby. No way would he chance black on an empty, post-drunken-night stomach.

"Thanks for last night." He leaned against the counter and watched Riley stir the pot. "And for not kicking me out. Sorry for making an ass of myself."

"Apology accepted."

Evan heard the words, but he didn't believe them. He put his coffee mug on the counter and moved the few feet to stand behind Riley, whose back stiffened even further. "I mean it, Riley," Evan murmured, running one hand across Riley's hip. "I acted like a complete idiot. Let me make it up to you."

Riley stopped stirring for a long moment. When the spoon starting moving again, Riley had relaxed maybe an iota. "There's an event tonight," he said. "A new exhibit at the art museum. My parents expect me." He took a breath and let it out slowly. "They don't expect me to arrive with a date."

Evan chuckled. "So you want to use me to shake up the folks a little?"

"Maybe."

"Deal." Evan leaned in and brushed his lips across the back of Riley's neck. "Do I need a tux or something?"

"Do you have one?" Riley's shoulders had lowered from near his ears down to something approximating normal.

"No, but I can find one." Evan kissed Riley's neck again and watched as Riley relaxed even more.

"No need. A suit would be nice, but dress pants and a nice shirt will work fine. Nothing showy." Riley glanced at him then, giving a wry smile over his shoulder. "I'll take care of that."

Evan lifted a hand and brushed his fingers across Riley's full lips. "I should probably go, then. I might need to do some laundry." He leaned away and lifted one arm to give himself a sniff. "Not to mention take a shower. Or three."

Riley laughed softly, sounding back to himself by then. "A shower wouldn't go amiss." He turned back to his oatmeal. "I made enough for two, though, so you should stay to eat."

That was an invitation Evan wouldn't turn down.

OVER BREAKFAST—the super-creamy oatmeal was sweetened with brown sugar and studded with blueberries and walnuts—Riley brushed aside Evan's attempt at more apologies and instead chatted about Cory's performance and how much Mikey had enjoyed the night. "I hadn't realized how little he'd gotten out." Riley shook his head. "I know his parents are conservative, though I haven't talked to them in years. I'm just glad he managed to break free. I'm trying not to hover. Let him make some mistakes if he needs to. Maybe it'll help him figure himself out."

Evan chuckled. "Cory's good at that," he said. "If it hadn't been for him, I don't know where I'd be now."

Riley raised an interested eyebrow. "You mean doing porn?"

The tone of the question had Evan reconsidering. Maybe it wasn't his drunken escapade that had Riley acting weird. Evan had completely forgotten about the little porn revelation the night before.

He swirled his coffee, unsure where to start that conversation. "I...." He trailed off, realizing he'd never told Riley about his military background. "I used to be in the Marines, until they found out I was

94

gay." He wasn't about to bring up Lucas. "And let's just say things didn't go well when I got home. Cory knew my brother from way back, and he kind of stepped in after Charlie died. When he found out what was going on, he offered me a place to stay. He and Jimmy had just started trying the living-together thing back then."

Riley nodded. "And they brought you in as a third?"

Evan chose his words carefully. "Not exactly. I mean, yeah, we had sex some, but it wasn't any kind of formal thing." Steeling himself, he lifted his eyes to meet Riley's gaze. "Doing porn was their idea. Jimmy was just retiring from the industry, so he knew people, and he's pretty savvy, so he also knew what not to do." He shrugged. "It's a living. I'm good at it, and it pays the bills."

Riley tilted his head. "I don't mind the job, honey, if that's what's worrying you." He lifted his coffee mug. "It just caught me off guard. I...." He paused, mug held in front of his mouth, and his next words were so soft Evan had to strain to hear them. "I don't often hang around long enough to get into details about day jobs."

Evan knew that feeling, but before he could say more, Riley swallowed his mouthful of coffee and smiled again. "So you've known Cory and Jimmy a while, then?"

Evan accepted the obvious change of subject. He could revisit the rest later. "Cory played high school football with my brother," he said, pushing aside the flash of pain thinking of Charlie always gave him. "And he is a mother hen like you wouldn't believe, so swooping in to take care of me was just second nature." He smiled. "He and Jimmy are good people."

Riley scooped up a spoonful of oatmeal. "Okay. But if they're a committed couple—"

"They are," Evan interrupted. He reached for his coffee again. "They love each other completely. But they love twinks too, so sometimes, they'll pick one up to share." His mouth twisted. "They've only had a long-term third once, for about a year, but they found out he'd been secretly fucking other people. And they might not be completely monogamous, but they don't hide things from each other."

Riley nodded. "So Cory taking Mikey home...?"

95

"…would not include full-on sex. And if it lasted for any length of time, it would end up as Cory, Jimmy, and Mikey." He watched Riley's face closely. "Would you have a problem with that?"

"I don't really know." Riley stirred his coffee idly. "I'm trying to stay hands-off and let him find his own way, but Mikey's just so new to all this. That sounds like diving into the deep end before you learn how to doggy-paddle."

Evan smiled. "Yeah. But they're good guys, and they're very protective. They'll be careful with him. Especially since they know you already."

Riley nodded and finished off his coffee. "Well, I need to get things moving for the day," he said, pushing back his chair. "Can you be ready at six thirty? Preshow cocktails start at seven, and if I'm going to freak out the parents, then I'd better be on time."

"Sure." Evan took the one last sip of coffee and set down the empty mug. "Should I come here, or…?"

"I remember where you live," Riley said. "I'll pick you up."

"I'll be ready." Evan stood and stepped up close enough to kiss Riley's cheek. "Thanks again for putting up with my drunk self last night."

Riley's cheeks pinked. "You're welcome," he murmured. "Try not to have quite so much tonight?"

Evan laughed. "I'll be on my best behavior. Scout's honor."

Riley eyed him. "Why do I doubt you were a Boy Scout?"

"Oh, but I was," Evan replied. "But that's a story for another day."

He gave a final smile and headed for the door, feeling lighter than he had in weeks. He had an actual date with Riley, even if he'd have to put up with stodgy, artsy-fartsy types and apparently Riley's parents. *Shit*. He'd better find his suit fast and make sure it would be okay….

RILEY'S BMW pulled up to the curb outside Evan's apartment at 6:29, less than five minutes after Evan got downstairs. His suit had needed to be pressed, but thankfully, the dry cleaner down the street had been able to do that in less than an hour. Evan paired the charcoal gray with a medium-blue dress shirt and one of only three ties he owned, this one a deep blue paisley. He'd polished his dress shoes with military precision, until even his old drill sergeant wouldn't have been able to find fault.

In short, he'd cleaned up nice.

He slid into the passenger seat of Riley's car and gave Riley a smile. "How'd I do?" he asked, waving a hand down his body.

Riley's lips curved up. "Very impressive," he said, checking the street before pulling out from the curb. "I hope you like beef Wellington. I didn't think to mention the menu for dinner earlier. They do have a vegetarian option, so if you'd prefer that, I can inform the catering staff when we arrive."

Evan lifted an eyebrow at Riley's formal turn of phrase. "I didn't realize dinner was included, but yes, that's fine. More than fine, actually. I haven't had beef Wellington in years." Not since his brother's high school graduation dinner, actually. His parents had spared no expense when Charlie graduated near the top of his class, unlike for his own graduation four years later. He tried to tamp down the lingering resentment. He'd graduated by the skin of his teeth, and that week had been the anniversary of Charlie's death. Of course his parents hadn't been up for a big celebration.

Evan forced his mind away from that line of thinking and took in Riley's appearance. He'd slicked down his blond curls, making him look older and much more formal than usual, which went well with the slim-cut black suit he wore. It wasn't a tuxedo, but close, and he'd worn a pale peach shirt and a tie swirled with a rainbow of pastel colors. A subtle statement, Evan guessed, one that few would likely pick up.

But his parents would get it, and that was the point.

"You look great," Evan said. "I like the tie."

One corner of Riley's mouth turned up. "I have one that's bright, wide stripes," he admitted, "but I thought I'd let my choice of date speak for itself."

Evan laughed. "Well, I'll be on my best behavior, then."

"I can't promise that, but I'll try to keep the snark to a minimum." Riley stopped at a light. "Have you been to the museum before?"

"Once, many years ago, on a school field trip. They had a special exhibit on local artists, mostly folk art and things like that." Evan thought for a second. "I do remember being entranced by a painting of a nude man. I guess that should've told me something, huh?"

Riley chuckled. "Well-done art can draw you in no matter your usual preferences, but yes, that might have given you a bit of a clue." He turned left and then almost immediately right, bringing the car to a stop next to a man wearing black pants, a crisp white shirt, and a bow tie. After a moment, Evan's door opened, and a similarly dressed man stood there.

"Nice service," Evan remarked as he slid out of the car. He stood and looked around, noticing the nearby valet lot appeared stuffed full of high-end vehicles, uniformly shiny and mostly black. Riley's dark blue coupe wouldn't stand out even among the sea of sedans and SUVs.

After an exchange of keys and retrieval of tickets, Riley joined Evan on the curb. "Shall we?" He gestured toward the entry, which featured a traditional red carpet leading up to the door but lacked the flurry of paparazzi that usually would accompany it.

Feeling a little reckless, Evan crooked his elbow at Riley. "We shall." Riley's lips curved up, and he slipped his hand through Evan's arm. They walked inside arm in arm, heads held high.

"OH MY God." Riley collapsed into giggles as soon as they got back into his car a few hours later. "Did you see the look on old Dr. Bancroft's face?"

"Was he the one with the Trump-worthy comb-over and the Barbie doll trophy wife?"

"That's the one."

"He took one look at us and turned green around the gills, I swear." Evan snorted. "Nearly put him off his beef Wellington to have a couple of *fags* at his table."

"The irony," Riley said, getting himself under control enough to start the drive back home, "is that I know for a fact that he's in the deepest, darkest reaches of the closet. I know at least three guys he's hooked up with. For money, of course," he added. "I don't know anyone who'd sleep with him for free."

"They earned their fees, that's for sure." Evan shook his head. "It's always the closet cases who yell the loudest about *the gays*."

Riley sighed. "Sometimes I almost feel sorry for them. They hate themselves so much." He giggled again. "I wonder how someone like Fred Phelps would've turned out if he'd just given in to the draw of the dick."

Evan shuddered. "Ugh. That'd be so much worse even than Dr. Comb-over. Can you imagine sticking your dick in that dried-up thing?"

"Awwwww, c'mon," Riley cooed. "With any luck, we'll both get old someday, and we'll still want the dick even then."

"Don't want to think about it. I'm going to stay young forever." Evan reached across to pat Riley's thigh. "Don't worry. I won't give you too much grief about being *so much* older than me."

Riley shot him a look. "I was going to ask if you wanted to come over," he said drily. "But I'm beginning to rethink the invitation."

Evan flushed warm. "Is your roommate home?"

"No." Riley arched an eyebrow. "He's still with your friend, though he's promised he's safe and sound and will be back tomorrow."

"Do I get to peel you out of that suit?"

"Only if I get to peel you out of yours."

"Deal." Evan let his hand wander back to Riley's leg, rubbing this time, brushing his fingers dangerously close to his crotch. "I'll even let you make me breakfast."

RILEY MADE good on his promise, starting as soon as they got into his loft by slowly sliding Evan's tie off and tucking it into his jacket pocket. Evan toed off his shoes, and Riley paused just long enough to slip out of his before going back to work on Evan's clothes. His jacket ended up laid over the back of the sofa, and Riley worked the buttons of his shirt open slowly, running his fingertips over each inch of skin as he uncovered it.

They didn't speak, their increasing breath rates and occasional moans doing the talking for both of them. Evan let Riley get his shirt off before he took his turn, gradually stripping Riley to the waist and then lowering himself to his knees before reaching to open Riley's pants.

He looked up as he slid the zipper open. Riley gazed down on him like a fallen angel, his hair curling out of its smooth style, the light in the entryway setting the golden strands glowing. His pale skin flushed with arousal, he watched Evan avidly as he pushed open the front of his pants and leaned in to nose along Riley's hard cock, outlined sharply against the snug, bright pink briefs he wore. Evan smiled. He should've known Riley would have a hidden message under his uptown clothes.

He pulled down the waistband of Riley's briefs, catching his cock in his mouth when it bounced free of its confinement. Riley's sharp flavor invaded his mouth, familiar but still new, and Evan sucked him in all the way, enjoying the uncontrolled moan Riley let out. Riley slid his hand across Evan's scalp, the sensation making Evan shiver, and he bobbed his head, sucking hard, playing his tongue along Riley's shaft.

God, he loved this. The first time he'd had a cock in his mouth—Lucas's cock—had felt like the answer to all the questions he hadn't even known to ask, and it had only gotten better from there. He loved fucking and getting fucked, but sucking a dick was the ultimate, all the flavors and smells added to the power of being on his knees, bringing another man to *his* knees.

"Oh God." And right on cue, there went Riley's legs. Evan held him up and got them turned so Riley could lean on the back of the couch. Evan was unwilling to let up until he had a mouthful of Riley's cum, and Riley seemed to be on board, using his newly settled spot as leverage to pump his hips in counterpoint to Evan's movements. Evan braced his hands on the sofa on either side of Riley's hips and opened his throat, nodding as Riley took an experimental thrust. Riley took the signal as the encouragement it was, wrapped both hands around Evan's head, and started fucking Evan's mouth.

Evan settled in, closing his eyes and letting Riley take him at his own pace. He didn't expect it to last long, but he didn't expect Riley to falter and then stop, just the tip of his cock inside Evan's mouth.

"Look at me," Riley murmured, and Evan opened his eyes, focusing on Riley's face. "I want you to know who's fucking you."

Evan's heart thudded as Riley shifted back into motion, and he couldn't look away from the gaze that pierced him. Something unnamed flowed between them, a thread of understanding and shared experience. Their paths may have been different, but they'd ended up much in the same place: isolated, so alone in so many ways, and yet here, together, sharing desire and intimacy.

Riley's eyelids eventually fluttered shut as his orgasm took him, but Evan couldn't look away. He watched the pink flush overtake the creamy skin on Riley's chest as he shook through his climax, watched beads of sweat pop up on his forehead, dampening the blond fringe of curls. Riley's mouth was open on a moan, lips pink and full, and he was beautiful, and Evan didn't *want* to look away.

He wanted to watch Riley come like that every day for the rest of his life.

The thought scared him so much he nearly lost his erection, which strained against his now wrinkled dress pants, but he did as he always did with unwanted thoughts and shoved it back to the darkest recesses of his mind. He licked off the last of Riley's cum and used his grip on the sofa to pull himself to his feet, dragging his body the length of Riley's as he rose.

"Bed?" he breathed out against Riley's mouth.

"Bed," Riley agreed before grabbing his hand and dragging him down the hallway.

EVAN FOLLOWED the smell of coffee to the kitchen at much-too-early the next morning. Riley stood at the stove wearing loose shorts. He tossed a smile over his shoulder.

"Breakfast will be done in a few," he said. "Help yourself to coffee."

Evan did, watching Riley the whole time. He'd fucked Riley hard the night before. He'd gone into the evening thinking he'd get Riley to fuck him, but he'd needed to erase the memory of the tender moment they'd shared earlier. He couldn't let himself start thinking that way. Happy endings were for other people.

He sat at the table and watched Riley, trying to reconcile all the parts of the other man. He looked like a twink, all slim body and tousled curls, but he had a genteel way about him, likely a product of his upbringing. He could snap off a snarky or dirty comment in one moment but then offer tenderness and empathy in the next.

How he'd handled his parents the night before was a perfect example of his inner dichotomy. They'd managed to avoid a face-to-face most of the night, though Riley had pointed them out discreetly, and it was clear that they knew he'd arrived with a date. A *male* date. After the dinner, while the crowd moved from the banquet hall to the gallery where the exhibit was on display, Riley had taken Evan's hand in a strong grip and crossed the room to where his parents stood. After a brief introduction, punctuated by false smiles and limp handshakes all around, Riley had excused them and moved as far away from the older couple as possible. They hadn't crossed paths again the rest of the evening.

Evan watched Riley as he scrambled eggs, feeling like something was off but unable to tell what. Riley held himself more stiffly than usual, but Evan didn't think their activity of the night before was to blame. He sipped his coffee and bided his time. Maybe once the caffeine woke him a little more, he'd figure it out.

His phone chimed, and he checked it to find an e-mail from Jordan about the Erato shoot, which they'd scheduled for Saturday. He'd nearly forgotten. Quickly, he set up a notification on his phone so he wouldn't forget again.

As he finished, Riley came over with a plate piled high with eggs mixed with cheese. "I have managed to run completely out of bread and bacon."

"This looks amazing, don't worry." Evan gave him a wide smile, which Riley returned only halfheartedly. To his surprise, Riley didn't join him at the table. Instead, he crossed to the sink and started washing up the few dishes.

Evan lowered his fork and cleared his throat. "So, the event last night seemed to go well."

Riley didn't turn around. "Yes. Thanks again for going with me."

"No thanks necessary. I got an amazing free meal, and Dr. Comb-over's hair for entertainment."

Riley flashed a smile over his shoulder at that. "The exhibit itself was nice too, wasn't it?"

Evan shrugged a shoulder and scooped up a forkful of eggs. "Some of the paintings were pretty," he said. "I'm not big on fine art. I just know what I like, y'know? And most of that wasn't it."

"It's always some kind of postmodern statement about a consumerist society," Riley agreed. "Can't a painting of a tree just be a painting of a tree?"

Evan swallowed his bite and laughed. "Exactly. But no, the tree has to be withered and dying, and it represents the failings of environmentalism and the coming global apocalypse. Or something."

Riley nodded in response but fell silent, now working on cleaning the empty sink. Evan ate a few more bites of his eggs, which were delicious, before finally taking the plunge. "Your parents seemed nice enough."

Riley's spine stiffened, but he kept washing the already shiny stainless steel. A voice in Evan's head told him it was probably a bad idea to push it, but he didn't listen. "I mean, they weren't exactly friendly, but they didn't have claws or pointed teeth or anything."

"Appearances can be deceiving." Riley's voice was low and the words sounded forced, as if spoken through clenched teeth. He clearly did *not* want to talk about his parents. Evan understood the inclination, but Riley had been so glib before about being the black sheep of the family. Evan figured he wouldn't have cared how his parents reacted.

Then the answer hit, and Evan felt like an idiot.

"You aren't over it."

"Over what?" Riley didn't stop, barely reacted, just kept scrubbing.

"Your family." Evan leaned forward. "You haven't gotten over the way they treated you."

Riley stilled.

"You act like you don't care," Evan continued, hearing the note of wonder, of dawning comprehension in his own voice. "You put on this devil-may-care, poor-little-rich-boy front, but that's all it is. Inside, you're wrecked. You miss your family. And you'd do almost anything to have them back. Maybe even go back into the closet."

Silence filled the air. Evan could hear his own heartbeat in his head as he waited. For what, he wasn't sure.

"Get out."

Evan jerked. That sound... he'd never heard anything so angry from Riley. He hadn't known the man had it in him. Okay, well, yeah, he had. But he never thought he'd hear it, and especially not directed toward him.

"I said *get the hell out of my house.*"

Stunned, Evan rose to his feet. "Riley—"

Riley spun around, eyes flashing, high spots of color on his cheeks. "Please," he ground out between clenched teeth. "Just go. I can't—"

Evan reached out a hand and flinched when Riley jerked back. "Riley," he tried again, watching as Riley once again turned to the sink.

"You know your way out." Riley's voice shook minutely, but his back was ramrod straight, and he might as well have been wearing a sign that said "do not touch." Evan didn't want to go, not like this, but he knew Riley must be feeling as if any wrong move would shatter him. He knew trying to stay would only make things worse.

So he left.

CHAPTER 11

EVAN STARED into his empty cup, the plate with the half-eaten bagel pushed aside. The sounds of the café seemed far off, as if he had his ears plugged up. He itched, inside and out, like a million tiny bugs were stinging at him from everywhere. The buzz in his brain would drive him insane soon, he knew it.

What he didn't know was how to make it stop.

He'd been running on empty since he left Riley's place the morning before. He'd made some phone calls, and he'd done laundry, and he'd tried to watch some TV, but that got cut short the third time an ad for his father's law firm came on. There was no way Evan could stare at Charles Day's fake smile as he urged potential personal injury clients to "Have a Winning Day!"

Most of the time Evan had stared at the wall. He'd been unable to sleep the night before, thoughts bouncing around inside his skull, elusive and fleeting. His parents. His family. His friends. His job. And through it all, the one thing he could never stop thinking about, no matter how hard he tried:

Riley.

He didn't know how the quirky, slight man had wormed his way into every part of Evan's life, but there he was, plopped down front and center, with no intention of moving. Evan hadn't thought he'd wanted more than a hookup, but now? Even after Riley's uncharacteristic behavior the morning before, he wasn't so sure.

From the first moment they'd met, Riley had been a flash of brilliant light against the dark gray of Evan's life, bringing back warmth and energy Evan hadn't even known he'd been missing. Riley felt real, more than anything else in Evan's life, and part of Evan wanted to wrap both arms around that and never let it go.

A pretty large part of him, actually.

Maybe even all of him.

The buzzing in his mind faded. He wanted Riley in his life, at least as a friend. But could Riley be more than that? Could Evan convince him to take a chance?

Was that what Evan wanted?

And if he did... how could he make it happen?

Evan shook his head to dislodge the thoughts. It was too much to think about all at once. He'd been following the same path for so long that the idea of all that change was more than he could handle.

He needed time, and he needed space. And only one place could give him both.

CORY DIDN'T ask, but he kept sending meaningful glances Evan's way as they headed east on the interstate. When Evan had shown up at Cory's place a few hours earlier and said he wanted to go camping, Cory hadn't even asked. He'd just made a phone call and packed a bag. Owning his own company gave Cory enough flexibility and income to take off on a random Wednesday without much issue. He'd call the office every day, and Evan would need to be back for his shoot on Saturday, but otherwise, three days of freedom stretched in front of them.

Their destination, naturally, was Jimmy's resort. Adults-only and clothing-optional, the place stayed busy thanks to word of mouth and a few strategically placed ads, but Evan knew that he could almost always get a place to stay, especially during the week like this. In addition to traditional RV spaces and an area for tents, Oasis had a small cluster of rustic cabins, short on amenities but long on privacy, and unless he was completely overrun with demand, Jimmy usually held one of those back for friends.

Evan kept his eyes on the road, one finger lightly drumming the steering wheel in time to the dance mix playing on the satellite radio. They'd taken Cory's car, as usual, with its lower mileage and greater comfort than Evan's older model, but Evan had grabbed the keys, not willing to sit back and relax while Cory drove.

Even though Cory and Evan had never been lovers in the traditional sense, no one knew Evan better. Sometimes Evan forgot there had ever been a time they hadn't been friends, and one of Evan's favorite things about Cory was that he knew when to shut up. He had a naturally bubbly personality, and when Evan needed it, no one was better at drawing him out, cheering him up, showing him a good time. But Cory also was that rare friend who could sit with Evan and *not* talk. And it was obvious he knew that was what Evan needed.

Leaving Atlanta at midmorning meant the drive to the resort took only an hour, instead of close to twice that if they'd been caught in rush-hour traffic. Evan took the lonely exit and turned right, driving another mile before he reached the entrance off to the left. A small, tastefully designed sign read "Oasis" in script lettering and shades of blue and green. It looked more like the entrance to a high-end spa than a gay resort, despite the accompanying black-and-orange sign reading "Private Property: Keep Out."

The paved entrance gave way almost immediately to gravel, and Evan steered his way carefully down the winding driveway and pulled up in front of the main building. Half office and half social space, the bungalow-style structure overlooked the small lake on the grounds from the back deck, and every weekend night, there was an open bar and dance music for anyone who wanted to come out of their love nests for a while before diving back in for the night. A second building next to it, attached by a wide walkway, held Jimmy's personal living space.

Evan waited in the car while Cory ducked inside to greet Jimmy and get the keys to their cabin. Evan knew the space would have little more than a bed, a bathroom, and a couple of chairs, but that was fine, since most guests only used the cabins for sleeping, showering, and fucking. Otherwise, they'd be at the pool or partying in the social area. A few well-maintained trails circled the lake, too, and there were even clearings where couples could indulge urges for outdoor sex.

Cory was back in minutes with a key in his hand, a smile on his face, and a spark in his eye that told Evan he'd have the room to himself that night. Living separately like they did, Cory and Jimmy rarely slept apart when they were in the same place, and it looked like they planned to take full advantage of Cory's impromptu visit.

"Cabin eight," Cory said. Evan restarted the car and headed down the path to the last cabin on the left, knowing exactly where to go from his previous visits. The cabin was right next to one of the hot tubs—the property had two—which was handy but also meant any late-night activity might keep him awake. No matter. He was here for the distraction, not the rest.

Cory wasn't going to let things go, though. They'd barely gotten inside with their bags and the cooler full of beer they'd brought along before Cory flopped down into one of the chairs by the window and pinned Evan with his bright blue eyes. "We might as well get the hard part over first, babe," he said. "You wanna tell me why you're running away?"

Evan opened his mouth, a denial on his tongue, but Cory lifted a hand. "Don't even try it. You might be able to pull the wool over the eyes of most people, but I know you better than that."

All the fight went out of Evan, and he flopped down on the end of the bed. "I don't even know where to start."

Cory gave him a small smile at that. "I hear the beginning is a good place."

AN HOUR and two beers apiece later, Evan stopped talking, his throat and emotions raw. Cory was probably the only person in his life who could get him to spill his guts with so little effort, in part because he so rarely tried to force anything. Not for the first time, a part of Evan wished he could've fallen for Cory. It had to be easier than feeling like he did about Riley.

It didn't take Cory long to respond to Evan's logorrhea. "You need to tell him everything, babe."

Evan rolled his eyes over the top of the bottle as he drained the last of his second beer. Swallowing, he set the bottle down on the table between them, harder than he intended.

"Easy for you to say." He folded his arms on the tabletop. "Even without all the family shit we're both dealing with, it's not like I've been on my best behavior around him. And that's without getting into the porn thing."

Cory snorted. "That 'porn thing' is a job, Evan, just like any other. It's what you do, not who you are. It doesn't define you unless you let it."

Evan knew that. He'd said the same thing to others himself over the years he'd been in the industry. He'd never been ashamed of his career before he met Riley, and Riley didn't seem to have a problem with it. Riley had teased Mikey about the amount he watched, but he'd never said anything bad about porn in general, or about the people who made it. Hell, he'd even slept with Evan again after he found out what he did for a living.

Evan lowered his head to rest on his arms. "I haven't felt this screwed up about anything in so long. I don't even know what it is about the guy. He's so far from my usual type." He barked out a short laugh. "Maybe he's an incubus or something. Got me under his spell."

Evan didn't have to see Cory's face to hear the grin in his voice. "Well, at least you're laughing about it. Better than the doldrums of the last couple of weeks."

Evan looked up then. "Shit, man, I'm sorry. I didn't realize I was bringing everyone else down." He felt like crap for that, but Cory waved off his apology.

"No worries, babe. Not like we haven't all had our turn being drama queens, some in louder ways than others." He pushed to his feet. "Why don't we forget all this for a while and hit the pool instead? It'll keep. Not like you'd be able to do much of anything about anything until we get back to the city anyway."

A wave of affection for Cory washed over Evan, surprising him. Had he been so numb for so long that something so simple could make him feel so much? And hell, if it could, then what else had he been missing out on?

One more thing to think about, but not now. Cory was changing into his swim trunks, and Evan reached for his duffel bag to get his. A little sun and fun would do him a world of good, and then he'd be better prepared to deal with the rest of it.

AN AFTERNOON spent poolside followed by a meal of grilled steaks and loaded baked potatoes—cooked by Jimmy and served on the deck by the lake, of course—left Evan pleasantly exhausted enough that he only woke once during the night. He didn't remember the nightmare, just the feel of his own heart pounding and the residual adrenaline of some nonspecific fear.

He woke the second time to Cory's voice.

"Wakey wakey, eggs and bac-ey!"

Evan groaned and pushed his face harder into his pillow, but Cory wasn't going anywhere. He opened the blinds facing the bed, flooding the room with sunlight. "Breakfast waits for no man, mister! Get your fine little ass up and moving."

Evan opened one eye and glared. "Whose ass you callin' 'little'?" He shook the backside in question, and Cory laughed and gave it a smack.

"All right, all right, so it's one of the most perfect bubble butts ever. Happy now? Get up, get up! I'm hungry!"

"Jesus." Evan rolled over and pulled the pillow over his face. "Why are you always so energetic after you spend the night fucking your brains out? Shouldn't you be worn out?"

"Endorphins, man! They're the best!" Cory plopped down on the mattress and rolled on top of Evan. "Get uuuuuuuup! Jimmy's not gonna move until he's got more than just me to cook for."

"Ugh." Evan shoved at Cory until he fell onto the mattress next to him. "How come *you* get the sex but *I'm* the one who gets yanked out of bed early?"

"You must've been a bad boy in a former life." Cory sprang up from the bed and headed into the bathroom. "I'll get the shower started for you." He disappeared behind the door. "Hurry it up!"

"Ugh," Evan repeated. He wanted nothing more than to curl up around his pillow and go right back to sleep, but Cory in postcoital mode was relentless. Hell, he was relentless about 90 percent of the time anyway, and if the past five years had taught Evan anything, it was that he wouldn't be denied.

Giving in to the inevitable, Evan rolled out of bed and headed for the shower, shoving off his shorts as he went. Cory had seen it all and then some anyway.

BREAKFAST WAS equal parts delicious and a little slice of hell.

"So are you in love with the kid or what?"

Evan laid his fork down on his plate and reached for his mimosa. He needed another dose of champagne to get him through this.

"First off, he's not a kid," he finally said. "He's twenty-seven. Two years older than me. And second of all, I'm not in love with him, okay? You can just back off of that. I like him, yeah. He's funny, and yeah, I know what he looks like, but he's not some vapid twink who can't see beyond reality TV and the latest Gaga single."

Cory nudged him with his knee under the table. "Bet he's a little monster in bed."

Evan kicked Cory in reply, but gently. "He's great in bed," he admitted. "And, um...." He hesitated to admit it. "And he's plenty aggressive, but...."

Jimmy sat straighter at that. "Wait, you're saying he hasn't fucked you?"

Evan shook his head, focusing his eyes on his plate. "I mean, we haven't had sex a lot or anything. Only twice, really. And he said he tops. But he hasn't made a move in that direction. He's pretty damn active, but...."

"Hmmm." Evan could feel Jimmy studying him. "Would you be okay if he never topped?"

Evan shrugged one shoulder. "I don't know. I bottom on camera, so I get it that way."

"And if you stop doing porn?"

Evan did look at Jimmy then. "Who said anything about quitting porn?"

Jimmy gave him a smirk and a raised eyebrow. "Honey, just about everyone quits porn eventually. Or quits doing *just* porn, anyway. How many guys over forty do you see still hanging around? Hell, how many guys last as long as you have? There's a reason they call it porn 'modeling.' The older you get, the less likely you are to get booked."

Evan shook his head. "I mean, yeah, I know all that. But I'm only twenty-five."

"And that's five years older than you were when you started," Cory pointed out. He reached for his mimosa. "We're not saying it's time to hang up your jockstrap, babe. Just pointing out that you will need to do something else eventually. And if you aren't getting fucked at home, is that gonna be a problem?"

Evan honestly didn't know. He considered it while he ate a piece of bacon. He'd thought of himself as mostly a bottom since the first time he and Lucas had sex, even though he'd topped sometimes. Riley had been the one to climb on board their first time around, and the second time, Evan had been feeling toppy. But Riley *had* made that flip-flop comment, after all.

"Have you considered asking Riley about it?"

Evan gave Jimmy a look. "I hadn't considered *any* of it until you two started digging into me," he retorted. "And it's all kind of moot if Riley decides he doesn't want me, isn't it?"

Jimmy snorted. "You're assuming that because he got pissed off one time. You haven't so much as tried to call him since then. You need to stop assuming and start doing."

Evan laughed. "I'm having that printed on a T-shirt."

Jimmy swallowed his last bite of eggs. "T-shirts, bumper stickers, tattoos, do whatever the hell you want with it. As long as you *do it*." He stood. "C'mon. Help me clean this shit up, and I'll give you a massage. You could use a little relaxation."

Evan lifted an eyebrow. "You gotta be kidding me."

Jimmy laughed as he set his plate in the sink. "Seriously. You gonna turn down a free massage?"

"Is this a straight massage, or—"

Jimmy cocked his hips. "Ain't nothin' about me straight, honeychild, you know that. And yeah, the happy ending's standard. Like I said, you need to *relax*."

Evan hesitated. It wasn't as if Jimmy hadn't seen it all. When Cory had first suggested that Evan try porn, Jimmy had been the one to offer to show him the ropes. "Break him in," as he'd said.

"You've only ever been with Lucas, babe." Jimmy had sat there in his boyfriend's living room, talking like he made offers like that every day. "Trust me, you don't wanna be on camera if you have a freak-out or anything halfway through. We can test it out in private, and I can give you some shooting tips at the same time, okay?"

Evan had still been stuck back on step one. "You want to fuck me."

Jimmy had barked out a laugh. "Hell, man, you don't have to make it sound like I'm sending you back into combat. Yeah, you're hot as fuck, or Cory wouldn't have suggested porn in the first place. And I'm not made of stone. But it's just sex, and even if it's bad, it's pretty good. I know what I'm doing, though, so it won't be bad."

And it hadn't been. In fact, it had been so damn good that Evan had ended up as a temporary third for Cory and Jimmy, the first time they'd tried that arrangement. It hadn't lasted, but thankfully, the friendship had come out stronger in the end.

Now Jimmy fixed him with a glare. "Look, honey, it's just a massage, okay? I do it all the time around here, you know that. No different from anyone else, 'cept you never took me up on it. But you need it bad, so you're gonna get your fine ass up on the table and let me at it."

Evan never had been able to tell Jimmy no.

CHAPTER 12

TWENTY MINUTES later, Evan shimmied out of his shorts and climbed onto Jimmy's massage table, settling on his stomach with his face in the cushioned ring at the end. Jimmy had been a masseuse at public spas for several years before he bought the resort. He'd paid for his training with his porn earnings. But while Evan had gotten a few of his garden-variety massages before, Jimmy was right that he'd never taken the full treatment. He was also right that Evan was strung tight as a bow, and while a massage would help, that extra bit of relief couldn't hurt.

The massage room sat at the end of the hall in the resort's main building, farthest away from the office but closest to the walkway that led to Jimmy's place. Painted a soothing medium blue, the room had low lighting, cherrywood cabinets along one wall, and a tiny bathroom with a shower for rinsing off afterward. A small stereo on the counter piped in soft, New Age-y music, and aromatherapy candles gave off the scents of vanilla and lavender. Built for relaxation. Evan tried to let it all seep in through his pores.

Jimmy started at Evan's shoulders, working out the knots down his spine and under his shoulder blades with firm, patient hands. Evan told his brain to shut the hell up and tried harder to relax, though he flinched when Jimmy hit particularly sore spots. And boy, were there a lot of those.

"You are one giant knot, honey."

Evan took a deep breath and let it out slowly. He used a trick he'd read about years ago, mentally concentrating on each section of his body, starting from the toes up, and consciously clenching, then relaxing the muscles. By the time he reached his neck, he felt more relaxed, and an approving sound from Jimmy confirmed it.

"Much better." Jimmy fell silent, and Evan worked on getting his mind to shut off by using the same method. He thought of Riley and then let the image go. He thought of his mother and let her go too. And then he thought of Lucas, and for the first time in years, he let the anger and the grief go and focused instead on the good.

EVAN'S FIRST deployment had been uneventful. He got letters and a care package from home, things stayed pretty quiet, and if it hadn't been for the unrelenting desert heat and the sand that found its way into every crevice, he'd almost say it was fun. He went home on two weeks of leave in the summer, and his reception there was nothing short of a hero's welcome.

Still, he'd felt separate from it all. His parents smiled and hugged him, but they didn't really see him. They didn't know who he was. Hell, Evan had barely figured it out himself.

He'd felt much the same during his first night with Lucas, part of him staying off to the side, watching the rest of him give in to everything he was feeling. When it was over, when they'd cleaned up and packed their things in the morning, Lucas caught hold of Evan with a hand on his arm.

"Look, you know we gotta keep this quiet, yeah? You know what happens if anyone finds out."

Evan nodded. "Not a word," he vowed, and Lucas gave him a wide grin.

"Good deal. Now let's get outta here before we get left behind. Germany's a hell of a lot nicer than Afghanistan, but I don't wanna have to explain AWOL to my CO."

All the way from Germany to Kabul, Evan had to fight to keep all the emotions buried. He couldn't keep from staring at Lucas. From replaying the night before, the way Lucas had touched him, wringing out every last bit of pleasure he could, even in the short amount of time they'd had. Evan wanted more. He wanted to explore Lucas's beautiful skin slowly, find every spot that made him gasp and moan. He wanted Lucas's hands holding his head and Lucas's cock down his throat.

More than anything, though, he wanted Lucas back inside him, pounding into him, giving him everything he had. Just the thought of it blew his mind. Lucas had been so careful with him. How would it feel to get fucked hard instead? To have Lucas put all of his strength into sending Evan soaring? Evan's whole body shuddered at the thought.

Arriving back in Afghanistan was like descending into the bowels of hell. Searing hot, dry air slapped Evan in the face as he stepped off the plane. The troop transport that would take them to the base waited nearby, and he watched as other Marines climbed on board to join the ones already there.

"C'mon," Lucas said from beside him. "Back to the sandbox with us."

For the first time dreading what awaited him, having had just a little taste of what he'd been missing, Evan trudged down the stairs and toward the vehicle that would take him back to work.

THE END had come suddenly.

Almost six months passed after that night in a generic hotel room in Germany. Six months in which Lucas had become Evan's best friend, in addition to his sometime-lover. Finding time alone together had been a challenge, but they'd managed it at least once every couple of weeks, even wrangling a two-day R&R pass in Kabul for Evan's birthday in January, hitching a ride in and back with a supply truck.

But the friendship had become even more important than the sex. Lucas understood Evan in a way that Evan didn't think he even understood himself. Lucas could pull him out of a bad mood with just a few choice words, drag him away from thoughts of the family he'd left behind, the brother he'd enlisted to honor. With Lucas around, the desert seemed like a sandy beach, and the dangers of war far away, unable to touch them when they were together.

They were two weeks from heading back stateside when it all came apart at the seams.

THEY WERE headed northwest, riding in an armored transport along a narrow road that had been cleared just a few days before. Even so, the drivers and sentries were on guard, eyes peeled for anything out of the ordinary....

EVAN SHOOK, but the tremors weren't as bad as usual. For the first time he could remember, he'd managed to drag himself from the nightmare of his memories before the horrific ending.

A hand smoothed down his spine. "You back with me, babe?"

Evan nodded into the ring that still supported his head. "How long was I out?"

"Not long." Jimmy's hand moved away. "Maybe fifteen minutes or so? I can finish up if you want, unless you'd rather nap? You can stay here if you don't want to go back to your room yet."

Evan shook his head. "You can finish. I mean...." He shrugged. "I feel pretty okay, so you can skip the happy ending. But the rest of the massage would be nice." He turned his head far enough to flash a small smile, and Jimmy laughed and laid his hands back on Evan's skin.

"All right, if you insist. But feel free to change your mind anytime you like."

Evan nodded and relaxed back into the table, mind calm for once. He closed his eyes and saw Lucas's smile, and maybe for the first time in five years, it didn't hurt.

WHEN THEY headed back to Atlanta on Friday, Evan thought maybe he could handle anything. Cory drove, at ten above the speed limit as usual, blasting a retro dance music station on satellite radio and singing along in full Coco Lamé voice. Evan joined in, though he kept collapsing into giggles whenever Cory would attempt a falsetto he hadn't quite gotten the hang of yet. Maybe Evan would buy him a helium tank for his birthday.

Evan didn't hear his phone ringing over the blasting music, but he felt it vibrate against his thigh. He dug it out of his pocket and glanced at the screen. "Fuck."

Cory reached to turn down the volume on Whitney. "What's up, hon?"

"Mom." Evan stared at the screen, torn, until Cory poked him in the leg.

"Answer it," he said. "She's being pretty persistent."

Evan wavered but then swiped to answer and lifted the phone to his ear. "Hi, Mom."

Gwen drew in air, as if surprised to hear him. "Evan," she breathed. "Oh my God. I was afraid you'd never speak to me again."

Evan blew out a breath and tipped his head back to rest against the seat. "I considered it," he admitted. He tossed Cory a glance. "A friend talked me out of it."

"Well, tell your friend I said thank you." Gwen paused and then let out a small laugh. "I'm so discombobulated I don't know what to say. I didn't really expect you to answer."

Despite himself, Evan smiled. "I didn't really expect it either, but you've got me now. I...." He grasped for the right words. "Can we maybe... try again?"

"Yes!" Gwen's response came immediately. "That's exactly what I wanted to ask. Evan, honey, I miss you so much. I didn't... I don't have any excuses for the way I behaved, but I want to find a way to make up for it if I can."

Jesus. Evan squeezed his eyes shut as he heard the words he thought would never come. He had no idea if there was any way for his mother to make up for the past five years, but just the thought that she might be willing to try made his stomach clench and his heart pound.

"Okay," he managed. He swallowed. "What about...." He couldn't finish the question, couldn't force the word out, but she knew.

"Your father has agreed to talk." Gwen's voice had steadied. "I can't make any promises on his behalf beyond that. Just know that whatever decisions you and I make are between us. Your father and I don't always see eye to eye on every subject, and I can only do so much. You know how stubborn he can be."

Yeah, Evan knew. He'd grown up with the man, after all. His father had never been abusive or cruel, but he'd been distant, at least from Evan. He'd worked long hours to get his law firm off the ground, but in the time he'd been home, he'd always seemed to favor his firstborn son. After Charlie died, he'd turned his grief inward and spent even more time in the office. Evan hadn't recognized that immediately, but he knew how hard losing Charlie had been on his parents. That had made their choice to turn their backs on Evan that much worse.

Evan needed to get off the phone before his anger got the best of him. "I'm on the road, Mom."

"Can you come for dinner on Sunday?" The words came out in a rush, and rather than argue, Evan agreed.

"I'll be back by then."

"All right, dear." Gwen sounded more her usual collected self. "I'll look forward to hearing from you. Take care."

"You too." Evan ended the call and slid the phone back into his pocket. Mind a million miles away, he jumped when Cory poked him again.

"You okay over there?"

Evan nodded. A lie. "She wants to see me again. They both do, I guess. Well, she said that, but I think she's the one pushing it."

Cory was quiet for a few long moments, and then, "Yeah. I can see that. She was a lot more torn up than your father when we went to see them."

God. Evan had nearly forgotten that visit. Repressed it would be more accurate. The memory came flooding back in vivid detail, and he flinched.

"I can't believe you would do this." Charles Day stood in the middle of his spotless living room, a shaft of sunlight cutting across the space between him and where Evan and Cory stood near the door. His wife sat in an armchair, half hidden behind her husband, ankles crossed demurely and a handkerchief twisted in her fingers. "You've

dishonored your brother's memory, behaving like this. What were you thinking, boy?"

"Hey!" Cory took a step forward. "Evan loved his brother, and Charlie loved him. Charlie would've done anything for Evan, and Evan felt the same way. Charlie only wanted Evan to be happy."

Charles's face reddened, and he pointed a finger at Cory. "You stay out of this, pervert. And you"—he transferred his attention to Evan—"you will get out of my house and never come back. You are no longer my son."

Evan's knees buckled. Cory caught him in strong arms. "I can't believe you would dishonor Charlie's memory like this," Cory spat out. "You don't deserve to call either of them your sons."

Cory had nearly had to carry Evan out the door after that. He'd gotten them both down the walkway and into Cory's car before Evan lost it, and he and Jimmy had been the ones to get Evan through the next few weeks. And then Jimmy had suggested a career in porn.

"So." Cory reached for the volume and tapped it back up a few dozen decibels. "Where were we before we were interrupted?"

The song switched from "Hot for Teacher" to "Girls Just Wanna Have Fun," and Cory gave a whoop as he cranked the volume even higher. Evan pushed aside everything else and joined in the sing-along.

CHAPTER 13

THE APARTMENT complex for the Erato shoot wasn't far from Trevor's place, and with traffic light on Saturday morning, he got there a little faster than he expected. At the entry gate, he punched in the code Jordan had given him, and a few seconds later, a tone sounded and the gates started to open. Trevor followed the directions to a building at the back of the complex and found the right apartment. When he knocked on the door, Jordan opened it with a bright smile.

"Hey, man, come on in," he said, stepping back out of the way. Trevor walked past him to the breakfast bar at the edge of the kitchen, where he stopped and set down his duffel bag. He turned just in time to be caught up in a big hug. He felt himself smile as he returned it automatically. Jordan was hard to resist, as much for his happy attitude and charisma as for his tight little body.

"Thanks for doing this," Jordan said as he stepped back. "I know it's a little less than your usual rate, but...."

Trevor shrugged. "Not that much less," he pointed out. Only about a hundred bucks, actually, and without having to travel. "And if you mean it about not directing every second of it, heck, it'll be worth every penny."

Jordan laughed. "Well, you know the usual stuff about not blocking shots. That's why I'm starting off with people who've been doing this for a while. I just want to give some setup and turn on the cameras and go for it. You guys know what works. We might need to do a few pickup shots here and there, but for the bulk of it, you'll be pretty much on your own."

Another man wandered in from the bedroom, and Trevor turned to see it was his scene partner, Adam. They'd never worked together, but they'd met briefly about a year earlier, and Trevor had heard good things about him from mutual friends. Tall and leanly muscled, Adam had sculpted arms peeking out below the sleeves of the snug workout shirt he wore. A pair of headphones hung around his neck, the wire plugged into the phone he held. When he smiled, his face transformed from ordinary to radiant, with deep dimples bracketing his white teeth.

"Hey, man," Adam said, holding out a hand for Trevor to shake. "Nice to see you again."

"You too," Trevor replied automatically as he shook hands. "This your first shoot here too?"

Adam chuckled and shook his head as he sat back down, and Trevor sat across from him. "No, I knew Da... I mean, Jordan before they launched the site, so I did one of the first scenes, with him. It'll go up in another couple of weeks, I think."

Trevor didn't acknowledge the near-slip with Jordan's name. He'd been there often enough himself, and besides, he knew Jordan's real name was Danny. "It's a different kind of take on things, that's for sure. I'm used to everything being bigger-better-faster-more. Not that there's anything wrong with that."

Adam grinned. "Yeah, I get it. I've done some pretty kinky shit, and I love it all. But sometimes simple is good too, y'know?"

Trevor agreed with a nod, though his gut instinct told him "simple" rarely was. Still, it was a new studio and a new look, and anything different was good with him. Worst case never changed: if he hated it, he'd just never shoot with them again.

"All right, guys, let's get set up." Trevor and Adam turned their attention to Jordan, who waved toward a doorway. "Bedroom's in there. Cameras are ready, so we'll just check the lighting and take some stills first. Not a lot, just for promo."

Trevor followed Adam into the room, which was decorated much like the other bedroom sets he'd worked on: neutral walls in a shade of medium beige, abstract artwork in muted tones, and a queen-size bed covered in a solid, dark green comforter. Tables on either side of the bed held matching lamps, which had lighter green shades and low-wattage lighting. The lights, camera, and reflective umbrellas were set up opposite the bed, with a couple of director's chairs crowded next to a table containing a laptop, a high-quality still camera, and a basket full of lube bottles, condom boxes, towels, and a container of wet wipes.

"All right, boys, hop on board." Jordan headed over to grab a light meter while Adam and Trevor climbed onto the end of the bed. Adam grinned at Trevor, eyes bright, and Trevor couldn't help smiling back.

A light flashed. "Cute! Okay, let me check that and do some testing." Jordan fiddled with the laptop for a minute and then crossed to the bed, holding the light meter under first Adam's chin and then Trevor's. He made a couple of adjustments to the umbrellas and switched out the meter for the camera.

"Okay, let's get some stills. No posing. Just… get to know each other. Smile, touch, kiss, whatever feels natural. I'll let you know when to take off shirts and such."

Trevor turned toward Adam, and they moved closer together, running their hands across each other's thighs and chests, sliding fingers down arms. Adam leaned in for a kiss, and Trevor met him halfway, lips brushing gently while the camera flash popped. They deepened the kiss, Adam sliding one hand behind Trevor's neck, and Trevor shifted closer still, conscious of the camera but enjoying the feel of Adam too.

"Okay." Jordan's voice broke in after a little more groping. "Whenever you're ready, shirts off." Adam and Trevor followed directions, hands moving to push at fabric. Trevor got Adam's shirt up to his armpits and discovered his left nipple had a gold ring in it, so he bent close to pull it into his mouth and give a little tug. Adam gasped, and Trevor smiled, licking over the hardened peak again before moving away and pushing Adam's shirt the rest of the way off.

They continued kissing and touching, first shirtless and then, at Jordan's direction, in just their underwear. Adam had gone with a black jockstrap that left his muscular butt on display, and Trevor took advantage, getting a double handful and kneading the firm flesh. Adam retaliated by sliding a hand under the back of Trevor's snug red briefs and a finger into his crack, pushing at Trevor's hole while his tongue worked Trevor's mouth.

Jordan laughed softly, and Trevor broke away from the kiss to find the director watching them. "Okay, boys, let's back up a little. Get back into your clothes, and we'll start filming. I might take a few more stills after we're done, but the rest I can get from the video."

Trevor backed away, body thrumming from the hot make-out session, and reached for his clothes to redress while he waited for the word from Jordan.

"You're doing great so far, but remember: think intimate." Jordan peered through the camera viewfinder and made an adjustment. "We want people to feel like they're watching a couple. It's not just about the sex. Don't worry too much about positions or where the camera is. I'll have two cameras going most of the time, this one and a handheld camera, so we'll get plenty for the scene. Holding off on cumshots until I can prep is great, but not a requirement. I'd rather have something that looks natural than a lot of edits, and I can work around almost anything. Okay?"

"Okay," Adam replied, and Trevor nodded. He tipped his head from side to side to loosen up, ready to dive in.

"All right. No action or cuts unless there's a problem. Just go for it whenever you're ready."

Adam turned to Trevor and smiled that great grin again. "Let's do it."

Trevor laughed and accepted Adam's kiss. *He's a good kisser*, Trevor thought as he ran his hands over Adam's sculpted biceps. Adam obviously spent a lot of time in the gym, but he didn't have the excessive bulk some guys developed. Still, he had a lot more than Trevor, who worked out enough to stay toned and defined but didn't try to build muscle at all. Trevor had a dancer's build, long and lean, which suited him, his employers, and his fans just fine.

The mattress shifted as Adam moved closer, deepening their kiss, and Trevor followed Adam's lead, letting himself be lowered to lie on his back with Adam lying half on top of him. In most scenes, clothes would have started coming off by now, but Adam didn't seem to be in any hurry, and Jordan didn't say anything, so Trevor went with it. Things were supposed to be a little different here, and he didn't have a problem with that.

Adam's hand ran slowly down Trevor's chest and abdomen, coming to rest just above where his cock was swelling under his shorts.

Adam's mouth still played with Trevor's, tongue teasing, teeth nipping at Trevor's full bottom lip. Trevor moaned and lifted his hips, begging silently for the touch that was just out of reach. Adam smiled into the kiss and gave it to him, just one too-soft, too-fast caress before he slid his hand under Trevor's shirt to touch the bare skin of his stomach instead. Trevor let one hand skim down Adam's arm and kept the other wrapped around the back of Adam's neck, scraping his fingernails lightly into the close-cropped strands at his nape.

Adam broke the kiss finally, just to dip his head down and lick one of Trevor's nipples, left bare by Adam pushing the shirt up under his arms. Trevor moaned and arched his back into the touch; nipple play had never done that much for him, but he knew viewers loved to see the men onscreen react to every touch. Adam didn't know him, though, so he took Trevor's reaction as encouragement and went from licking to sucking, with a few nibbles thrown in for good measure. That worked better for Trevor, and his next moan was more natural.

Adam paused again, this time to push at Trevor's shirt, and Trevor took his cue, lifting up enough to pull it off and then reach for Adam's. They came back together, on their sides, facing each other this time, and Trevor rolled them farther, until he lay half on top of Adam. He rubbed his hardening cock against Adam's hip and his thigh into Adam's groin, where he could feel a nice-sized erection filling out to match his.

Adam kept kissing him, mixing up deep, wet tonguing with light brushes of his lips until every touch sent a shiver down Trevor's spine. If the site was going for intimate, then they'd be getting what they wanted in spades, because things sure felt intimate to Trevor.

Maybe a little *too* intimate.

Unbidden, Riley's face flashed into Trevor's mind, and he broke out of the kiss to get away from the thought. Riley didn't belong here. Riley was Evan's, and *Evan* didn't belong here. Trevor closed his eyes and started moving down Adam's body, licking at his nipples, hard peaks surrounded by a wide, flat ring of deep brown. He paused to play with that nipple ring again, knowing the audience would love it. And just the fact that Adam had the ring meant he probably got more out of nipple stimulation than Trevor did.

The rest of Adam's body was honed to pure perfection, with hard pecs and ab muscles standing out in sharp relief. "Cum gutters," the guys called the creases running along Adam's hips toward his groin, and Trevor's mouth watered at the idea of licking them clean at the end of their scene.

He tongued his way down them now, pausing to suck and nip a few spots here and there, listening to the steady stream of moans flowing from Adam's mouth. They sounded natural, not forced like so many guys did on camera. Adam slid his big hand across Trevor's scalp, fingers tightening and relaxing in time with Trevor's movements.

Trevor popped the button of Adam's shorts with one hand and pulled the zipper down, never letting up on his mouth's exploration of Adam's skin, and Adam lifted up to give him room to skim the shorts down and off, leaving Adam in nothing but his black jockstrap, front distended by his erection. Trevor smiled a little to himself as he mouthed his way down the hard length. The new site touted itself as by and for gay men, and over the years, Trevor had learned the signs of when a model was gay for pay. Adam's reactions, especially his rock-hard cock, showed his sexuality was pretty damn clear. Trevor didn't mind gay-for-pay guys, as long as they were into everything, but he much preferred knowing his scene partners were just as into men as he was.

Adam lifted his hips again, a silent signal to Trevor to move things along, and Trevor did, leaning up far enough to use both hands to pull the waistband of Adam's jock out and down. His cock popped up to lie against his abs, and Trevor went down on it immediately, not even bothering to get the underwear the rest of the way off. Adam was big but not huge, slender enough that Trevor could deep-throat him almost from the start. Adam loved that, from the sounds Trevor heard drifting down at him, but then, who wouldn't?

Trevor bobbed his head and sucked, tongue working the full length of Adam's dick. The flavor of precum filled his mouth, salty-bitter like sweat and skin, and he moaned, sending vibrations into Adam's body. Adam groaned and jerked, and Trevor pulled off, giving that beautiful cock one last lick before moving back up to Adam's mouth.

Adam's kiss was voracious. He brought both hands to hold Trevor in place as soft sighs and moans worked their way out of his mouth.

Adam rolled them over, and Trevor let himself fall back against the mattress, Adam on top, their cocks rubbing together between their bodies. Trevor lost himself in their kiss, forgetting for a few moments that he was in the middle of a scene, until Adam pulled away and dove for his waist, pushing his shorts and underwear out of the way so he could get his mouth around Trevor's cock.

Trevor nearly shouted in surprise, a sound that fell off into a moan as Adam went to work, bobbing his head fast and sucking hard. Trevor got his hands onto Adam's head and held on for the ride, glad for the reprieve. He liked his blowjobs slower and with more buildup, so Adam's technique, while not lacking in sensation—or in appearance, for the cameras—actually made it easier for Trevor to keep his body under control.

Adam soon slowed down, though, working Trevor's cock with more deliberation, lifting his gaze to meet Trevor's. The spark of mischief underlying the lust caught Trevor's attention. Adam gave the impression of a man who knew how to have fun with this business of sex, and Trevor found himself wondering how Adam would be in private—one-on-one, without the crew and the cameras.

But that idea just brought Riley right back into his mind, so he pulled himself out of that line of thinking in a hurry. Besides, he never had slept with scene partners off camera, and he wasn't about to start now.

He reached for Adam's arms, pulling him up and off his cock, and shifted away long enough to get his shorts and underwear out of the picture. Adam took the moment to lose the jock that was still hooked on one of his legs before coming back toward Trevor, pressing him into the mattress and kissing him again. This kiss was slow, deep, mouths open wide. Adam pulled back to tease with his tongue before diving back in. Trevor followed Adam's lead, letting his hands wander the expanse of Adam's back, feeling those muscles shift and bunch under his skin. Trevor got a handful of one firm asscheek and squeezed, smiling into the kiss as Adam moaned.

"Not just a top, hmmm?" Trevor murmured against Adam's lips, and Adam laughed just as softly.

"Not even mostly," he admitted. "But that's what he wanted…."

Trevor knew all about that. Personal preference had little to do with on-camera work. But as Adam said, he was the top today, so Trevor went with it. He spread his legs, bringing them up to hook his thighs over Adam's hips, and thrust his pelvis up into Adam's.

Adam pulled out of their kiss and laughed softly again. "Okay, then." He started working his way down Trevor's body again, more slowly this time, pausing to suck at his nipples and even nose into his armpits. Trevor moaned as Adam licked there, swirling his tongue in the clean hair, scented only with Trevor's natural musk.

Distracted by the unusual sensation in a spot that didn't usually get much attention, Trevor jumped when Adam closed one large hand around his dick. He didn't stroke, just squeezed gently, fingers working in time with his tongue. Trevor shifted on the mattress and moaned again as Adam licked his way across his chest to his other nipple, where Adam latched on and sucked hard, in contrast to the light brush of his thumb across the tip of Trevor's dick.

Oh, holy shit. The contrasting sensations nearly drove Trevor right over the edge, and dammit, it was way too soon for that. Hell, even if they hadn't been on camera, it would've been way too soon. *What is this guy doing to me?*

Trevor bucked up again, knocking Adam's mouth loose, and pushed at his shoulder. "Come up here so I can...."

Adam took the hint and flipped around, planting his knees on the mattress on either side of Trevor's head, his cock dangling enticingly an inch from Trevor's mouth. Trevor licked the drop of precum off the tip before cupping Adam's ass in both hands and drawing his dick inside. Adam hummed out a low sound as he lowered his own mouth around Trevor's dick, and they both went to work.

Trevor arched his back and lifted his head from the mattress so Adam wouldn't need to push farther down and risk blocking the camera's view as he sucked Adam deeper. Better for a sixty-nine would be lying on their sides with the camera above them, but that would mean stopping and restarting, and Jordan had said he didn't want that. Trevor shifted instead, bringing his camera-side arm down to prop himself against the mattress and using his other hand to wrap around the base of Adam's cock. That gave him room to work Adam over with his mouth and tongue without their bodies getting too close for a clear shot.

More settled into the position, Trevor let his mind soak in the parts of his job he loved best. Adam's skin smelled fresh and clean, overlaid with the enticing musk of his arousal and the dark places between his legs. His sounds were muffled with his mouth full, of course, but he moaned deep in his chest whenever Trevor hit a particularly sensitive spot, and Trevor felt the vibrations against his tongue.

Adam slid his mouth, hot and wet, over Trevor's cock, snaking his tongue along the bottom side, flicking the tip against his frenulum. Trevor let out a moan of his own and sucked Adam harder, but not deeper, letting his fist cover the ground his mouth wasn't reaching. He backed off, stretching things out, the professional in the back of his mind reminding him that Jordan needed as much film as he could get.

Adam moved then, planting both of his ripped arms on the mattress and dipping his head all the way down until his mouth hit Trevor's pubic hair. Trevor grunted in surprise and nearly choked on his mouthful before he pulled off and let out a groan. "Fuck," he called out, hand still working Adam's dick while Adam deep-throated him. *Jesus*, this guy knew what he was doing. Trevor could hear Adam's breath rasp in and out through his nose and then stop as Adam swallowed around the head of Trevor's cock.

"Fuck!" He yelled it that time, holding onto his last shred of control to keep from erupting right down Adam's throat. Adam took the shout as warning, though, and backed off, though Trevor felt him smile. Trevor leaned up to nip at the crease between Adam's groin and thigh, getting a flinch and chuckle from his partner, before he went back to suckling at the head of Adam's dick.

They kept up the sixty-nine a little while longer, neither of them going for anything strong, a silent agreement to let Jordan get in some extra film before they moved on. Soon, though, Adam slid his mouth off Trevor's cock and licked it all over like an ice cream cone before pulling away and turning his head to look up at Trevor.

"Flip over," he murmured, and Trevor's ass clenched. He nodded and followed orders, quickly settling onto his hands and knees. Adam draped himself over his back, knees between Trevor's, and reached out both hands to tangle their fingers together where Trevor had braced himself on the mattress. Trevor could feel Adam's cock rubbing against the back of his balls, and he let himself moan at the sensation.

"You smell good." Adam spoke louder that time, clearly for the cameras, though from the nose nuzzling behind his ear, Trevor guessed it probably wasn't just for show. Adam ran his tongue along the shell of Trevor's ear, drawing out another shiver, and then licked his way down Trevor's neck. He shifted back, tongue still in motion, drawing lazy patterns along Trevor's spine. Trevor let his head drop on another moan, breath coming quicker in anticipation as Adam's mouth continued moving lower.

Adam gave him a thorough rimming, dividing his efforts between licking across and around Trevor's hole and sliding his tongue in deep, fluttering inside Trevor's body. Trevor gasped and twitched under Adam's assault, pushing his hips back, begging for more. By the time Adam pulled free and reached for the lube on the nightstand, Trevor's arms had given out, and he lowered himself to rest on his elbows instead, hips tilted up high.

Adam took his time prepping Trevor for his cock, longer than Trevor needed by far, but he reminded himself that the vibe for the shoot was different, and slower was better. He let himself relax into it, focusing on each sensation as it happened, rather than anticipating the next, and trying to find the balance between enjoyment and professionalism.

He knew Jordan would stop them if anything went too off course, so that wasn't a concern, but for the first time since he'd started in the business, he was having difficulty remembering that this was work, not personal. Adam stroked his fingers inside him like a lover, not a coworker, seeking out every delicious spot, prolonging his pleasure until he was nothing but shivering need. By the time Adam slid on a condom and pressed his cock against Trevor's hole, Trevor was ready to beg to be fucked.

Adam didn't do that, either. He pushed inside slowly, so slowly that Trevor thought he would scream, and once he was all the way in, he started to rock gently. He didn't pull out, didn't slam in hard, just shifted his hips in tiny movements that sent shockwaves through Trevor. It wasn't until Trevor whimpered and started to shake that

Adam pulled back, slowly, before slamming in so hard he nearly knocked Trevor off his knees.

Trevor's mind shut off. He couldn't think about cameras, or what might come next, or anything but the delicious feel of Adam's beautiful prick pounding his hungry hole. His fingers curled into the comforter, as if that could keep him from falling apart. His cock bounced with every thrust of Adam's hips, touching nothing but air, but Trevor couldn't even collect himself enough to grab it. He couldn't do anything but feel.

"God, you've got a sweet hole." Adam's voice came from just behind Trevor's ear. "Sucks me in so good. Are you gonna come like this? Just from my cock?"

Trevor groaned and nodded. He was. Another few minutes of Adam fucking him, dragging his cock over Trevor's prostate on every thrust, and he would spray all over the bed.

"Good." Adam leaned away and grabbed Trevor's hips with both hands. Then he must have hit a hidden turbo button, because suddenly he was pounding in so hard that Trevor danced on a knife's edge between pleasure and pain. Trevor let out a shout and dropped his cheek to the mattress, vibrating from sensation, so close that he could taste his climax in the back of his throat. Adam dug his fingertips in harder, nails cutting into Trevor's skin, and that extra bite of pain was just enough to send Trevor flying.

When he came back to his senses, Adam was stretched out over him, half lying across Trevor's back, kissing across Trevor's shoulders. "Mmmmm." Trevor smiled into the pillow and was a breath away from reaching back to run his fingers along whatever skin he could reach when the slice of heaven he'd fallen into shattered around him.

"Cut! That was amazing, guys. So fucking hot."

Jordan's voice sliced through Trevor like a razor. He jerked as he realized he'd thoroughly forgotten what he was doing, had lost the thread so completely that he didn't even know if his scene partner had finished. He shifted and felt wetness on his back, so he assumed Adam had pulled out and jerked off to finish, but he didn't remember it.

He *did* remember how totally he'd fallen under the spell of intimacy the scene had woven. He'd *never* lost track of himself before, never let his professional shell crack like that. He felt exposed in a way that had nothing to do with his nudity and everything to do with *him*.

The memory of the last few seconds before his climax played back, and neither Adam nor Trevor were there. He'd been Evan, and the body pounding into his had belonged to Riley.

Oh shit. Please *tell me I didn't yell out Riley's name.*

He jerked upright on the bed, pulling away from Adam and refusing to look at Jordan. "So, that's it?" His voice wavered, so he didn't say anything else.

"Yeah, it's a short scene, so we're done. I'll loop some of the best parts."

"Great." Trevor climbed off the bed and grabbed a towel off the chair in the corner to wipe himself down. "Great job, guys," he added, though he still wouldn't look at them.

There was a long pause, but even though he could feel them staring, Trevor didn't look up. He needed to get out of there, the faster the better.

"Okay, well." The bed squeaked, and Trevor assumed Adam was climbing off too. "That was pretty awesome. Glad to work with you, Trevor."

Trevor nodded, still not looking at them. "You too. Thanks." His clothes lay on the floor nearby, so he started pulling them on.

After another long pause, Jordan spoke again. "Let me get my checkbook, and I'll take care of the fees. Meet me in the living room when you're dressed, guys."

Trevor's stomach plummeted into his feet. *Holy shit*, he'd totally forgotten about getting paid. If Jordan hadn't said something, Trevor would've been dressed and out the door without payment.

What the fuck is wrong *with me?*

He held it together long enough to get dressed and even managed to look Adam and Jordan in the eyes as he shook their hands. Check in hand, he jumped into his car and headed for his apartment.

A few blocks from home, though, he changed his route.

CHAPTER 14

EVAN PUSHED the button and bounced on his toes as he waited. Thoughts careened around inside his head, none of them slowing down enough for him to catch them.

"Yes?" Riley's voice came from the speaker, and Evan jumped to respond.

"Yeah, hi, Riley, it's Evan. Can I come up? I just need to talk to you."

The delay before Riley's response was so long Evan thought it would never come. "All right," Riley finally said. "You know where it is."

The door buzzed and Evan jumped inside, heading for the elevators. A door opened immediately when he pushed the call button, and inside, he pushed the button for Riley's floor and then held the door-close button until it worked. The ride took a year, but when he finally arrived, Riley was there waiting, standing just outside the elevator door.

Evan didn't think. He reached Riley, wrapped his hands around Riley's face, and pushed him back against the wall opposite the elevator before kissing him.

For a long, perfect moment, Riley submitted, opening his mouth and letting Evan inside. But then he stiffened and started shoving at Evan. It took another few moments for Evan to realize it, and by the time he did, he had to duck away to barely miss taking a knee to the groin.

They stood in the hallway, Riley still plastered to the wall, Evan two feet in front of him, both breathing hard but clearly for different reasons. Anger mixed with lust painted Riley's face in hard lines, so different from his usual smiling self. As the adrenaline leeched away, Evan's gut churned, and shame crept in.

"I'm sorry," he started, but he only got a half step toward Riley before Riley's hand flew up to ward him off.

"Don't." Riley's face smoothed as he straightened up, steel in his spine. "I don't know what's going on here, but I can't do this. I like you, and I'd like to see you again, but I can't deal with you out of control. First you came here drunk, and now you come here like this, and…." He dropped his hand to his side, and some of the fight went out of him. "I'm sorry for the way I behaved last week. It wasn't fair to take out my issues on you. But—" He lifted his gaze to meet Evan's. "I just can't deal with you this way, okay?"

Evan opened his mouth to reply but realized he didn't have a response that wouldn't involve either jumping Riley again or starting an argument for no good reason. And even if he hadn't been in a high-end building with on-site security, even if Riley hadn't been part of a family rich enough for Evan to end up buried under the jail, he was not that guy. He was not going to force himself on anyone, ever.

Instead, he nodded his agreement, turned, and quick-stepped to the stairwell a few feet down the hall. He didn't look back.

AFTER A mostly sleepless night fueled by horrific dreams, Evan knew following through on his agreement to go to his parents' house was a bad idea. He went anyway. He needed to get it over with, and if it ended in disaster again, well, it wasn't likely to make him feel worse than he already did.

He arrived at noon on the dot, and his mother greeted him at the door with a tremulous smile and a small hug. She had on her June Cleaver best—a simple, tailored dress, pearls, and low heels—and it wasn't until then that Evan realized they'd probably gone to church that morning. It had been long enough that he'd forgotten they preferred the earliest Mass to avoid the crowds and leave time to cook dinner.

"Come in, dear. I made a pot roast today, so it can wait a bit longer for us to have time to catch up." Gwen led Evan into the living room, which he entered with a heavy dose of dread, remembering the last time he'd been in there. But it didn't look the same now. The walls had been painted a different color, and the furniture was new, laid out differently than he remembered. It didn't feel like the same room, which lessened his anxiety a bit.

At least, until his father unfolded himself from his easy chair and rose to his feet.

At six-foot-one, Charles Day stood only two inches taller than Evan, but he outweighed Evan by a good fifty pounds. His muscular build was much more like Charlie's had been, though with age, Charles was developing a bit of a paunch.

He did not look comfortable in the least at the situation in which he found himself, but he stood tall and held out a hand. "Evan."

Evan steeled himself and reached out to take the offering. "Charles."

His father's face twisted, but before he could respond, Gwen fluttered into Evan's view. "Can I get you a drink, dear? Your father is having his usual."

Evan dropped his hand back to his side but held his father's gaze. He knew what his father drank. "Maker's Mark," he said. "Neat." He'd learned the words long before he'd had any clue what they meant.

"Is that what you'd like, dear?"

Evan turned to his mom and gave her a small smile. "No. Did you make tea?"

Her hand lingered where she'd lifted it toward his arm. She smiled. "I did. With lemon?"

"Is there any other kind?"

Gwen laughed softly and turned to head toward the kitchen. Evan looked around the room, taking in the few familiar elements, like his parents' wedding picture on the sofa table and some knickknacks on the mantel he remembered from childhood. He considered the second chair and the sofa, but he knew his mother would prefer the former, so decided he'd go with the latter.

His father resettled himself into his chair as Evan sat. The two men just looked at each other until finally Charles nodded, as if he'd made some silent decision.

"You're looking well."

Evan waited to see if he'd go on. Maybe add "son" to that. But he didn't. Evan held on to his temper. "Thanks," he replied.

That was as far as they got before Gwen returned, a glass of tea in each hand. "Here you are, dear," she said, holding one of the glasses out to Evan. He took it, and Gwen reached for a coaster from the basket on the table and placed it in front of Evan. She did the same with a second coaster, placing it on the table between her chair and Charles's, next to Charles's own drink.

Once Gwen had seated herself, she crossed her lower legs in the familiar position Evan remembered and folded her hands into her lap. "I'm sorry we didn't get a chance to talk longer last time," she said. "I apologize for upsetting you."

Evan took a swallow of his tea to soothe his dry throat before setting the drink onto the coaster. "I apologize for flying off the handle," he replied. "I guess there's more built up there than I'd realized." He glanced around the room. "I like what you've done in here. I assume it's your design work?"

Gwen glowed from the compliment. "Yes, it is. It's one of the first things I did, actually. I've made a few tweaks here and there over the past few years, but the basic design is the same."

"Well, you did a great job." Evan smiled, starting to relax for the first time since he'd agreed to come for Sunday dinner. In some ways, his mother's obvious nerves about their meeting helped ease his. At least he knew he wasn't the only one having a tough time.

"She's been doing a little of this kind of work along and along." Charles picked up his drink in its heavy, leaded crystal glass and took a sip. "We don't need the money, of course, but she enjoys it, and it keeps her as busy as she'd like to be."

Evan bit back his first inclination, which was to blast his father for belittling his mother's talents. Yes, it was probably true that they didn't need the income from her work, since Charles made plenty off the settlements he raked in for his clients. But she clearly enjoyed it, and the results were nicely done. Couldn't he just be supportive?

Evan forced a smile. "It's very good work." He turned his attention back to his mother. "I have a friend who does some design work. I bet the two of you would have a lot to talk about."

Charles made a low, derisive sound, but before he could say anything, Gwen reached over and laid her hand on his arm. "Charles," she chided, and he glanced at her and gave a small nod.

"We wanted to talk to you about something," Gwen said, turning her head back to Evan. "It's kind of... well, it's kind of big. We were going to wait until after we ate, but I think maybe it's better to get it out of the way."

Evan's stomach roiled. "Um, sorry. I think I need to visit the bathroom first."

Gwen nodded. "You remember where it is?"

No, Mom, I only lived here for eighteen years. "Sure do." Evan pushed to his feet and headed into the hallway, taking the first right into the bathroom he'd shared with Charlie growing up. The location was all it shared with that bathroom, though. It had been gutted at some point, the old fixtures and flooring replaced with newer styles, fixtures and tiles in stark white and cabinets in cherry with silver handles. A sage-green shower curtain hung across the bathtub, and matching towels were displayed on the towel bars. Evan relieved himself quickly, and while he washed his hands, he stared at his reflection in the mirror.

"Keep it together," he muttered. "See what they want from you before you throw it back in their faces."

Finished, Evan slipped out of the bathroom and headed back toward the living room. A glint from the dining room to his left caught his eye, and he paused to take a look. This room had been repainted and had new curtains, but the furniture was the same as he remembered, dark wood with curved accents, and the glass chandelier remained. The dimmer switch had been turned low, but Evan saw that the table was set for three, and that next to the place setting at the head of the table sat a long manila envelope.

Curiosity got the best of Evan almost immediately. He walked over to the table and picked up the envelope, realizing as he did that it had his name on the front, along with his last military APO address, though the envelope didn't appear to have been mailed.

Well, it's addressed to me, Evan justified to himself as he opened the envelope and pulled out the sheaf of papers inside. He flipped the pages around the right way and skimmed the top sheet.

His heart nearly stopped beating.

Evan lowered himself into a chair at the table as he stared at the information he held. A quarter of a million. He had a *quarter of a million dollars*. For four and a half years, since the day he turned twenty-one, he'd had a fortune sitting in an account, just waiting for him to collect.

And his parents had never told him.

His hands started to shake.

"Evan?"

Evan's head snapped up. His mother stood in the doorway to the kitchen, his father just to her left. Evan jumped to his feet.

"What the *fuck* is this?" His mother flinched. Evan ignored it and waved the paper at them. "Money? I had *money* all this time, and you never told me?"

"Son—"

"Don't you *son* me." Evan's vision blurred. "Do you have any idea...? No. You don't have a clue. Do you know how I've been making a living since the Marines threw me out? *Do you?*" He laughed, but even to his own ears, there was no humor in the sound. "Your son has been doing *porn*, Mommy and Daddy. Oh, and it gets better. It's *gay* porn."

He watched with no little satisfaction as his parents' expressions went from confused to stunned. "That's right. I've been whoring myself out for five *fucking* years since you and the US military dumped me like yesterday's trash. You know how hard it is to get hired for a real job with a 'Don't Ask, Don't Tell' discharge and no education?"

His mother was crying by then, her hands over her face. His father's face had passed red and was headed quickly toward purple. Evan ignored them and crumpled the papers in his hand. He threw them against the wall.

"You can keep your fucking blood money," he said. "I'd rather spend the rest of my life getting fucked on camera for money than take a fucking *penny* from you people."

"That's enough!" His father took a step toward him, arm raised, and Evan barely had time to prepare himself for impact before everything seemed to happen at once. His mother jumped forward, grabbing for his father's arm, and his father flung his hand out, catching her across the cheek. She reeled backward and fell, cracking her head on the corner of the sideboard against the wall. She landed on the floor and lay still.

Evan and his father froze for a long moment before they both jumped to her side. "Don't touch her!" Evan demanded, his military medical training kicking in. "Don't move her. Call 911!" He looked up to find his father in a crouch, staring down at his wife, tears welling in his eyes. "Snap out of it!" His father looked at him. "Call 911! Tell them we have a head and possible neck injury and need an ambulance with a backboard. *Now!*"

Charles snapped out of his fugue and jumped up to rush around the corner to the kitchen. Evan bent close to his mother, checking to be sure she was breathing, reaching for her wrist to check her pulse. A trickle of blood from the injury on her temple grew into a steady stream running down the side of her face to drip onto the carpet below. He wanted to move her, wanted to check her out more carefully, but he couldn't risk causing more damage if she'd hurt her neck.

He could hear his father talking, but the sound was muted, like his ears were stopped up. Then he realized they were, because he was crying. Tears streamed down his face, dripping onto the carpet, landing next to his mother's blood.

In the distance, he heard sirens, and he pushed back the tears, wiping an arm across his face to clear his vision. He had a job to do, an injured person to help, and he'd be damned if he was going to fail one more time.

EVAN STOOD just outside the curtain that hid his mother's emergency room bed. The doctor had arrived a few minutes earlier, and the tiny space hadn't allowed for Evan to stay during the examination. To his relief, his mother had roused briefly when the paramedics arrived at the house, and though they'd still taken every precaution, strapping her to a backboard before moving her to the stretcher, she'd been able to answer a few questions as they took her to the ambulance.

There had never been a question of who would ride to the hospital with her. Evan had given his father one hard look, and Charles Day had backed away toward his own car.

Evan didn't know where his father ended up after that. He tried to tell himself he didn't care, but he looked around anyway. A few dozen feet down the hall, he could see the edge of the waiting room, mostly deserted at midafternoon. His father sat in the first row of seats, looking like a washrag that had been wrung out and tossed, crumpled, into a corner.

Despite everything, Evan felt a stab of empathy. He knew his mother's fall had been an accident, a stupid accident, but the image of his father's hand striking his mother would not leave his mind. He couldn't forgive and forget, not yet. Maybe not ever.

"Mr. Day?"

Evan focused on the young woman who stood holding the curtain open. He didn't know if she was a doctor, a nurse, or some random person off the street, and at that moment, he couldn't care less. "Is she okay?" he asked, taking a step closer. He felt someone else step up next to him, probably his father, but he didn't shift his focus.

"The bleeding stopped, but she's in and out of consciousness. We're having a portable X-ray brought over, but you can see her for a minute if you want."

His father took a step forward, and Evan almost reached out to stop him on pure instinct, but he managed to hold back. Yes, he was still pissed as hell, but the fact was that this was his wife in the hospital, and Evan couldn't actually stop him from seeing her.

Instead, he followed behind. The young woman, apparently a nurse, warned them not to touch her or jostle the bed, since they were still concerned about a possible neck injury.

His mother looked tiny in the bed, her skin pale even against the stark white sheets. A stabilizer had been wrapped around her neck, an IV inserted into her arm, and a clip-on monitor attached to her finger. Machines beeped, and the noises of the ER drifted in, but the sounds faded as Evan watch his father bend close, careful not to touch, even as Evan could see him straining to hold himself back.

More of his anger drained away. He still didn't know why they'd hidden the money from him, and he couldn't *think* about forgiveness for that until he knew *why*, dammit. But he knew his parents loved each other, even if he wasn't so sure how they felt about him. He couldn't hold that against them, could he?

I sure as hell can, he thought.

Something bubbled up inside him, a well of emotion so tangled and dark he couldn't sort it out. Anger, resentment, and frustration swirled together into a blackness he couldn't fight. Didn't know if he wanted to fight.

His skin crawled, and he had to get out of there *right that second* or the top of his head was going to blow right off his body.

He spun on his heel and fled.

HEAVY METAL blasted from the speakers in Evan's car as he drove. He didn't know how long he'd been in the car, and he didn't really give a shit. Hours, at least, since darkness had fallen, a huge full moon hanging in shades of orange over the treetops. But Evan knew the highways and back roads around Atlanta well after spending most of his life in the city, so he just kept driving.

He'd just taken a left at a T intersection to head back toward the interstate, and the music searing his ears had switched from AC/DC to Black Sabbath, when his phone ringing cut through the noise. Glancing down, he saw a number he didn't recognize and almost ignored it before he thought that it could be the hospital. He stabbed the button on his steering wheel to answer, cutting Ozzy off in midscream.

"Hello?"

"Is this Trevor?" The voice was unfamiliar, but the name he used showed clearly it wasn't about his mother, either.

"Yeah. Who's this?" Trevor slowed down, looking for a place to pull over in case he needed to write down information.

"Sorry, this is Billy Hart," the man said. "I run a new website called Extreme-X, and I'm in a bind. I had a model for a shoot tomorrow flake out on me, and I need someone to fill in for him. It'll be some pretty heavy BDSM, and you'd be the sub. Standard rates, with some bonuses for extras. You up for it?"

"Sure." Evan didn't let himself second-guess. Residual energy and adrenaline still thrummed through him, and he needed to burn it off somehow. Getting flogged and fucked for pay should do the trick. "Can you text me the info? I'm in the car."

"No problem. You have recent test results?"

"Yeah. I just did a shoot yesterday." God, that seemed like years ago.

"Perfect. We're starting around noon. I'll shoot you a text with all the info in a few. Thanks, man."

"No problem." Evan ended the call and music blasted out at him. He hit the volume button to bring down the level. He still felt wired, but the anger had ebbed to a more manageable level. He needed to do something to burn through the leftover adrenaline.

A predatory smile crossed his face, and he hit the gas, heading back toward the city. He knew exactly where to go.

TREVOR STALKED into Panther like the eponymous animal. Need vibrated through him, driving him to the bar for a double whiskey, which he shot back like water. He scanned the gyrating dance floor, looking for likely prey, and zeroed in on the one.

He pushed away the empty glass, warmth spreading through his veins, and walked over to where the young man danced, alone in the crowd. Sliding one hand around his target's hip to settle on one asscheek, Trevor pulled him in close and began to move.

The other man didn't even look surprised at Trevor's aggressive approach. He melted against Trevor's body, hands gliding up Trevor's arms to grasp his biceps, hips shifting right into the rhythm Trevor set. Dark eyes flashed up in clear invitation. The hair across the young man's forehead was plastered down with sweat, and the smell of his cologne and skin filled Trevor's senses.

They danced until the song changed, until no air remained between them. The smaller man laid his tongue at the base of

Trevor's neck and licked up to his mouth. "Wanna get out of here?" he breathed against Trevor's lips, and Trevor didn't hesitate.

THE OTHER man, who told Trevor his name was Cooper—not that Trevor cared—lived in a tiny studio two blocks from the club, in an area populated by preppy young gay men. Cooper's bed took up most of the open floor space, which made things easy when they stumbled through the door wrapped around each other. Cooper barely paused long enough to lock up behind them and pull a strip of condoms and a bottle of lube out of the bedside table. Clothes flew in all directions, and they came together again in the middle of the mattress, skin to naked skin.

It wasn't often that Trevor felt the need to dominate. He switched between top and bottom readily, but rarely did he just want to hold someone down and fuck the hell out of him. Tonight was one of those nights.

He'd picked well. Cooper rubbed up against him like a cat, following Trevor's lead, eager and pliant. Trevor sucked at his mouth, wrapping one hand around both their dicks and stroking hard and fast, needing it *now*, dammit.

Cooper pulled away just before Trevor did, twisting sinuously to turn over onto his stomach. Trevor leaned back and watched, lust gripping him at the view, Cooper's ass turned up and his back arched, his face pressed flat against the mattress.

"Fuck me," Cooper groaned, and Trevor didn't hesitate. A scant few minutes of prep later, he was driving in deep, fucking into the man beneath him with all the pent-up energy in his body. Cooper took it all, groaning and cursing, writhing and thrusting back, matching Trevor's rhythm, stroking his own dick so Trevor didn't have to spare a thought or a hand. Need drove him on, the smell of sex and the sound of skin slapping together ramping up his lust until there was room for nothing else.

When he came, everything left his body at once. All the anger, the confusion, the pain he'd channeled into lust drained away, leaving him shaking and shaken. He hardly noticed Cooper finding his own release. The other man had been nothing more than a prop.

Not that it mattered, since it seemed Cooper had done the same with him. A more polite version of "go away now" followed the sex, and Trevor was back on the street less than an hour after they'd met.

He walked back to retrieve his car, mind blank, soul empty.

CHAPTER 15

JUST BEFORE noon the next morning, Trevor pulled into the lot outside the shoot location, fueled on nothing but coffee, nicotine, and adrenaline. He hadn't even tried to sleep, and with only a handful of hours the night before, he was running low on reserves. Pausing to stub out his sixth cigarette in the past twelve hours, he pulled himself out of the car, venti quad-shot Americano in one hand and his duffel in the other.

The studio sat in a warehouse district a few miles from Trevor's place. He'd been to the neighborhood before—a nearby set of buildings held a popular gay dance club and a shop that sold everything from the most basic sex toys to leather harnesses. Trevor thought this building might have had a club in it years ago, too, though he'd never been there himself.

He followed the directions he'd been texted around the side of the building, to the door with a 303 over it. He rang the bell and waited to be let inside, deliberately not bothering to take deep breaths to calm the inevitable nerves that came before every shoot. This time, he needed to hold on to that rush, the energy running through him, if he wanted to get through the shoot and get out of here.

Noises on the other side of the door must have been locks disengaging, because a couple of seconds later, the door opened and Trevor found himself looking at a short, muscular man with a bit of a pot belly and a full, bushy beard.

"Glad you made it, man!" The man's overly loud voice and, at closer look, the brightness of his eyes made Trevor wonder what he'd spiked his morning coffee with. "C'mon in. I'm Billy. Emmett is over there finishing the setup with Griffen. He's your scene partner. Oh yeah, you got your test results?"

Jesus. Trevor hoped whatever had Billy running on fast-forward wasn't being brewed up in a back room somewhere. "Yeah, it's in my bag," he said, following Billy over to the side of the room, where a long folding table sat against one wall with a laptop and some random gear on one end and an oversized black duffel on the other. Trevor set his own bag down in between and dug out the paperwork showing his STI status, but by the time he turned to hand it to Billy, the man was over by the wall, chittering away at the two taller men working next to a St. Andrew's cross.

Trevor ignored them and took a minute to look around the space. Standard fare for a kinky shoot—industrial and barren. One of the reflective umbrellas looked like it might collapse at any moment, but that wasn't his problem, as long as it wasn't anywhere near him at the time. Another long table against the other wall held a camera, a case of bottled water, and a beat-up cardboard box full of folders, which Trevor assumed must be the required paperwork for the shoot.

Fuck. He hadn't expected high-end glamour, but he'd seen worse only once, with a studio that shut down a month after his shoot. At least the check had cleared. Maybe he should insist on payment in cash this time. He didn't know if he'd trust a check from these guys.

"Okay!" Billy came skittering back over. "Emmett's got everything ready to go. So here's the setup. Griffen is gonna drag you in on a leash—acting, y'know, not literally." Trevor managed not to roll his eyes. "And he's gonna strip you, strap you to the cross, flog you some, and then fuck you. Can you come hands-free?"

Trevor lifted an eyebrow. "Probably not today." Only a handful of times total, counting the shoot with Adam, and he doubted seriously he'd get far enough into anything these guys pulled to manage it.

Billy pouted. Literally. "Okay. Um, then Griffen will probably jerk you off after he's done. That work?"

Trevor nodded. "Sounds fine." Not a whole lot of *fun*, but that's why this was a job.

"Be right back." Billy disappeared through a door in the side wall, closing it firmly behind him, and Trevor tried not to think about what he might be popping or snorting or shooting in there.

"Trevor?"

He turned to face his scene partner. "Yeah," he said, holding out a hand. "Griffen, right?"

"Right." Griffen stood about two inches shorter than Trevor, but he had muscles on top of muscles, and his dark eyes and severe haircut gave him the look he needed to play the Dom role. Trevor had seen one scene Griffen had done with another studio, but he'd never met the other man before.

"Billy went over the scene plan with you?"

Trevor nodded. "Sounds pretty straightforward."

"You've been flogged before?"

Trevor thought the fact that he had was kind of the point of his being here, but ignored the ridiculous nature of the question and nodded again. "Did a few scenes with Kinksters. Got flogged for two of them."

"Oh." Griffen scowled, suddenly looking a lot meaner than before. "With Jeremy?"

"Yeah." Trevor didn't have a problem with Jeremy, who'd seemed to be a good guy, but it looked like maybe Griffen did.

Griffen snorted. "Amateur," he muttered. Then he shook himself. "Well, I'll be pulling my strokes, of course, for the camera. Nothing too rough. But we'll want to get you pinked up pretty well, so it shows up before I fuck you. I'll get a safeword from you during the scene, so go ahead and pick something, but you won't actually need it."

Trevor gave another mental eye roll. He didn't think much of Griffen's attitude. Every BDSM scene needed a safeword, whether it got used or not, and Trevor had enjoyed his shoots with Kinksters, even though he wasn't that much into the rougher stuff.

A moment from his shoot with Adam crossed his mind, soft tongue and fingers teasing him until he shivered, but he shook it off. *Not much into the super-gentle stuff either*, he told himself, focusing back on the scene in front of him.

Billy bustled back in, looking redder-nosed for the wear, and scampered around the room, checking the lights and adjusting the umbrellas. Emmett moved the tripod camera in closer, and Billy paused for a millisecond to check the view before grinning at Trevor and Griffen.

"Okay! Let's get things rolling!" Energy practically vibrated the air around him as he grabbed a light meter and hurried over into the scene space. Trevor and Griffen turned automatically to face the lights, and Billy hummed bits of some almost familiar dance tune while he and Emmett finished setting things up. Trevor waited, not patiently, but it wasn't as if he had much choice about it.

"Got it!" Billy tweaked some settings—*almost as hard as* he's *tweaking*, Trevor thought—and gave them a too-huge grin. "Ready when you are, boys!"

Griffen moved off to the side, where Emmett waited, holding a collar and leash. Trevor followed, stripped down to the black sport briefs he'd been instructed to wear, and let Emmett buckle the collar on, grateful that he double-checked to make sure it wasn't too tight. Griffen gave him a raised-eyebrow glance. "On three," he muttered, and then he counted them down: "One, two, three."

Even with the countdown, Trevor was caught off guard by how firmly Griffen yanked at the leash, but he kept his feet and followed the other man into the scene area. Griffen pulled him to a stop in front of the St. Andrew's cross and gave the leash another pull, this time down. "On your knees, boy," he barked.

Trevor obeyed, going to the floor with practiced ease. Griffen held the leash too tight, though, so he had to keep his head up and neck extended so it wouldn't cut into his skin. He pulled against Griffen's hold as a hint, and Griffen lightened up his grip a little, but not enough for comfort. Trevor opened his mouth to complain, but Griffen pulled the leash tight again.

"You don't talk, boy," he growled out. "You can scream all you want, but you don't get to talk."

Trevor waited for him to ask for a safeword, but the question didn't come. Instead, Griffen fumbled for the fly to his leather pants with his free hand. "You're gonna suck me, boy. And then I'm gonna beat the fight right out of you and fuck you into next week. Then after I'm done with you, *maybe* I'll think about letting you come."

Griffen loosened the leash, but just enough that he could turn Trevor and himself at the right angle for the camera to catch every moment when he shoved his cock into Trevor's mouth. Trevor fought back the urge to bite down and got to work instead, sucking and licking every inch. *At least he's got a nice cock*, he thought, *even if it's not all that big.* He didn't taste like overripe funk, either. The only time Trevor had ever stopped a shoot had been to insist that his scene partner take a bath, not just a shower, and wash *everywhere* this time.

Trevor relaxed his throat and took Griffen in deeper, swallowing around the tip before pulling back to suck all the way up the shaft. Griffen moaned above him, tugging lightly at the leash, his free hand grabbing the back of Trevor's head and forcing him back down.

"Suck it, bitch," Griffen panted. "Suck it harder."

Trevor was glad his mouth was stuffed full of cock. Otherwise he might've started laughing. He hoped there were people out there who found that kind of thing hot, because Trevor sure didn't get much from it. But he followed orders and sucked harder, hollowing his cheeks, bringing one hand up to pull at Griffen's balls. Griffen groaned again and moved to put his other hand on Trevor's head, but he must not have realized how tight he still had the leash, because the attempt made Trevor jerk his head back with a gasp.

"I said suck it, bitch!" Griffen yanked again, until the collar cut into Trevor's windpipe, and Trevor fought him then, ripping at the leash until he got it unwound from Griffen's hand one turn, leaving enough lead that Trevor could breathe. Griffen realized he'd overstepped and let him get comfortable, to some degree, before he shoved his dick back at Trevor's mouth.

"Yeah, suck me hard." Griffen thrust his cock deeper, and Trevor's throat burned from the combination of nicotine, caffeine, and deep-throating. But he held out until Griffen finally withdrew and yanked at the leash, directing Trevor without words to stand and then pulling him toward the St. Andrew's cross. Trevor stopped in front of the equipment and waited until Griffen reached for a hand to strap him in. He resisted.

"Safeword," he whispered sharply. Griffen paused. "Ask me for a safeword or I fucking swear I'm out of here."

Griffen yanked his hand to half turn Trevor toward the camera. "What's your safeword, bitch?"

Trevor almost left anyway. He also almost said Kinksters, just out of spite. Instead, what came out of his mouth surprised him.

"Mason," he said. For a moment, he had no clue where that word came from, but then he remembered. Riley. His full name was Mason O'Reilly Yeats.

He might have walked out then, an image of Riley's smile filling his mind, but before he could react, Griffen had him turned around and started buckling him into the restraints on the cross. Bound by wrists and ankles, Trevor took a deep breath and reminded himself that he had a job to do, and the rest of it could wait. Right now, he needed to finish the scene.

He could see Griffen in his peripheral vision, but it didn't prepare him for the hard yank on the leash he still held. "You're going to learn to behave, boy," he growled. "Your punishment this time is a good, hard flogging. Next time I won't be so easy on you."

He tossed the end of the leash over Trevor's shoulder so that it hung down in the front, out of the way of the flogger that was about to work Trevor over. Trevor realized then that he hadn't asked to see the implement that would be used on him. But then, he'd never had to ask before. He hadn't done that many BDSM-themed shoots, but always before, he'd been shown any paddles, floggers, plugs, clamps, or anything else that might be used. He'd never gone into a hard-edged shoot blind like this.

The vague uneasiness about the shoot that had bothered him since he arrived slipped toward full-fledged terror. He fought it as hard as he could, but with his hands and feet tied, and having no clue what was about to happen, he couldn't come up with anything to stop his heart and mind from galloping out of control. He began to shake, and just at that moment, the first stroke of the flogger hit his ass. He arched away on instinct, an unbidden gasp coming out of his mouth. That was no easy, warm-up stroke. If this was Griffen pulling his strokes, Trevor never wanted to experience his full strength.

Before he'd even straightened back up, the flogger came down again, just as hard, and within seconds Trevor was crying out and twisting almost continuously, trying to get away from the searing pain. He panted, unable to catch his breath, not even to use his safeword.

Griffen paused, and Trevor opened his mouth to yell "Mason!" but two more strokes hit him across his upper thighs and he could only suck in air. He fell forward against the cross, trying again to get out the word that, he hoped, would make it all stop, but then the flogger came down again, harder than ever, and right across his lower back.

"No!" he screamed, surging into action, twisting and fighting against his bounds. Even the least experienced floggers knew that the lower back was always, *always* off limits. Without the ribcage for protection, the kidneys sat fully exposed to every strike, and it didn't take much force to leave them bruised or even permanently damaged.

"Hold still, boy!" Griffen's hand landed on the back of Trevor's neck, holding him flat against the cross, and the flogger hit his ass twice before returning to stripe his lower back. Trevor struggled even more.

"Mason!" he finally got out. "Stop, dammit!"

Griffen laughed. "We stop when *I* say we stop, boy."

A voice yelled from off camera, and a switch inside Trevor flipped. He went from mental terror to full-out panic, yanking at the cuffs on his hands, trying desperately to escape from the hell he'd been shoved into.

The hell he'd been living in for five long, desperate years.

Trevor fought against his bonds, grabbing at the chains holding him to the cross and pulling hard, and suddenly, something gave. The cross shuddered and shook, and then, as if in slow motion, it began to topple over.

And Trevor toppled right along with it.

CHAPTER 16

MOMENTS FLASHED like photographs across Evan's vision: The blurry view of the warehouse's metal ceiling high above him. The weight of the wooden cross lying on his body. The throbbing in his head and the searing pain in his wrist. Then, people scrambling around him, unbuckling the restraints, lifting the cross away so he could breathe again. Emmett crouching beside him, telling him in a soft drawl to be still and that help was on the way. Emmett disappearing and an EMT appearing in his place, asking questions Evan couldn't answer.

He felt the prick of a needle in his arm, and then everything faded away.

He opened his eyes to dimmed lights, distant noises, and the smell of antiseptic. His head and wrist still throbbed, and when he tried to move, so did his back. Hell, everything hurt. It was just a matter of degrees.

"Ev?"

Evan turned his head, slowly, to see Cory sitting by his bed. Cory smiled. "Hey there. How're you feeling?"

Evan blinked. "Hurts," he murmured, his mouth dry. It took too much effort to say more than that.

Cory grabbed something on the bed. "Let's get the nurse in here to check on you, okay?"

Call button. Evan would've nodded in acknowledgment, but the concept of how much pain that would likely cause kept him still. It only took a few moments for a nurse to come bustling in anyway.

"Mr. Day," she said, her voice bright but soft. "I'm Carla. You took quite a spill, I hear. How do you feel?"

God, she expected him to talk? He licked his lips and made his best effort. "Head hurts," he whispered. "And wrist. Back." He coughed out a poor attempt at a laugh. "Just... everything."

"I can imagine." Carla took a look at some monitors. "We're going to be taking you down to radiology in a few minutes to get some X-rays, and then we can get you something to drink, at least."

The memory of the lashing his lower back had taken pushed Evan to speak again. "Kidneys," he whispered. "Check them?"

Carla gave him a look and then shared one with Cory. "The EMTs didn't mention anything about your kidneys or lower back," she said. "But they did bring you in on a back board, so they probably didn't turn you over. Did something else happen?"

"Yeah." Evan swallowed. "Got hit. Before the fall."

He couldn't talk anymore. His throat was still raw, remnants of his rough night and even rougher treatment at Griffen's hands, and every word made the pain in his head worse. He closed his eyes.

"We'll check, honey," Carla said. After a pause, she added, "Your friend here took care of your insurance information and all that."

"So you won't go bankrupt or anything," Cory chimed in. "Though I might charge you for the heart attack I nearly had when the EMT called me. Honey, once you're feeling better, we have got some talking to do."

Feeling better. Oh shit. Evan's eyes popped open. "Mom," he rasped out. "Where am I?"

Cory laughed softly. "Not your mom, honey, but you're at Piedmont."

With extreme effort, Evan waved his good hand toward the curtain. "Mom's here," he forced through the fire in his throat. "Got hurt yesterday. Need to... find her...."

He started to move, but a big hand came down in the middle of his chest. "You're not going anywhere, honey." Cory's voice managed to be both soothing and firm. "If your mom's still here, then I'll find out what's going on for you, okay?"

Evan relaxed and nodded before he thought about it. Pain exploded through his head, and he cried out despite his best efforts.

"Shhh, honey, it's okay." Cory cupped his cheek. "You took a pretty nasty spill, from what I hear, and you hit your head. Just lie still and let the doctors and nurses take care of you, and I'll take care of everything else."

Evan couldn't respond. It took all of his focus to concentrate on breathing and *not moving*, dammit.

"All right, Mr. Day." A new voice entered the room, but Evan had squeezed his eyes shut and couldn't pry them open. "We're gonna take you down to radiology and get everything checked out."

"I'm going to check on another patient while he's gone, okay?" Warm breath brushed his ear, and a soft kiss landed just in front of it. "I'll be back just as soon as I can, okay?"

Evan stopped himself just in time from nodding again. Instead, he forced out an "okay." A minute later, his bed lurched into motion, and his stomach went with it. He bit back the nausea, everything in him recoiling at the thought of how much it would hurt to throw up. Things seemed to settle once the bed was rolling down the hall, and a few minutes later, they came to a stop in another hallway.

"Just a little backed up here, Mr. Day. They'll get you taken care of soon."

"Okay. Thanks," Evan added, though he kept his eyes closed. He could see through his eyelids how bright the lights were here, and he didn't think that would be much help with his headache.

The sounds and smells of the hospital surrounded him. Someone in another bed nearby moaned, clearly in pain, and the scent of stale urine seeped in around the astringent in the air. He hadn't been a patient in a hospital in years—four years, he figured, when he'd been checked out at the public hospital, Grady, after he was rear-ended and the airbag in his car smacked him in the face. The ER there had been much busier and noisier than this one.

He drifted, maybe even dozed, for who knew how long before another voice spoke up from beside him. "Okay, Mr. Day, we've got you ready now."

"Evan," he said. He cleared his throat. "Call me Evan?"

"All right, then, Mr. Evan. Here we go."

Evan had to smile at the woman's phrasing. Her slow drawl gave away her Southern roots anyway, but the "Mr." before his name sealed it.

The bed clanked as she unlocked the wheels and got him moving again. His stomach stayed quiet this time, and soon he was in another room with what looked like a gigantic camera overhead. X-ray, apparently.

"All right, Mr. Evan. We're going to get some shots of your wrist, and then we're gonna help you turn over so we can get some shots of your head too. Then we'll take you over for the CT scan."

Evan took a deep breath and braced himself for the pain he knew would follow. It wasn't as bad as he feared, even as they removed the temporary brace from his wrist and moved his arm into several different positions, the giant camera rumbling and clicking to take each shot. Turning over was an adventure in nausea, but he made it, and he lay there and breathed as more shots were taken.

Once that was done, they let him stay on his stomach while they rolled him a few doors down to another room with another huge machine in it. It took three people to help him transfer to the narrow bed, and getting his arms positioned was a challenge because of the wrist injury. By the time the tube had finished scanning over his head and abdomen, Evan ached all over and felt like he could sleep for a week.

They kept waking him up, though. He dozed again on the way back to his spot in the ER, but the nurse roused him to ask questions and finally, thank God, to give him a few sips of water. She injected something into his IV for pain too, and he lost track of time after that, not that he had any way to keep up with it. No phone or watch, and no clocks that he could see. Distantly, he thought that the fact he could see, no double vision, probably was a good thing, at least.

Finally, the curtain slid back and a new person stepped up to his bed. "Mr. Day, I'm Dr. Patel," she said. "How are we feeling?"

"Evan," he replied. "And I dunno about you, but I feel like crap."

She laughed softly and turned to the computer. "We should have results from your tests, so let me pull those up and we'll see what we can do." She fell silent, and Evan went back to not thinking and not moving.

"Okay." Dr. Patel moved back to his bedside. "So, here's what we have. Your ulna is broken just below the wrist, but it's clean and looks pretty well aligned, so you shouldn't need surgery. We'll have an orthopedist confirm that before we apply a permanent cast, though. You do not have a skull fracture, but there is some fairly severe bruising, and you've got a concussion to go along with that. So you're going to have a pretty bad headache for a few days, and we'll need to admit you to be sure you don't develop any more serious bleeding. That will also put some limits on your medications and food. You'll probably be on liquid nutrition for the first twenty-four hours, mainly because you'll probably have more bouts of nausea, and vomiting would make things worse."

She paused then. "I know this is a lot to digest, especially when you've taken a good knock on the head. You still with me?"

"Yeah." Evan fought the instinct to nod. "Anything else?"

Dr. Patel grimaced. "The CT showed some insult to your right kidney. We'll need a urine sample, and if that's not a problem, then we won't need to place a catheter. Either way, though, we'll need to catch and test your urine for blood, make sure the kidney gets better and not worse."

Evan winced, hoping the catheter wouldn't be necessary. "How long will I be in?"

"That depends on you." Dr. Patel lifted her eyebrow. "If you're a good patient and follow all the rules we give you, probably two to three days. That's if nothing gets worse and you don't need surgery. The good news is that we have some open beds, so it shouldn't take us long to find you a spot and get you settled in. Is someone here with you?"

"Yeah," Evan answered. "He went to check on my… on another patient we know."

Dr. Patel nodded. "Okay. Let me get my notes written up and put in the admission order so they can get you assigned to a room, and a nurse will be over to get the urine sample. You probably won't see the orthopedist until you're up on the floor, and we're limited on what we can give you for pain because of the head injury, but we're doing the best we can on that front."

"Okay." Evan was relieved when the doctor moved back to the computer and started clacking away again. His head throbbed, and he hoped he'd remember everything she told him. Two to three days in the hospital sucked, but it could be worse. He could be heading in for emergency brain surgery, for example.

Soon Dr. Patel stopped typing. "All right, Mr. Day. We should have someone moving you to a room before too much longer."

"Thanks," Evan said.

"You're welcome. Take care." The doctor left, and Evan stared up at the ceiling for a while. At some point, a nurse came in and checked his monitors and IV, and he had to pee into a container shaped like a deformed milk bottle, but at least that wasn't a problem, so it looked like a catheter would be off the table. He didn't know how long "before too much longer" turned out to be, but eventually, Nurse Carla came back in, followed by a tall black man wearing scrubs and a bright white smile.

"We've got your room ready," Carla said as she started unplugging wires. "Otis here will take you up, and the nurses on four will take over from there." She reached up to unhook the bag of saline from the stand and then laid it on the bed next to Evan's hip. "If you'll keep an eye on that, then we should be good to go. You take care, Mr. Day."

Evan didn't correct her this time. "Thanks, Carla," he said, closing his eyes as the bed started to move. He hoped Cory would find him soon. He wanted to know about his mom.

"EVAN?"

Cory's voice roused Evan from a light doze. He was so fucking sleepy, but he forced his eyes open and held out his good hand. "How is she?"

Cory dropped the bag of Evan's things next to the bed and dropped himself into the chair. "She's doing all right. Lord, I had no idea it would be like talking to a brick wall to get your daddy to tell me anything. I mean, I've dealt with him before, but man, he's a tough nut to crack."

A sound something like a laugh escaped Evan. "He always was." He swallowed, his throat dry. "Need some water."

"Oh, sure, honey." Cory grabbed the big plastic mug with the straw from the side table and maneuvered it to a spot where Evan could get the straw to his mouth without moving his head. A little water spilled, but Evan didn't care. The cool liquid felt *so* damn good going down.

Evan's stomach twisted, and he stopped himself from drinking too much. With the headache he had and the way his back hurt, he didn't need to make himself sick. He lay back against the pillows and concentrating on breathing until the nausea faded.

"I didn't even think about it until I got to her room," Cory said, "but he asked why I was there. Well, to be specific, he said, 'What the hell are *you* doing here?' I think the only reason he didn't bellow it was that it's a freaking hospital."

Oh, man. Evan hadn't even thought about Cory having to explain his showing up like that. "What did you tell him?"

Cory shrugged. "That you were here with a friend and asked me to check on her. I figure it's enough truth for now."

Evan started to nod, then realized that was a bad idea. Slowly, he turned his head toward Cory and opened his eyes just a slit. "Did they say when she'd get to go home?"

Cory shook his head. "No, all I got out of him was that she'll be fine. I don't even know what happened to her."

That was a story Evan had no desire to tell. "She hit her head," he murmured. "It… it was bad. I shouldn't've gone."

Cory frowned. "To dinner? Honey, what happened?"

"They lied." Evan lay back against the pillow and stared at the ceiling, unwilling to close his eyes because he'd just see the blood on his mother's head. "They had… *I* had money. A trust fund or something, I dunno. I should've gotten it when I turned twenty-one. They never told me."

"Fuck." Cory fell silent. "How much?"

"Over a quarter million."

"Fucking fuck!" Cory jumped to his feet, and pain forgotten for a moment, Evan turned his head to stare. "You mean to tell me you could've had *$250,000* coming to you? And your parents didn't tell you?" Cory's face turned nearly as red as Evan's father's had during their argument. "How dare they? Bad enough they turned you out like a stray dog. But *fuck!*"

Evan seriously thought Cory was going to punch something. He'd never seen his friend this angry, not even during the confrontation with his parents after Evan came home. "Cory—"

"No!" Cory cut him off. "I'll kill him. I'll strangle him. I'll wrap my fingers around his scrawny little neck...." His hands curled in the air in front of him, recreating the movements he described, and Evan did the only thing he could do.

He laughed.

It hurt, but hell, what *hadn't* hurt the past few days? He wrapped his good arm around his stomach, and he laughed until he coughed.

And then he cried.

It was like a switch flipped inside him, and the absurdity that had become his life morphed into tragedy. All the pain and sorrow he'd been carrying for so long welled up and spilled out of him. He cried for his brother, the boy he'd idolized and the man he missed desperately. He cried for Lucas, his first love, the man who'd taught him who he really was. He cried for his mother, who'd loved him but wouldn't stand by him. He cried for his father, both the man he was and the man Evan wanted him to be.

And he cried for himself. The child who'd wanted to be loved. The teenager who'd lost his beloved brother. The man who'd lost his lover, his career, and his family, all in one swift blow. The shell who'd been walking through his life for five years, hiding everything inside so deeply that nothing reached below the surface.

By the time the tears ran dry, he ached all over. His head and back throbbed, and his mouth was a desert. He came back to himself to realize that Cory sat on the side of the bed, holding his good hand in both of his and making wordless, soothing sounds. Evan's breath shuddered in and out, but he managed to make his mouth work.

"Water?" he rasped.

Cory reached for the mug again. He didn't say anything, but after he'd helped Evan take a few sips, he put the mug back and grabbed the box of tissues, pulled a few out, and handed them to Evan. Evan used them to dry off his face and wipe his nose, and Cory didn't even flinch as he took the wet paper from Evan's hand and tossed it toward the trash.

He tilted his head and gave Evan a soft smile. "Feel better now?"

Evan almost laughed. "Kinda." He breathed in as deeply as he could before the pain kicked in and then blew it out. "Sleepy."

"I bet." Cory leaned forward to press a kiss against Evan's damp temple. "You rest. You've earned a nap."

Evan nodded once and closed his eyes. Sleep claimed him quickly.

WHEN EVAN opened his eyes again, the light from the window told him it was daytime, but it took him a few moments to realize that, no, his eyes weren't playing tricks on him.

Riley sat in the bedside chair.

He had a book in his hands and appeared to be engrossed, which gave Evan a chance to study him. He looked older, somehow, more like his actual age than his usual barely legal appearance. His blond curls were smoothed behind his ears, and his eyes were shadowed, circles under them so dark he looked bruised. He wore a simple T-shirt and jeans, snug-fitting but not skintight.

Just looking at him made Evan's heart feel lighter.

A pang in his back forced Evan to move, and Riley's head popped up immediately. His gaze met Evan's, layers of emotion laid bare by that one simple look.

"Hey." As conversation openers went, it was far from brilliant, but Evan had plenty of excuses.

"Hey," Riley replied as he leaned to set his book on the floor. "How are you feeling?"

Evan shifted again, the pain in his back not letting up. "Like hell," he admitted. "Kind of hurts everywhere. Some places worse than others."

Riley scooted forward in his chair. "The nurse was in about twenty minutes ago. She said she'd check on you again soon, but I can call if you need painkillers?"

"No." Evan reached out his good hand, and Riley hesitated only a moment before stretching his own out to meet it. Evan folded his fingers around Riley's and sighed, just that simple touch relaxing him.

Evan lifted his head from the pillow and raised an eyebrow. "How'd you know I was here, anyway?"

Riley chuckled. "A long, complicated story running from Cory through Mikey and then to me," he replied. "I got here about thirty minutes ago."

Evan could just imagine that process. He lowered his head and just looked at Riley, and after a long pause, Riley spoke again. "I'm sorry."

Evan blinked. "For what?"

Riley shrugged one shoulder. "For everything. For pushing you away."

He stopped short, and Evan waited. Finally, Riley took in a breath and blew it out. "You were right," he said, lifting his gaze to meet Evan's. "I never got over the thing with my parents. I talk a big game about how I'm the black sheep and all that, but the truth is, it hurt. It still hurts, that they treat me like some kind of sideshow freak instead of their son."

His voice cracked on the last word, and Evan wanted to wrap his arms around Riley so much that he nearly climbed out of the bed, despite the throbbing in his back and head and all the tubes and wires attached to his body. He tightened his grip on Riley's hand, feeling wholly inadequate and wishing he could do so much more.

Riley took a few deep, cleansing breaths and then gave Evan a tremulous smile. "So it seems we're equally fucked up," he said. "I guess that's as good a place as any to start, right?"

Evan had to smile at that. "Yeah. Maybe we can help each other get to not-fucked-up from here."

Riley leaned in, and Evan let his eyes fall shut as Riley kissed him softly. "It'll be okay," he murmured. "We'll make it okay."

And Evan believed him.

THE NURSE did come in shortly after their conversation, and another dose of painkillers meant Evan fell asleep again. This time, though, he slept with Riley's hand still in his.

He woke with his hand empty and his father sitting at his bedside.

Evan's heart jumped into his throat. "Mom! Is she…?"

"She's fine." Riley stepped in front of Charles. "Cory told your parents about you, and your father came to tell you about her. I'll be right outside, okay?"

Evan almost begged Riley to stay, but he had no idea what his father might come out with this time, and he didn't want Riley caught in the crossfire. He nodded, and Riley smiled softly and left.

Evan turned his attention to Charles Day. The man looked crumpled, and not just because of the wrinkles in his clothes. Lines that hadn't been apparent two days earlier were etched deep into his face, and he looked much older than his fifty-five years.

"How is she?"

Charles sighed. "She'll be fine. She had a hairline fracture and some swelling underneath, but they've been monitoring her closely, and the swelling is almost gone. They'll keep her another couple of days to be safe, and she'll need to take it easy for a few weeks, but…." He trailed off, and something deep inside Evan relaxed, a knot he hadn't even been aware of.

"Thank God," he breathed. "Jesus. I was so…."

He didn't know how to finish that sentence. Scared? Worried? Guilty? *All of the above*, he thought.

His father shifted in his seat, drawing Evan's attention back. "Look," Charles said. "I know we got off on the wrong foot the other day. I let my temper get the best of me, and your mother is paying the price." He met Evan's gaze for the first time. "We're sorry that we never told you about the money. We set up the fund for you, and when your brother—" He cut off and swallowed hard. "Anyway, all the money is yours, and we want you to have it. No strings. We can put that in writing if you want."

Evan didn't want to talk about this now, but then, he doubted he ever would. "I don't know if I can trust that," he said. "I lost *everything* five years ago. I know you don't want to hear it, but I was in love with Lucas, and I lost him, and then I lost my job and my family. I had *nothing* left. And now you're telling me I can have almost all of it back, and I don't know if I can believe it. You cut me off five years ago. How do I know you won't pull me in and then do it again?"

Charles nodded. "I understand completely. We haven't exactly been trustworthy so far." He leaned forward. "But I mean every word of it, Evan. The money is yours. I want you to use it to go to college. I want you to get out of that business you're in now. You can do so much more with your life."

Evan reined in, barely, his first instinct, which was to defend "that business" and his role in it. *Keep it together*, he told himself. "That business is the reason I'm not starving on the streets," he pointed out. "If it hadn't been for Cory and his boyfriend—"

"I know." Charles deflated a little. "That came out wrong. I…. Well, I'd be a hypocrite to say anything against adult entertainment. I'm no saint."

Evan did *not* need the image of his father watching porn in his brain. "It's a job like any other," he said. *And I'm good at it*, he thought, but he didn't need his father to hear that any more than he wanted to think about the man watching porn. He held back a shudder.

"I understand. I… I overreacted. I didn't expect to hear anything like that from you, and I lashed out." He lifted an eyebrow. "Though I think you do owe your mother an apology for the language you used to break that news."

Evan dropped his chin and nodded. "I was angry too," he replied. "And I will."

"She's been caught in the middle. Getting back in touch with you was her idea. I didn't want to do it." Charles barked out a soft laugh. "Damn pride. It sinks its teeth into you and doesn't want to let go."

That, Evan understood all too well. "We wasted a lot of time."

Charles gave him a small smile. "That we did." He leaned in closer, forearms resting on his thighs, and rubbed his palms together. "How about we start over? The money is yours if you want it. We won't dictate what you do with it, but we hope you'll use it to go to school. Or maybe start a business, if that's what you want. Hell, you can blow it all if you want." He grinned, and he looked so much like Charlie in that moment that Evan's breath stopped. "Though we'd draw the line at bailing you out after the fact if you went that route."

Evan let out a soft laugh. "I've thought a few times about taking some classes," he admitted. "Having the money would make it easier."

"Definitely." Charles's smile fell away. "And like I said, no strings. But it would be a load off our minds if you stopped...."

He didn't finish, and Evan rolled his eyes. "It's called 'porn,' Dad. It's okay to say it out loud."

Evan didn't understand the expression that crossed his father's face. Charles rubbed his eyes with his thumb and forefinger and then dropped his hand and smiled at Evan.

"You haven't called me 'Dad' since you were fourteen years old," he said.

Since before Charlie died, Evan's mind supplied. He bit his lower lip to keep from losing it again.

"I guess I haven't acted like much of a dad since then." Charles folded in on himself again. "I know I can't make up for it. It's far too late for that. But I want to start fresh, son. I want my family back."

Evan wanted that too, more than he could have imagined. He nodded and held out his uninjured hand, and without hesitation, his father reached out to take it in a firm grip.

For the first time in five long years, Evan felt hope creep in.

CHAPTER 17

TALKING TO his father exhausted Evan. He fell asleep again even before his next dose of painkillers. The nurse roused him briefly when she came in to check on him, and he was otherwise alone in the room. The next time he woke, though, two people were waiting for him.

"Hey there, gorgeous." Jimmy had apparently seen Evan's eyes open first and bounced up from his seat to lay a big smooch on Evan's cheek. He smiled, his eyes soft. "How are you feeling?"

"Groggy." Evan managed a half smile as Cory appeared next to Jimmy. "Hey," he said, and Cory leaned in to kiss his other cheek. Then Evan frowned and turned his attention back to Jimmy. "Wait, I thought you were busy this week?"

Jimmy shook his head. "Just 'til yesterday, hon. The last of the stragglers cleared out this morning and I left the place in Shaun's capable hands." He cocked his head to one side. "What's this I hear about a kink scene gone wrong? Do I need to roll some heads?"

Evan rolled his eyes. "Mine, for starters. I ignored way too many warning signs with the whole thing. Oh." He lifted his head off the pillow. "It'd be nice to get paid, though. We didn't finish the scene, but I figure after that mess, they owe me."

Jimmy's smile was feral. "I'm pretty sure I can arrange that. Just give me the info."

"It's all in my phone." He looked around. "Which I guess is still in my bag?"

"Yep," Cory confirmed. He turned toward the storage cabinet in the corner. "The one good thing those idiots did," he said over his shoulder, "other than calling 911, was put your duffel in the ambulance with you." He turned back. "Phone, wallet, clothes, all accounted for. Oh, and your keys." He set the bag on the foot of the bed and rummaged through it for the phone. "I guess your car's still in the parking lot over there, but now that Jimmy's here, we can go fetch it for you."

He produced the phone and handed it over, and Evan turned it on, waiting for the screen to light up. He hoped it still had enough charge for him to get the information for Jimmy. Good thing he'd turned it off completely before the shoot.

Within a couple of minutes, he'd found the e-mail and forwarded it to Jimmy so he could deal with it. Evan knew if there was any way to make the studio pay for any of this, Jimmy would figure it out. Jimmy gave Evan another big kiss on the cheek and headed out to make some calls. Cory dragged a chair close to the bed and settled in. "So. How are you really feeling?"

Evan shrugged one shoulder. "Sore. Stiff. Beyond ready to get out of here."

Cory nodded. "And your parents?"

Evan sighed. "Dad and I talked. It was... rough. But good. I'm.... Things might be okay there."

"What did he say about the money?"

Evan's wrist throbbed, and he moved it to a different position. "It's mine. I mean, I guess part of it was Charlie's to start with, but now they say it's all mine, and they won't tell me what to do with it. They want me to go to college, but he says no strings. I don't know if I believe it, but...."

"But you want to."

"Oh God, yes." Evan blurted it out without hesitation. "You have no idea."

"I can imagine." Cory studied Evan's face. "I mean, the money's a big enough deal, but if your parents are actually willing to start making up for the way they treated you, then that would be fuckin' amazing."

Evan nodded, then turned as a soft knock came at the door. Riley's head appeared at the opening. "Oh," he said when he saw Cory. "We'll come back."

"No, honey, come on in." Cory pushed to his feet. "I need to go track down Jimmy anyway." He glanced over Riley's shoulder. "You said 'we'?"

Riley smirked. "Mikey's in the hall."

Cory grinned. "Well, then, *we'll* go track down Jimmy. It's time he got an introduction anyway, and we can go get Evan's car too."

Riley's hesitance was obvious, so Evan stepped in. "They'll be good," he said. "They might be dirty old men, but they're not predators."

Cory glared. "Thanks for the backhanded compliment."

Evan winked at him. "You know you like it like that."

Cory winked back and headed for the hallway, pausing to drop a light kiss on Riley's cheek as he passed by. Riley lifted a hand to touch the spot, looking a little shell-shocked as he crossed the room to the chair Cory had vacated.

"They really are harmless." Evan thought Riley could use a little more assurance. "They're a handful, but they wouldn't hurt a fly. Or a twink."

Riley lowered himself into the chair. "I just worry, you know? I'm trying not to hover, but Mikey's been pretty sheltered. I didn't tell you that whole story, but suffice to say when his parents moved to Florida, they were happy to get Mikey away from me."

"What? Why?"

Riley huffed out a breath. "We lived next door to each other. Mikey's a couple of years younger than me, and his parents are really conservative. His dad's a preacher, and his mom was ridiculously protective, so he's always seemed even younger. By the time we were preteens, it was obvious to everyone that I was not exactly straight. Mikey's parents thought it would rub off or something ridiculous. His dad got an offer to help run a big church in Florida, so off they went."

"Wow. That seems like a bit of an overreaction."

Riley's grin was evil. "The punch line is that it didn't work. Mikey's 100 percent gay, maybe even gayer than me." He deflated.

"But he's hidden it for so long. He just turned twenty-five years old and dated women until about two years ago. He started working at an amusement park while he was still in high school and then got on at Disney and worked his way up some, so he got his own place eventually. But he's still living under his parents' thumb. Or was."

"Until you got him out."

"Yeah." Riley gave a lopsided smile. "It took me years to convince him, first just trying to get him to admit to himself that he's gay. He still acts a lot younger than he is. I hope getting him away from his parents will help with that."

Evan smiled. "Well, Cory and Jimmy are good at helping with things like that. I told you they're the ones who took me in after I got kicked out of the Marine Corps, right?"

Riley shook his head. "You told me a little, but I bet there's a lot more to that story."

"You know it. Hell, Jimmy not only got me into porn, he broke me in. When he found out I'd only been with one guy, he told me he'd help me practice." Evan laughed. "I figured he was just trying to get into my pants, but he was for real. Cory helped convince me." He smiled. "They taught me a lot about sex and a lot about my body, and a whole hell of a lot about how to have sex on camera."

Evan realized at that point that he was telling the guy he hoped would be his boyfriend about all the sex he'd had before they met, and maybe Riley didn't want to hear it. He bit his lip. "Sorry," he said. "Probably TMI."

"No," Riley replied. "I'm glad to hear it. You always hear bad stories about porn. People getting forced into it, or not knowing what they're doing and getting ripped off. Or getting sick."

"It's not like that for most people," Evan said. "But I got luckier than most. Cory and Jimmy have been there for me from the start. I don't know where I would've ended up without them." *Dead on the streets somewhere, probably*, he thought, even though he knew that was probably an overly morbid conclusion.

"Well, then I'm glad you had them." Riley cleared his throat. "So, have the doctors given you any idea when you might get out of here?"

Evan dropped his head back against the pillow. "Couple of days, is all they'll say. I've been sleeping so much that it hasn't mattered. This is the first time I feel almost human again." He glanced at the clock on the wall. "It feels like it should be Friday or Saturday, but it's only Tuesday night, right?"

"Right." Riley tilted his head. "What about your mom? Will she go home soon?"

"Same answer. A couple of days. I hope I can get out before she does so I can help get her home."

Slowly, hesitantly, as if he thought he'd be rebuffed, Riley reached out and took Evan's hand in his. "I'd like it a lot," he said, "if you'd consider staying with me for a few days once you're released."

Just like that, tears sprung up in Evan's eyes. He blinked them away and nodded. "I'd like that," he answered, voice gone raspy. Riley smiled then, that wide, brilliant smile that had drawn Evan in from the beginning. And Evan felt himself returning it in kind.

WEDNESDAY AFTERNOON, Evan decided he was strong enough to go visit his mother.

Her room wasn't far, at the other end of the same floor as Evan's. Riley, who'd been by his side since their conversation the day before, except for a trip back home to shower and bring fresh clothes, insisted that Evan go in a wheelchair, which Riley pushed.

When they got to Gwen Day's room, she looked so tiny in the big hospital bed that it made Evan's heart hurt to look at her. Riley carefully navigated his chair to the side of the bed, and Evan lifted his good hand to lay it over Gwen's. "Mom?"

Gwen's eyes fluttered open, and when she saw him, she smiled. "Oh, my beautiful little boy."

From the corner of his eye, Evan saw Riley slip out of the room, but he let that go for now and focused on his mother. "How do you feel, Mom?"

She smiled, a shadow of her usual self. "My head hurts." She fluttered her free hand. "The obvious." She laid her hand across her stomach, reaching toward him again. "How are you, dear? Charles tells me you had a bit of an accident as well?"

It occurred to Evan that neither of his parents likely knew the source of his injuries. If he had anything to say about it, they never would.

"I took a fall too," he told her. "But I'm doing okay. I should be out of here tomorrow. I hope you will be too."

"I think so. I had a tough time at first, couldn't remember anything from one minute to the next." She lifted her hand to her forehead. "But it's all right now. Just the headache left."

Evan shuffled forward in his seat. "I guess you know Dad came to see me."

Gwen brought her hand down to cover his and squeezed. "He told me you'd talked. I understand you've worked everything out?"

"Mostly." Evan bit his lip, choosing his words carefully. "It's hard, Mom. I don't…. It's hard to believe all of this is real, you know?"

Gwen focused on him fully, her gaze piercing through him. "I understand, dear. We behaved terribly, and I've been just sick about it. It took me a while to wear your father down." She shook her head. "I love him dearly, but he's always been so very proud. He made himself out of nothing, and it's very difficult for him to admit when he's wrong about anything."

Evan nodded. "We talked about that. I think he's trying, but—"

"I'm more than trying." Evan's head snapped to the right, and he saw his father standing in the doorway. He held a manila envelope in one hand, very much like the one Evan had found in their dining room on Sunday.

"I've already set up the transfer," Charles said. "You have an escrow account in your name alone, and it contains the full principal and interest from the trust fund. The total is just over $262,000." He held out the envelope. "No strings. Just like I promised."

Evan rose slowly, sliding his hand free from his mother's, and took the two steps necessary to take the envelope from his father's loose grip. He returned to his seat and pulled out the small stack of papers, skimming quickly over the basic information. Everything seemed to be exactly what his father said, though of course he wouldn't have confirmation until he actually tried to access the money.

"Evan." He raised his head and found his father had pulled up a chair close to him and sat perched on its edge, leaning toward him. "I swear to you, everything is exactly what I'm saying. I may have made many mistakes, including not telling you up front about this money. But I have never lied outright. I would never lie about something like this."

"Please, Evan." He turned his head to his mother, who held out her hand to him again. Tears shimmered in her eyes. "Please give us another chance. I don't want to lose you again."

Evan swallowed back the emotion that made his throat suddenly tight. "I don't want to lose you either." He looked at his father. "Either of you."

Charles smiled at him, and Evan found himself believing it would all be okay.

CHAPTER 18

IT WAS late afternoon on Thursday when the hospital finally let Gwen go. Evan had gotten his walking papers two hours earlier, Riley there to take him home—home to Riley's—but he'd stayed with Evan in the lobby until Gwen could leave too. He needed to be sure she got home okay. He knew his dad could've handled it on his own, but he just… he needed to be there.

Once Gwen was loaded into his parents' Town Car, Evan climbed into the passenger seat of Riley's BMW and settled in for the drive. In rush-hour traffic, it could take a good hour to get to his parents' home. Riley waited until they were stopped at a traffic light to talk. "Your mother is a real Steel Magnolia, isn't she?"

Evan chuckled. "Right down to the football-helmet hair," he agreed. "I think she always wished she'd had a daughter just so she could dress her up in lace like Shelby and send her off down the aisle."

"In some ways," Riley said slowly, "she reminds me of my mother. Putting on a good face even when things are crumbling around her. Being the perfect hostess and wife." He gave Evan a wan smile. "I think my mother missed the part about still having a heart underneath it all."

Evan reached over to lay his hand on Riley's thigh. "Everyone has their own battles to fight."

Riley lowered his hand to entwine his fingers with Evan's. "Not necessarily, but we can hope that maybe they'll eventually recover from their cases of craniorectal inversion."

It took Evan a second to parse what Riley meant, and then he laughed. "Removing heads from asses would be helpful, yeah." He lifted their hands to his mouth so he could kiss Riley's fingers. "Working pretty well for us so far."

Riley smiled, eyes on the road. "Clear skies as far as I can see."

Clear skies and smooth sailing, Evan thought, keeping Riley's hand clasped in his.

GETTING GWEN from the car and into the house turned into a production worthy of a sitcom. First she wanted to walk under her own power, but when she got out of the car, a wave of dizziness had Charles wrapping a strong arm around her waist to hold her up. Evan tried to do the same from the other side, but he managed to bang his bandaged arm into the doorframe, and it took all the self-control he could muster not to burst out in a string of curses at the jolt of pain.

Riley stepped in for him. "Mr. Day, if you'll help Mrs. Day inside, I'll get the car closed up for you, and Evan and I will be right in. If that's okay?"

"Yes, yes, that's fine." Charles's focus was on his wife, and the two of them started up the walkway toward the front door, moving slowly but steadily. Evan stepped away from the car, his broken wrist resting in his good hand, and Riley leaned in to hit the lock button inside the door before pushing the door closed.

"All right," he said as he turned to Evan. "Let's see if we can get you inside without any more injuries."

Evan growled under his breath, but he was smiling as he did it. He let Riley lead him to the door, though he walked under his own power. He had a broken wrist, not a broken leg.

The inner door stood open behind the storm door, so Evan reached for the outer handle and waved Riley in ahead of him. They got into the living room to find Charles fussing over Gwen, getting her settled on the sofa with pillows around her and a throw pulled over her legs.

"I'm okay, Charles. Good heavens. You'd think I'd had major surgery or something." She waved a hand. "I'm fine! I'm resting! Watch me rest!"

Riley shot Evan a look, and Evan bit his lip to keep from laughing. Steel Magnolia indeed.

Charles blew out an exasperated breath. "At least let me get you something to drink. I don't know if there's sweet tea, but I believe we still have a few bottles of that green tea you like."

"Yes, fine, that would be lovely." She fluttered her hands at him. "Shoo."

Charles grumbled but disappeared around the corner toward the kitchen. Evan crept forward, hesitant to say anything. She turned her head and saw him.

"Evan, dear! Do come in. Is your friend…?" She caught sight of Riley. "Please, come in, both of you. Would you like something to drink? Charles would be happy to bring you something."

"We're fine, Mom," Evan assured her. He slid into one of the side chairs, and Riley moved to stand behind him. "We won't stay long. You need to rest."

She gave him a glare. "And so do you, dear. You took a pretty nasty knock on the head, didn't you? And your poor wrist."

Evan shrugged. "It's not that bad. I'm cleared on the head injury. It wasn't nearly as bad as yours. And they sent me home with some pain meds, so I can take those if I need to."

Charles reappeared holding a tall glass filled with ice and a golden liquid and moved to place the glass within Gwen's reach, with one of her coasters under it. He retreated to his favorite chair but turned to face Evan. "Son, you know you're more than welcome to stay here while you finish recuperating. I'll be taking a few days off to stay home with your mother until she gets the all clear from her doctors, so it won't put us out at all."

Evan appreciated the offer, but he shook his head. "Thanks, Dad, but I already have a place to stay."

He glanced at Riley, who smiled at him. "Yes, I told Evan I'm happy to keep an eye on him for a few days." He turned that smile on his parents, and Evan could almost see them melt under the onslaught. "I'll take good care of him, Mr. and Mrs. Day. I promise."

Charles turned his head to look at his wife, who lifted her chin, silently urging him on. He looked back at Riley. "It looks like you're going to be a part of our son's life," he said, his words slow but firm. "Please, call us Charles and Gwen."

Evan blinked in surprise. That was much more than he'd expected from his parents. Welcoming Evan back, working on rebuilding their relationship—that had been hard enough to accept. But to have them welcome Riley as well? Evan didn't know what to say.

Except…. "Thanks, Dad." The words came out in a whisper, but they filled the room like a roar.

Riley laid a hand on Evan's shoulder, and Evan shivered, suddenly cold. Riley squeezed lightly. "Maybe we should go," he told Charles. "I think our patients both need to get a little more rest."

Evan almost protested, but his body was starting to throb again, and the idea of a nap sounded like heaven. He nodded and stood, Charles following suit a second later.

Evan stepped over and bent carefully to kiss his mother's cheek. "Feel better," he said, and she lifted a hand to squeeze his arm.

"I love you, my darling," she murmured back, and Evan had to force himself to pull away.

"Mr.—I mean, Charles." Riley held out his hand, and Charles didn't hesitate before shaking it. Riley turned to Gwen. "Gwen, I hope you'll recover quickly. Please feel free to call if you need anything at all."

She gave him a shadow of her usual smile. "I will. Take care of Evan for us."

"I will." Riley turned to Evan, who stood looking at his dad.

"Riley," he said, "could you give me a minute?"

He turned to Riley. Riley's gaze searched Evan's, and after a long moment, he gave a small smile and nodded. "I'll wait in the car."

"Thank you." Evan squeezed Riley's hand and then let go, and Riley went outside, pulling the door closed behind himself. Evan took in a deep breath and blew it out.

"Evan—"

"Yes," Evan interrupted. "Yes, I'll take the money. Yes, I'll use it to pay for college first. And yes, I'll give you both another chance. I can't make any long-term promises, but I…." He trailed off and had to swallow to be able to go on. "I want my family back."

Despite his best efforts, his voice broke and tears filled his eyes. He bit his lip to try to get himself under control, but in another moment, his father pulled him into a hug.

"It's okay, son." Charles's usually deep, booming voice sounded like a shadow of itself. "We'll figure it out, okay?"

Evan nodded, wrapped his uninjured arm around his father's waist, and took the comfort being offered. In that moment, he felt like the young boy he'd once been, the one who'd idolized his older brother and adored his father, the man who'd taught him to throw a baseball and catch a fish and taken him camping and to Disney World. The memories flooded back, buried so long beneath pain and anger, and he shook as they flowed through his mind.

He'd lost so much, but he was getting so much of it back again.

A choked sob came from somewhere nearby, and Evan forced himself to pull back far enough to look at his mom. She was crying openly, and Evan slid away from his father's embrace and took the few steps to the side of the sofa. He dropped gingerly to his knees and reached for her, drawing her into a gentle but heartfelt hug, mindful of both her injuries and his own.

Eventually, they collected themselves, and Evan gave her another lingering kiss on the cheek before he pushed carefully to his feet. Once he was standing, his father stepped in front of him, looked him in the eye, and held out a hand to shake. "I'm proud of you, son."

Evan copied his father's posture and accepted his hand. "Thank you, sir."

They held their positions for a long moment before Evan released Charles's hand and took a half step back. "I'll see you soon."

Charles nodded. "We'll look forward to it."

As Evan walked down the sidewalk toward Riley's car, he was happy to realize that he looked forward to it too. But what made him smile was seeing Riley leaning against the side of the car, watching him approach. Their gazes locked, and Evan flushed as he saw Riley's eyes dilate. He didn't stop until he was inches away, and without a pause he pulled Riley into a kiss.

Riley went willingly, opening his mouth to let Evan inside, wrapping his arms around Evan's shoulders. Evan pressed Riley against the car, careful not to bump his injured arm, and rotated his hips against Riley's. The reaction he felt made him smile into the kiss, and Riley's lips curved up.

Evan pulled back and lifted an eyebrow. "Take me home?" he asked, knowing the answer.

Riley slid his hands down Evan's arms, ghosting lightly over the cast, and tangled their fingers together. "Home," he agreed.

RILEY BARELY paused to breathe on the drive back to his place. He talked about the job interview Mikey had just done, the design work he was doing for a friend, anything other than Evan's hospital stay or the way his hand kept finding its way to Evan's leg, each time another inch closer to his crotch. Evan sat back and let Riley's lilting voice and gentle touch flow over him, warming him from the inside out.

Evan's phone buzzed in his pocket just as Riley pulled into his parking place, and he pulled it out just long enough to see it wasn't his parents and hit ignore. He didn't really care who it was. That was why God gave him voice mail. He unfolded himself from the car to find Riley waiting for him, Evan's duffel bag in his hand. Evan moved to Riley's side and jumped when Riley squeezed his left buttcheek.

"I like these jeans," he said, his voice as casual as his fingers weren't. "They'll go nicely with the rug on my bedroom floor."

Jesus. Riley had never been one to mince words about what he wanted, but with everything that had happened, Riley's open display of want shot through Evan like a drug. He followed Riley inside like a puppy, and the second he'd locked the door of his loft, Riley grabbed Evan's uninjured hand and led him down the hallway. Evan had hardly set foot into the bedroom before Riley pinned to the wall with his body.

"Get your clothes off," he said against Evan's lips. "I want to see it all before I get inside it."

Riley kissed him then, hard, and it took a few seconds for Evan's brain to catch up with Riley's words. His body and cock jerked at the realization that he had Riley in top mode, ready to take charge and make things happen. Aches and pains forgotten, Evan and his cock were fully on board with that plan.

Riley started pushing at his clothes with one hand, and Evan reached out to still him while deepening their kiss. Riley made a sound of protest low in his throat but didn't pull away, which Evan took as a victory. He wanted Riley to fuck him so much he could taste it, but first, he wanted to kiss.

He kissed Riley thoroughly, soft and hard, rough and gentle, bodies rubbing together until their cocks were stiff and their breathing ragged. Evan slid his hand into Riley's hair, the curling strands smooth as silk against his skin. He shivered, the movement making his finger tighten, and Riley groaned into their kiss at the inadvertent but sharp tug.

Evan smiled against Riley's mouth. "Like that, huh?" he murmured, giving another little pull. The length was perfect, just enough to get a good grip on, and the even louder moan Riley let out and the jerk of his cock against Evan's thigh told the story without words.

In a flash, though, Riley turned the tables. He ducked away from Evan's touch and grabbed Evan's wrist to hold it against the wall. He didn't touch Evan's injured hand, but he pressed his full weight into Evan's body, grinding against him, not giving an inch.

"Yeah, I like that," he muttered, his usually soft voice gone raspy with arousal. "But I'm the one in charge tonight."

A full-body shudder went through Evan, and he surrendered to Riley's lead. Riley kissed him, touched him, undressed them both, and when Riley led him to the bed, Evan went to lie down, ready to take Riley's weight on top of him despite the way his body still ached from his injuries.

"No." Riley stopped him with a hand and climbed onto the mattress next to him. He lay back, propping his head up with several pillows. "I want to watch you ride me."

And Evan did. Riley got him ready, helped him balance with his one good arm, and guided his cock to Evan's hole, but once Evan had Riley inside, he let his body take over. Riley ran his hands down his legs, up to tweak his nipples, and Evan tilted his head down to meet Riley's gaze. Riley's lips curled in a wicked smile and he thrust his hips, holding Evan steady as he fucked up into him. Evan couldn't look away from Riley's eyes, gone dark with arousal and soft with emotion. A million unsaid words flowed between them. Time stretched out as if nothing else existed, holding them there together in a cloud of sensation, until Evan couldn't stand it any longer and reached for his dick.

Riley got there first. "Come on," he murmured, licking his lips as he tightened his fingers around Evan. "I want to feel you come on my cock."

Evan moaned and rocked faster, his orgasm hovering just out of his reach. He leaned forward, still unwilling to look away from Riley's face, and braced his good arm in the center of Riley's slim chest.

"Riley," he gasped. "Oh God."

"Yeah." Riley lightened his touch and focused in on the tip of Evan's throbbing cock. "Yeahhhhh...."

Evan groaned and jerked, his body shuddering as his climax rushed through him. He shot hard, and Riley's fingers loosened even more but didn't move away. Evan shivered as the last vestiges of his orgasm slid over him, his skin flushing and goose bumps popping out everywhere.

When he opened his eyes—he didn't remember closing them—Riley smiled up at him. "That was one of the hottest things I've ever seen," he said, and Evan laughed roughly. He realized then that Riley was still hot and hard inside him and he tightened his inner muscles, watching as Riley's eyes widened and a soft groan left his mouth.

"It's your turn," Evan said, rocking his hips, ignoring the twinges of overstimulation and the body aches that were making themselves known again despite the flood of endorphins. "Want to watch you like you watched me."

Riley wrapped both hands around Evan's hips. "It won't take me long."

Riley thrust up into Evan, and Evan tried to look everywhere at once, at the sweat-dampened curls across Riley's forehead, the half-lidded eyes, the full red lips parted to let moans escape. Evan wanted to touch, wanted to run his fingers across Riley's slim chest, twist and pluck his pink nipples, but more than that, he wanted to keep his balance so Riley could take what he needed.

More than anything, Evan wanted to see Riley come apart beneath him.

In just minutes, Riley's mouth opened wider, the rhythm of his hips stuttered, and then he came, shouting, jerking so hard Evan was almost unseated. He grabbed Riley's forearm with his good hand to steady them both, but he never looked away from Riley's face, his youthful features darkly beautiful in the throes of pleasure.

Gorgeous, Evan thought, and he smiled.

LATER, AFTER they'd cleaned up and eaten a quick dinner so Evan could take his pain meds—Riley insisted, after their activities, and with the way he felt, Evan wasn't about to argue—Riley drew Evan back into bed, but this time with nothing more than rest in mind.

"We have plenty of time for sex." Riley plumped the pillows and straightened the covers, his movements as brisk as his words. "You just got out of the hospital. You need to rest."

"Yes, dear." Evan got the reaction he'd hoped for with that, a huffed-out breath and an eye roll, but he'd also seen the curl of a smile touch the corner of Riley's mouth.

"Get in bed," Riley ordered. "Or I'll throw you in and hold you down."

Evan laughed at the teasing words. "Promises, promises," he shot back, stretching out on the mattress and feeling his body start to relax immediately. He sighed. "God, it feels like a year since I've slept in a real bed."

Riley slid in beside him and curled in close. "Hospitals do seem to be designed to keep you from getting any rest."

Evan rolled onto his side and wrapped an arm around Riley's waist, tugging him even closer. "They're trying to get you out the door fast. They don't want you to get too comfortable."

Riley brushed his nose against Evan's. "Well, my goal is the exact opposite. You just settle in and stay a while, okay?"

Evan smiled and kissed Riley, deep and sweet. "There's no place I'd rather be."

Watch for:

Wayward Son

by Shae Connor
Book Two in the Sons series

Family isn't just about blood—it's about heart.

After his move to Atlanta and away from the influence of his conservative parents, Mikey O'Malley finally feels free to be himself: art student, aspiring animator, and out gay man. He has friends, a new job, and not one, but two men interested in him. Cory Lassiter and Jimmy Black have been a happy couple for years, occasionally bringing a twink into their bed, but only for a brief roll in the hay. When Mikey meets the pair, the attraction is immediate, and it runs three ways. Mikey just can't believe they'd have room in their lives for a permanent addition.

When Mikey's newfound life is shattered by a lawsuit that accuses him of molesting a child years earlier, he's determined to face his troubles on his own, but Cory and Jimmy are just as determined that he not have to go it alone. To reconcile his need for independence and his desire for love, Mikey has to learn that being a man isn't just about standing on your own two feet. It's about letting yourself lean on the ones who love you.

Coming soon to
http://www.dreamspinnerpress.com

SHAE CONNOR lives in Atlanta, where she works for the government by day and reads and writes about people falling in love by night. She's been making up stories for as long as she can remember, but it took her a long time to figure out that maybe she should start writing them down. She usually has far too many stories in progress, but when she does manage to tear herself away from her laptop, she enjoys running, hiking, cooking, and traveling, not necessarily in that order.

Shae is on Twitter pretty much 24/7 at @shaeconnor and posts snippets, updates, and thoughts on writing and editing at her website, http://shaeconnorwrites.com. You can contact her at shaeconnorwrites@gmail.com.

Marshall Ramirez isn't looking to fall in love, but from the moment firefighter Brad Flannery walks through the doors of Marsh's veterinary clinic, he's smitten. Marsh treats Fuego, the cat Brad rescued from a house fire, and convinces Brad to take her on as a foster—along with the three kittens Marsh helps her deliver. What Marsh really wants, though, is for Brad to keep him too.

http://www.dreamspinnerpress.com

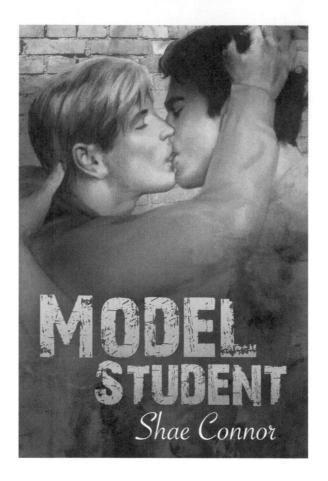

Making his living as a model allows Aaron Stevens to pay his way through film school at NYU. While on a photo shoot, he meets Matt Carson, a journalism student who wants to interview Aaron for his senior project, and they feel an instant connection that catches them both off guard. As their relationship develops over the next week, they open up to each other about their pasts, but attraction won't be enough to keep them together unless they can share their secrets too.

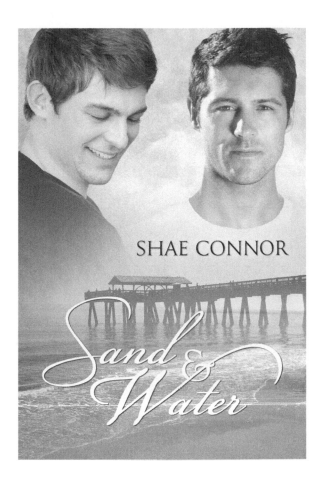

SHAE CONNOR

Sand & Water

Widower John McConnell gets along fine raising his daughter on Georgia's Tybee Island, though he wouldn't exactly say he's happy. Haunted by the memory of his dead wife, John hasn't considered dating again until he meets Bryan Simmons in the park. It isn't long before John realizes that what he feels for Bryan could be something real, but how will he know he's ready to move on?

As John soon discovers, Bryan carries some heavy emotional baggage of his own. With John's help, Bryan starts to put his demons to rest, and together they lay the foundation for a relationship. It looks like they might finally leave their tragedies behind them—until John takes a misstep that could turn a magical night together into their last.

http://www.dreamspinnerpress.com

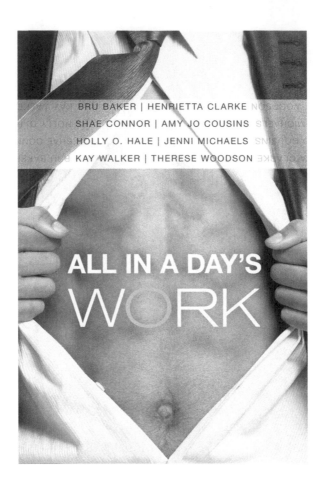

BRU BAKER | HENRIETTA CLARKE
SHAE CONNOR | AMY JO COUSINS
HOLLY O. HALE | JENNI MICHAELS
KAY WALKER | THERESE WOODSON

ALL IN A DAY'S WORK

A guy's got to make a living. He can do it the conventional way—by selling cars, scooping ice cream, or delivering sandwiches—or he can earn his money as a spy, a historical interpreter, or the host of a myth-busting television show. Whether the men in this anthology are working hard to build their own business or performing in drag at a dance hall, every day has the potential for surprises and the chance to satisfy their lust or maybe find something more permanent. For the guys in these stories, what's all in a day's work might be anything but what they expected.

http://www.dreamspinnerpress.com

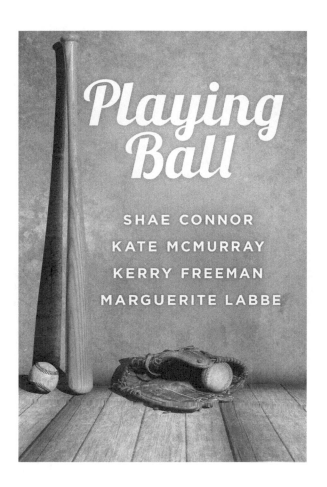

Baseball—America's favorite pastime—provides a field wide open for romance. A "Home Field Advantage" may not help when Toby must choose between the team he's loved all his life and the man he could love for the rest of it. In 1927, Skip hides his sexuality to protect his career until he meets "One Man to Remember." Ruben and Alan fell victim to a "Wild Pitch," leaving them struggling with heartache and guilt, and now they've met again. And on "One Last Road Trip," Jake retires and leaves baseball behind, hoping to reconnect with Mikko and get a second chance at love.

http://www.dreamspinnerpress.com

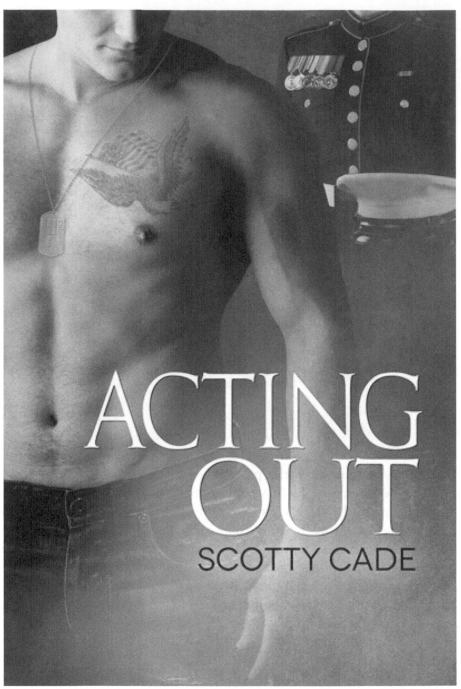

ACTING OUT

SCOTTY CADE

http://www.dreamspinnerpress.com

CPSIA information can be obtained at www.ICGtesting.com
Printed in the USA
LVOW01s1546220315

431550LV00015B/882/P